T0031013

I HEARD
A FLY BUZZ
WHEN I
DIED

ALSO BY AMANDA FLOWER

Because I Could Not Stop for Death

I HEARD A FLY BUZZ WHEN I DIED

An Emily Dickinson Mystery

AMANDA FLOWER

BERKLEY PRIME CRIME

New York

BERKLEY PRIME CRIME
Published by Berkley
An imprint of Penguin Random House LLC
penguinrandomhouse.com

Copyright © 2023 by Amanda Flower
Penguin Random House supports copyright. Copyright fuels
creativity, encourages diverse voices, promotes free speech, and
creates a vibrant culture. Thank you for buying an authorized
edition of this book and for complying with copyright laws by
not reproducing, scanning, or distributing any part of it in any
form without permission. You are supporting writers and
allowing Penguin Random House to continue to
publish books for every reader.

BERKLEY and the BERKLEY & B colophon are registered
trademarks and BERKLEY PRIME CRIME is a trademark of
Penguin Random House LLC.

Library of Congress Cataloging-in-Publication Data

Names: Flower, Amanda, author.
Title: I heard a fly buzz when I died / Amanda Flower.
Description: First Edition. | New York: Berkley Prime Crime, 2023. |
Series: An Emily Dickinson Mystery
Identifiers: LCCN 2023009693 (print) | LCCN 2023009694 (ebook) |
ISBN 9780593336960 (trade paperback) | ISBN 9780593336977 (ebook)
Subjects: LCSH: Dickinson, Emily, 1830-1886—Fiction. |
LCGFT: Detective and mystery fiction. | Novels.
Classification: LCC PS3606.L683 I4 2023 (print) |
LCC PS3606.L683 (ebook) | DDC 813/.6—dc23/eng/20230306
LC record available at https://lccn.loc.gov/2023009693
LC ebook record available at https://lccn.loc.gov/2023009694

First Edition: November 2023

Printed in the United States of America
1st Printing

This is a work of fiction. Names, characters, places, and incidents
either are the product of the author's imagination or are used
fictitiously, and any resemblance to actual persons, living or dead,
business establishments, events, or locales is entirely coincidental.

In memory of my beloved parents,

Rev. Pamela Flower and Thomas Flower

Our time here on earth together was shorter than

we wanted, but in heaven, it will be eternal

I heard a Fly buzz—when I died—
The Stillness in the Room
Was like the Stillness in the Air—
Between the Heaves of Storm—

The Eyes around—had wrung them dry—
And Breaths were gathering firm
For that last Onset—when the King
Be witnessed—in the Room—

I willed my Keepsakes—Signed away
What portion of me be
Assignable—and then it was
There interposed a Fly—

With Blue—uncertain—stumbling Buzz—
Between the light—and me—
And then the Windows failed—and then
I could not see to see—

—Emily Dickinson (591)

I HEARD
A FLY BUZZ
WHEN I
DIED

CHAPTER ONE

I THRUST THE tip of my spade into the earth and had images flash through my mind of digging a grave, a grave dug in stone. The tiniest bit of dirt came loose from the combination of my force and the steel blade. The small amount of soil hardly seemed worth the effort. I closed my eyes for a moment. Trying to plant these daylilies in August was a bad idea. This was the driest and hottest month of the year, not a good time for planting much of anything. However, when my mistress, Emily Dickinson, saw the lilies growing on the side of an abandoned road, she had to have them for her new garden at the Dickinson homestead. One way or another, I had to get them in the ground before they languished in the heat.

Sweat trickled down both sides of my face. My only recourse was to wet the ground and then plant the daylilies. I knew Emily would not want to change the location of the plants. When she made up her mind about something, it was as good as done. The only trouble being when I was the one who was supposed to make sure it got done. At least I wasn't alone on this particular assignment.

Cody Carey, the family's yardman, stood a few feet away and looked as hot as I felt. He wiped at his brow. The pair of us had toiled in companionable silence for a long while. Cody was a few years younger than my twenty-one years. He had a dusting of freckles across the bridge of his nose and cheeks. The blond mustache on his upper lip could only be seen when the light hit it directly. His attempt at a mustache was the same straw color of his hair. He had just started to work at the Dickinson home that summer, and Emily hoped to train him up as a proper gardener, both for the homestead and for the Evergreens, the neighboring property that was home to Emily's brother and his new wife.

"Willa!" a breathy voice called.

I jumped and dropped my spade onto the hard ground. The handle bounced and struck me in the ankle. I bit my lip to keep from crying out.

"Willa!" Emily called again. "Susan and Austin are home!" The jubilation in her voice was clear. My mistress Emily wasn't one to do anything by halves. If you were someone she loved, like her family, then it was wholly and fiercely.

Emily's brother, Austin, had married Susan the month before in a private ceremony. Not even the Dickinson family had been included.

Susan Dickinson née Gilbert was Emily's dearest friend, and I thought, as such, Emily would be thrilled to now be able to call Susan not just her friend but her sister. However, when she'd learned that Susan and Austin were to marry privately, she had seemed relieved.

"I don't think I could bear to watch. It's like a death. Death causes division and change, and I sense that coming," she'd told me.

To this day, I don't understand why she felt that way. Did she fear losing her brother to marriage or did she fear losing her friend? In any case, they were both with her now, living in a grand house that Emily's father had built for the newlyweds. I could not fathom what the loss, or "death" as Emily called it, could be.

Perhaps I was looking at this from the perspective of my own pain. Over a year ago, my brother, Henry, had been brutally murdered. He'd been the only family I had left in this world . . . the only family worth mentioning at least. I'd experienced real death and loss, so the comparison chafed at my own grief.

"We must go over to the Evergreens to greet them," Emily declared. "I know they will be tired from their journey, but it cannot be helped. I have to see them straightaway. I can't wait until the evening meal. That is hours from now."

"You should go," I said.

"I want you to go with me."

I picked up my spade and noticed that Cody had wandered off when Emily appeared. I hoped he didn't think I was going to plant all these daylilies myself. He was the yardman, not me. "I don't know why you'd like me to go with you."

"They will want to see you," she insisted.

I wiped sweat from my brow with the back of my hand, certain I would have dirt on my face. I doubted Austin Dickinson and the newly married Susan Gilbert Dickinson would be so eager to see me upon their return to Amherst.

Austin had spoken less than twenty words to me in the last year and a half I had been under the Dickinson family employ, and Susan scoffed at my friendship with Emily like I was her competition. This I could not quite understand. Susan was Emily's dearest friend and now her sister. I could never compete with that, nor would I want to. I was a maid. I knew my station. Emily may be amused by my friendship, but I was still a servant first. I was there to do her bidding and the bidding of the family.

"Please, Willa, come with me." Emily's small hands fluttered in front of her face. Emily was a petite woman with a tiny waist, reddish hair, and deep-set dark eyes. At the moment those eyes were afraid. Maybe not afraid, but certainly anxious. What could possibly strain her nerves about seeing her brother and Susan, two people whom she knew and loved best in the world?

"Are friends delight or pain? Could bounty but remain," Emily said.

I had become accustomed to Emily speaking so. When she spoke in that tone, she wasn't speaking to me but to herself. She was working through a poem. She murmured the words again and added, "Riches are good."

I picked up my spade and set it into the metal pail I used to carry my gardening tools around the yard. "I will come, miss. If it will be a help to you."

Emily's eyes cleared. The faraway look that seemed to overtake her every so often faded. "Thank you, Willa. You are a true delight."

I glanced at the large yellow house where I lived with the

Dickinson family and their head maid, Margaret O'Brien. "I should go wash up. I have been digging in the garden for the better part of an hour. I'm sure I'm covered in dirt."

Emily waved this idea away. "Do not bother. It is my brother and Susan. There is no reason to keep up appearances. Now come. Just remove your apron and you will be presentable enough."

I glanced up at the house, where it seemed to loom over the garden. "I can't be long. Miss O'Brien was expecting me to come in soon to assist with dinner. She will be quite upset if I'm not there on time. Your father likes to eat at the same hour every evening for his digestion."

"I have already told Miss O'Brien that I have need of you and you will clean the kitchen top to bottom after dinner to make up for the lost time."

I dug my fingernails into the palms of my hands. I typically cleaned the kitchen top to bottom every night, but with Miss O'Brien's help. Without her help it would take twice as long, which meant I wouldn't have any time to read *The Scarlet Letter*, the novel Emily lent me. When she'd learned of my love of reading, she'd given me access to her personal library. Many nights, I had to force myself to blow out the candle and go to sleep. I would have much rather stayed up and read, but the time I had outside of working was limited. My only day off during the week was Sunday. Often after church, I would walk through Amherst with a book under my arm.

At times, I would allow Matthew Thomas, a local police officer and friend, to accompany me on my walks. He would like to join me every Sunday, but as much as I enjoyed his companionship, I wanted nothing more than friendship from him. He felt differently and had made his intentions known. For his sake, I wished he would look elsewhere for a wife. I did not want him to waste his time on me when he could find happiness with someone new.

I removed my apron as Emily instructed, folded it, and placed it neatly onto the garden stool I used while weeding. Perhaps while I was gone, Cody would return and finish planting the daylilies. That would be a great gift.

Emily grabbed my hand. "Come, Willa. There's not a moment to waste." She pulled me along the grass and released my hand when we reached the younger Dickinsons' property. I slowed and took in the new house.

Just like the homestead, where Emily lived with her parents and younger sister Lavinia, the Evergreens was an impressive home. It was so new that the paint on the shutters gleamed in the sunlight. I'd heard Emily say it was an Italianate-style home, which made me think it must have been inspired by grand buildings in Italy. I'd never seen any structure like it. It was large, but the most impressive thing was the tower that rose out of the middle of it. It looked like a clock tower looming over the joint grounds of the Evergreens and the homestead.

Emily called the house a "bribe tied into a threat." Her brother had wanted to move west after his marriage to make his own way in the world and discover his fortune. Miss Susan had not wished for that. She wanted to stay in Amherst near friends and most of all near Emily. Mr. Dickinson made his son an offer that he couldn't walk away from: a grand new home and work at the family law firm. He would find nothing like this house in the wilderness. It was a gilded cage meant to keep him close, and Mr. Dickinson had succeeded.

Emily was running now. She was so eager to greet her brother and new sister. It made me wonder why she insisted I come along at all. It was clear she didn't need me. I had found Emily always had a purpose for everything she did, even if she was the only one who understood it.

Austin Dickinson stood next to a carriage and offered a hand to his new bride as she stepped out. Miss Susan looked up at the house, and her lips curved with pleasure as if some sort of dream had been fulfilled. It must have been a great comfort for her to know she was now secure and would always have a home. From the snippets I had overhead from the family, I gathered Miss Susan hadn't had the same upbringing as the Dickinson children. Her parents were dead, and she'd been handed off from aunt to aunt. As luck or providence would have it, she and Emily struck up a friendship several years ago, and from that relationship, Miss Susan became acquainted with Austin. Now, she was a member of one of the most prominent families in Amherst. It was a great change of fortune.

"You're home!" Emily cried, and ran to her brother and Miss Susan. "I thought I should die before you returned. It was so long, and you did not write me nearly as much as you should have."

"Emily." Her brother laughed. "We are to dine at the homestead tonight and greet you properly then. There is no reason to make a scene."

From the light shining in Austin's eyes, he was pleased to see his sister.

Emily hugged her brother and Miss Susan in turn. "I don't need a proper greeting. I could not wait one more second without seeing you. You can greet Mother and Father under the stiff confines of the dining table. But me, I want to be greeted in the open air with only heaven looking down."

"Oh, Emily, Sister," Miss Susan said. "I have missed you so. I'm certain I longed to see you as much as you longed to see me."

Austin wrinkled his brow. "Yes, we have *both* missed you, Sister."

The porter removed the couple's trunks from the back of the carriage, and Austin seemed to accept this as a time to escape. "I will show you where to put those. The house is still being put in order, and not all the furniture is in place."

"Yes, sir," the man murmured. His thick Irish accent was noticeable when he spoke. Austin led the green-eyed porter into the house. It was then that Miss Susan noticed me for the first time. "And why did you bring the maid with you?" Miss Susan asked. Her intelligent eyes bored into me.

"She was in the garden and wanted to welcome you home too. I see no reason to turn a warm welcome away, do you, dear Sister?" She sighed happily. "What a thrill it is for me to call you that. I feel as if I have been waiting for this day for so many years. I have dreamed it, prayed for it, and now it is here. We will be together each and every day, as we were meant to be."

Miss Susan's gaze softened when she looked at Emily. "This is what I have wished and prayed for too. I'm grateful to be married to your brother, but I wish ..." She trailed off and then looked at me again. "It is no matter. This is the best solution." Miss Susan's demeanor changed. "We have news."

"You are with child already?" Emily gasped.

Miss Susan clapped her hands as if Emily's thought were a fly that must be squashed. "Heavens no. We're going to have our first guests to the Evergreens here in just a week's time. There is a literary society meeting at the college just before the new term begins, and Mr. Emerson will be the honored guest. I learned of this while we were on our wedding trip, and wrote to extend an invitation. He accepted, and he and his secretary will be staying here with us."

Emily laid a hand to her chest. "Ralph Waldo Emerson, the writer?"

Susan chuckled and lovingly touched Emily's cheek. "My girl, yes, is there any other Emerson of literary importance in this world? He will be arriving from Concord by carriage a week from today. As you can imagine, this does not give me much time to prepare. My own maid is in a complete panic over it because, yes, I expect everything to be perfect. I will not have my first esteemed guest reporting back to the wider world that I neither knew how to keep a home, nor was a proper hostess." She lowered her hand from Emily's cheek.

Emily rested her own palm in the place where Miss Susan's had been, as if she missed its warmth.

Miss Susan looked to me. "I could use an extra maid this week. I have only the one. It is a shame considering this is such a large home, but Austin is not one to overspend. He is too afraid of following in your grandfather's footsteps in that regard."

Emily made a face. "Austin has good reason to be concerned. Everyone says he is much like our grandfather in temperament and thought."

"Yes, and now as his wife it is my job to keep him on a more practical path." She said this with more than a little pride. "In no time at all, the Evergreens will become the cultural center of Amherst, and Mr. Emerson will be the first guest to make that dream happen."

"Willa should help you," Emily said. "Just for this week, to ensure everything is ready and prepared for Mr. Emerson's arrival. I'm sure Mother and Father will agree. How you impress Mr. Emerson will reflect on them as well. I believe it will benefit the entire family if you can put on a nice show for such a learned man."

Miss Susan pinched her lips together. "Very good. Willa," Miss Susan said. "I expect you to report to the Evergreens at five in the morning. We have just a few days to make the home welcoming to Mr. Emerson."

"But what about Miss O'Brien?" I asked. "She will be left alone in the homestead to care for it herself."

Miss Susan scowled as if she was annoyed I would dare question her. She was the lady of a house now and wanted to be treated as such.

"Miss O'Brien will be fine," Emily said. "She has made do with no help many times before. It's only a few days, and you can help her in the evenings when you're finished at the Evergreens."

Help in the evenings, after putting in a full day's work starting at five a.m.? I was certainly game to help this family, regardless of which house required more immediate assistance, but I didn't want to think about doing double the work for the next week.

I folded my hands in front of myself and said nothing, just like any servant would in my place. It sounded as if the visit of Mr. Emerson was going to mean one thing only. Trouble. At the time, I had no idea just how much trouble it would actually become.

CHAPTER TWO

WHEN I RETURNED to the homestead, I dreaded telling Margaret O'Brien that I would be working at the Evergreens from morning to night for the next week. I was already walking on eggshells with the head maid because of how much time I spent tending Emily's flowers and plants in the garden. Margaret was very much looking forward to the first frost, when I would not be helping in the garden any longer.

Thankfully while I was at the Evergreens, Cody finished planting the daylilies with the help of the gardener, Horace Church. Horace was a tall man in his thirties with a full beard and a long list of convictions. If you got the gardener on a topic he was passionate about, he would speak about it for days if allowed. He cared deeply for the Dickinsons' gardens and was also the sexton at the Congregational church on the other side of Main Street, where all the Dickinsons except for Emily attended.

"Wet the ground first, Willa, if your mistress gets the idea in her head to plant during the hottest part of an August day," Horace called grumpily.

I waved to let him know that I had heard him. I was too nervous about the conversation that I had to have with Margaret to stop and chat.

The news that I had to share with the head maid would not go well. This I knew. I sympathized with her. When she left for a few days to care for her ailing mother, it was all I could do to keep the house running. Being responsible for such a large home right after the family had moved in and didn't know where all their belongings were was daunting. Thankfully both Emily and Miss Lavinia chipped in to help with the cooking during that time.

However, Miss Lavinia did it with a scowl on her face. Miss Emily's younger sister didn't care for me. With so much activity at the Evergreens, I didn't think that Margaret would receive their help this time. The entire family would be in a flurry preparing for Mr. Emerson's arrival. The meals at the homestead would be Margaret's problem and hers alone.

I tentatively stepped into the kitchen and grabbed my spare apron from the hook. My other apron was still in the garden. I hoped Margaret wouldn't notice it was missing. I promised myself that I would run out and collect it the first chance I had.

Margaret was at the stove stirring a summer soup as the Dickinsons' first course. Since Austin and Miss Susan had returned home, the family was having a formal meal all together in the homestead's dining room.

I washed my hands quickly and jumped into the work of preparing the meal. I began slicing the crusty bread that Emily had made that morning. Emily baked most of the bread for the family, and she was quite talented at it. Many times, I had thought if she had been born lower class, she would have made an excellent baker. Her father refused to eat any bread in the home that wasn't made by his eldest daughter.

It came as a surprise to me when I learned Emily enjoyed baking. Baking was all about time and precision, and her mind seemed to meander from thought to thought. Often it was as if Emily was unaware of her surroundings because she was so arrested by a thought or a word or a line of a poem that she wished to write.

I could feel Margaret watching me out of the corner of her eye. I didn't say a word and concentrated on slicing bread like it was the most important task I'd ever been given.

Margaret selected a wooden spoon from the canister by the stove, dipped it into the soup, tasted it, and gave a satisfied nod. She then removed the boiling pot from the hot burner and placed it on a cast-iron trivet in the middle of the table. "I take it you and Miss Dickinson were out gallivanting again. When I went to the garden to collect herbs for the soup, you were not there."

Heat rushed to my cheeks. "She asked me to go with her to greet her brother and Miss Susan, who have just returned from their wedding trip. She told me she asked you."

"She did," Margaret replied. "However, I did not think you would be gone quite so long."

"Nor did I," I admitted.

"I'm grateful you will be cleaning the kitchen tonight. Since I have done the majority of the cooking, it only seems right," she sniffed.

I nodded and again thought of the unread novel under my

pillow in my little room. There would be time to read later. Perhaps not in the next week, while I would be working at the Evergreens. As of yet, I could not think of a way to tell Margaret this news. She was already in a foul mood.

"I'm sorry I was gone longer than I expected. Em—Miss Dickinson was quite insistent I go with her."

If Margaret noticed that I almost slipped and referred to Emily by her given name, she gave no indication, but I was wise enough to know she would stow that fact away in the back of her brain for the proper time to use it.

Instead, she spoke of Austin's new bride. She wrinkled her nose. "She is no longer Miss Susan. She is Mrs. Dickinson and the mistress of the Evergreens, but it would be far too confusing to call her such as we already have one Mrs. Dickinson. We will continue to speak of her as Miss Susan, but only when away from the family. When you address her directly, I expect you to call her Mrs. Dickinson or Mrs. Austin Dickinson."

I nodded, having come to the same conclusion.

"The pie should be ready to take from the oven. Miss Emily made it, but I'm sure that she's forgotten all about it in her excitement. She lets so many things distract her. It's a wonder she gets anything done." She shook her head like a woman who would never dare succumb to a distraction.

I picked up a tea towel and opened the oven's blackened door. Steam billowed in my face. The pie was blackberry, made with berries grown in the Dickinson garden. It smelled heavenly. I wished that Margaret and I could try a piece of it, but I knew that it would have to be saved for the welcome home dinner for Austin and Miss Susan, and with so many family members at the dinner, there wouldn't be a single crumb left.

"That does smell good," Margaret said even if a bit reluctantly. It was no secret she preferred that the Dickinson sisters stayed out of the kitchen. Emily in particular made a terrible mess when she baked. It was left to Margaret and me to clean it up.

"After tonight," my superior went on to say, "I hope the family can finally settle into the two homes and we can have some peace. There have been so many changes in the last year with Mr. Dickinson leaving politics, moving here, and Mr. Austin's wedding. We all deserve some calm."

I bit the inside of my lip. Margaret wasn't going to like Miss Susan's plans for the Evergreens, then. I tidied the kitchen, stalling for time, trying to think of the very best way to tell her. Truthfully, it didn't matter how I told her, it would not be welcome news. It was best just to get it out in one breath, like pulling off a day-old bandage.

I opened my mouth to speak, when Emily appeared in the kitchen doorway. I wasn't the least bit surprised that I hadn't heard her coming. She had the ability to move around the house like a butterfly on the wind. She fluttered soundlessly from room to room.

Emily clasped her hands in front of her pale yellow summer dress. "Oh, Willa! You are a true friend for pulling the pie from the oven for me. I would hate for Austin and Susan's welcome home dinner to be marred by a burnt blackberry pie. Could there be anything else more bitter?" She leaned over the pie and inhaled deeply. "Perfect. This is Austin's favorite dessert. He will be surprised I went to all the effort for him. Do we have an ice cream to go with it? Homemade vanilla would be just the thing."

Before Margaret or I could respond, Emily went on to say, "Margaret, I trust Willa has told you that my brother and new sister will need her assistance at the Evergreens all week long to prepare for the arrival of their first guests."

Margaret glared at me. "She has not."

I swallowed. "I was about to tell you."

Even to my own ears my response sounded weak.

Margaret narrowed her eyes at me. "Who are these guests? Is it wise to invite people into their home when they themselves are new to it? I believe it is much wiser to wait."

"Whether it is wiser to wait or not does not matter. Susan has extended an invitation, and she cannot take it back."

Margaret looked down at her soup as if she wanted to hide her disapproval. "Whom did she invite?"

"Mr. Emerson," Emily said. "I can't believe he will be coming here to Amherst. And not just in Amherst but right next door in my brother's home. As you said, Susan and Austin are themselves new to the home. They need help to prepare. I'm sure you understand how much pressure this is on poor Susan to present her home and hospitality in the best possible light. It will be the first time she is entertaining as a wife. It could set the tone for all the guests she will have at the Evergreens for years to come."

Margaret looked up from her soup. "Who is this Mr. Emerson? I have never heard of him."

If I had asked Emily a direct question with such a sharp tone, I would have gotten her disapproving stare in reply. However, when it came to Margaret, it seemed the Dickinsons took her bouts of churlishness in stride. Except for Mr.

Dickinson, of course. Not even Margaret would speak to the patriarch of the Dickinson family in such a way.

Emily put her hand on her chest. "Do you not know the name Ralph Waldo Emerson and his work?"

Margaret gave her a blank stare.

"He is only the most influential writer of our time," Emily said somewhat breathlessly, as if she had trouble getting the words out. "He's lecturing to the Amherst Literary Society symposium at the college in a week's time. Of course, he would be staying either at the Evergreens or here. We are one of the most important families in Amherst," she said with not a bit of conceit. She had simply stated a fact she knew to be true.

"I see," Margaret said. "It is important that such a man stays with the family. I would think the homestead would be a more suitable place for him, as it is well established," she added with a bit of disdain.

Emily wrinkled her nose. "You know Mother could not handle such a guest in our home. Susan is far more equipped for the stress of entertaining."

Margaret nodded. Mrs. Dickinson was of a sensitive nature. It was not uncommon for her to go to her bed before dinner with complaints of a headache.

"Yes, the younger Mrs. Dickinson will make a good hostess," Margaret conceded. "She certainly has her ways of impressing the right people." Margaret's last comment didn't sound like a compliment. If Emily noticed her tone, she made no mention of it.

"However, she has her own servants. She has a domestic in that home. Why does she need Willa?"

"She's just arrived home and is still setting up her house. She needs all the help she can get. We understand that you have to stay here and take care of the homestead, but surely you can spare Willa for a few days in order for the family to make a good impression on such an important man."

Margaret looked at me. "It seems I don't have a choice."

CHAPTER THREE

A WEEK LATER, AN ornate carriage came to a stop, and Jeremiah York, the Dickinsons' stable hand, grabbed the bridle. "Whoa," the driver said to the horse, and large wooden wheels ground to a halt in the gravel.

I stood on the steps of the Evergreens with the other servants, ready to welcome the esteemed guests. Margaret had also been invited to be there for their arrival, but she had declined, claiming she had to tend to Mrs. Dickinson, who was afflicted with one of her headaches again. That might have been true, but I also knew Margaret was still upset that I had been away from the homestead so much this week as I helped the Evergreens staff prepare for Mr. Emerson's arrival.

In front of me the three Dickinson children and Miss Susan waited for the guests to disembark from the carriage. Emily stood a little off to the side from her family, and she stared at the carriage door with rapt attention. Her back was so rigid that it was as if a piece of iron bar had been pressed up against her spine. She held a large bouquet of flowers from the garden in her arms. Emily believed in gifting flowers from the garden whenever possible. She gave bouquets to neighbors and friends in town, and she pressed flowers from her garden in letters to friends and family who lived farther away. I was not surprised that she wanted to give flowers to Emerson. I saw that she picked the very best blooms that the garden had to offer this time of the summer. In her arms she held sunflowers, dahlias, black-eyed Susans, zinnias, and daylilies. It was a burst of large blossoms and bright colors.

Miss Lavinia stood next to her and was also tense, but her nerves perhaps came from what she thought of her appearance. She continuously smoothed her hair and felt the lace of her collar as if to reassure herself that it lay flat.

Austin and Miss Susan were arm in arm and looked very much like the young, fashionable couple they were. I had a feeling it wouldn't be long before their home became a place of importance in Amherst, even more than the homestead.

Austin clapped his hands. "Very good. Jeremiah, will you help the driver unload?"

The young man nodded and peered over his glasses at me. I gave him a small smile in return. Jeremiah had been my brother Henry's closest friend before his death. They had worked at the Amherst stables together as stable hands. After Henry's death, Emily convinced her father to hire Jeremiah to care for their horses in the homestead barn. I was glad. I knew Jeremiah still dabbled in the dangerous work he did for the Underground Railroad, but at least he had a safe, secure job, and a good family that could protect him. And he was no longer sleeping on the floor but in a proper bed in a small cabin on the property.

The hired driver hopped out of the carriage seat and opened the door, allowing a tall, austere man in a dark suit to step out. His dark hair was parted at the side, and he had long sideburns reaching to the bottom of his chin. However, the most interesting aspect of his features was his nose. I couldn't say I had ever seen one like it. It was rather large, filling most of his long face, and reminded me of the drawings of Roman emperors I had seen in the history books within the Dickinson family library. It suited him. On anyone else, a nose like that would have been overpowering, but on Mr. Emerson it was just right.

Mr. Emerson held out his hand to Austin. "Mr. Dickinson, it is a pleasure to see you again. I have very much enjoyed your thoughtful correspondence. If you were not a lawyer, I would say that you should have been a writer."

Austin chuckled. "Oh no, not me. My sister, Emily, is the writer in the family." He nodded at Emily.

Mr. Emerson glanced at Emily, who nodded at him. I had expected that Emily—who loved to speak of her writing—would have taken her brother's lead and told one of the best known writers of our time about her work, but she said nothing.

"What do you write, Miss Dickinson?" Mr. Emerson asked with an arched brow.

"Letters. I write many letters to friends and family. It gives me much joy to share my life and verse with them."

He nodded his approval. "I, too, enjoy letters. I fear

someday it will be a lost art. Everyone is in such a rush. They can't take time to scribble more than a mere note. All good things take time, patience, and practice. Those are the virtues that seem to be lacking in our society."

Emily nodded. "I have always thought the same with my po—letters."

Miss Susan stepped forward. "I'm Mrs. Dickinson, Austin's wife, but you can call me Susan. I'm also a longstanding member of the Amherst Literary Society. We are thrilled you have agreed to come and speak to the group this week. We're all so much looking forward to the wisdom of your newest work. I have read it and enjoyed it immensely."

Mr. Emerson took her outstretched hand. "I'm very happy to be here. Small literary societies are the backbone of literature, so it is a great pleasure to share my work and observations with you."

"Mr. Emerson, you came at the perfect time too," Austin jumped in to say. "Classes at the college for fall term don't begin for another month. However, many of the professors are back and preparing their lectures. I would expect most of them also plan to come to the symposium to hear you speak. It is quite an honor to have such a well-known author on campus."

"It would be my pleasure," Mr. Emerson said. "And please call me Waldo. When we are in your home, the pleasantries of Mr. and Mrs. are far too stuffy. Formality has its place. I don't believe it's among true friends."

Miss Susan nodded her acceptance of his offering to use his given name.

Emily stepped forward and held out the flowers to Mr.

Emerson. "I hope this bouquet will bring you joy and inspiration during your stay. The flowers are from our garden."

"They are lovely," Mr. Emerson said. "You can give them to my secretary to hold."

A moment later, a man exited the carriage. While Mr. Emerson was refined, well-spoken, and reserved, this man sparkled. His eyes were the bluest I had ever seen, and he had a full head of golden hair that was not marred by a hat. His clothes were crisply pressed, if a little worn, and he carried a large satchel with the initials "RWE" embroidered on the flap. "Good afternoon, everyone," he said in a cheerful voice as he smiled broadly, showing off a full set of ruler-straight teeth.

"Luther, I'm glad that you have decided to exit the carriage," Mr. Emerson said with just a touch of irritation. I do not know if the others would have even noticed it, as they had neither worked in service nor been on the receiving end of such a condescending tone.

Mr. Emerson turned to the Dickinsons. "This is my secretary, Mr. Luther Howard. He will be staying here as well, just as I wrote ahead to inform you."

"Yes, of course," Miss Susan said with the authority of a lady of the house, even though she had been such for only half a fortnight. "We have a room all ready for him as well. We're glad you are with us, Mr. Howard."

"Luther, please." He flashed those teeth again. "And it is my pleasure to be staying with such an esteemed family like yours. The Dickinsons have been instrumental in Amherst, but also in the commonwealth. I am glad to make your acquaintance."

Austin straightened his spine at these compliments. "Yes, well, we have always been taught that we must contribute to society. If we want this to be a great commonwealth and nation, we, too, must do our part for advancement and stability."

Mr. Howard looked up at the rising pillars of the Evergreens. "This is a grand home. Is it not true that it was given to you as a wedding gift from your father?"

Irritation flashed across Austin's face. Because Austin was a young man, I supposed he would have felt better if he had built the house with his own fortune instead of accepting the gift from his father, especially considering Austin's previous desire to travel west and make his own way in the world. However, Miss Susan had convinced him to accept the gift and stay, her argument being that she wanted her future children to grow up with family, which was something she herself had never had as a child.

Of course, Miss Susan would never have shared all of this with me, but Emily recounted it all one evening when she was practicing recipes for entry at a local fair. Margaret had asked me to stay up with Emily in the kitchen.

"You know she is going to make a terrible mess. She is the messiest baker I have ever seen. I'm actually shocked she's able to have a finished cake by the end. Her recipes are wonderful, but sometimes the cost to my floors is too much to bear," Margaret had said to me at the time.

"I'm so looking forward to seeing your beautiful home," Mr. Howard said now. He smiled at Emily and Miss Lavinia in turn. "These must be the young Miss Dickinsons. A pleasure."

Emily stared at him with a blank face, but to my surprise Miss Lavinia blushed. Mr. Howard must have noticed, because he smiled at the youngest Dickinson again.

"Luther," Mr. Emerson said. "Will you take those flowers from Miss Dickinson and bring them up to my room?"

Mr. Howard's eyes went wide. "I can't, sir."

"Why not?" Mr. Emerson asked, sounding quite annoyed over the matter.

"As I have told you before, I have terrible hay fever. Flowers in particular cause me to sneeze and cough." As if to prove his point, he sneezed. "You will excuse me."

Miss Susan wrinkled her nose. "We will have our maid, Katie, take the flowers to your room." Petite Katie, who stood next to me, hurried down the steps and collected the flowers from Emily's arms without a word.

As she carried the flowers away, Mr. Howard placed a handkerchief to his face and sneezed again. "Horrible things, flowers."

Emily scowled at him, and I knew there was little hope of her taking a liking to Mr. Howard now.

"We would like to settle in before dinner, and I'd like to take a bit of time to review my notes before my lecture tomorrow," Mr. Emerson said.

"Of course," Miss Susan said. "Katie will show you to your rooms. Dinner will be at seven, so you will have some time to yourself."

As the men walked up the steps, I watched Mr. Howard, and it seemed to me all the ladies present studied him closely as well. I noticed as Miss Lavinia in particular observed the young man walk into the Evergreens as if she were one of her many cats eyeing a chipmunk in the garden.

He was very handsome. However, I was more fascinated by his demeanor. The way he walked, the way he spoke, was not the manner of a person who had worked their whole life in service. He was confident. He did not hesitate to look anyone in the eye, not even Austin or Mr. Emerson. Something about his confidence unsettled me. Perhaps because I, as a servant, was all too aware of my place. My brother, Henry, had been in service, too, and he'd exuded confidence. However, he'd never been so forthright as Mr. Howard's self-assuredness seemed.

After the family and guests entered, the Evergreens cook and I entered the house. I was the last to go inside. As I stepped through the doors, I inhaled the sweet scent of roses from the bouquet on the side table. It almost completely masked the smell of furniture polish, vinegar, and lemon. Almost. Even though the home was brand new and clean, Miss Susan had insisted everything had to be gone over again. She wanted to make the very best impression. Over the last several days, the house had been scrubbed top to bottom, and Miss Susan had held the house staff to the highest standard of cleanliness.

The interior of the Evergreens was spotless. I should know, as I felt like I had touched every last inch of the new home in my cleaning efforts. The windows sparkled, the woodwork shone, and the carpets were brushed to perfection.

The family retired to the parlor. "I'm very much looking forward to getting to know Mr. Emerson. He is a brilliant man." Austin accepted a cup of coffee from Katie, the housemaid, a quiet Irish girl whom I'd heard speak less than ten words since we met.

Susan nodded and accepted a coffee of her own. "He is. I'm grateful he agreed to come to Amherst so soon after his new book was published. I enjoyed *English Traits* immensely. It was enlightening. I am looking forward to his lecture on it. It will be fascinating to hear his point of view on the work and see it his way."

"I don't believe that you can truly see anything another person's way," Emily said. "If you could, you would have had all the same experiences as that one person across a lifetime, and Mr. Emerson's lifetime is twice as long as yours thus far."

"This is true, Sister," Austin said. "But we can also try to understand."

Emily seemed to consider this. "I do not know what someone would think of my work. It's very likely every person who might come across it will have a different interpretation or feeling. However, if it does indeed invoke feeling, then the purpose is secure."

"I don't know why you didn't share with Mr. Emerson that you write more than letters, Emily," Miss Lavinia said. "You do not know what the symposium will hold. You might not get another chance."

Emily sighed. "I can't believe I acted like such a fool myself. I was tongue-tied. I'm quite embarrassed."

"He will be here for the entire week. That will be plenty of time for you to share your work with him," Miss Susan said soothingly. "Vinnie, please don't give your sister the idea that she missed her chance."

Miss Lavinia rolled her eyes.

Austin folded his arms. "Emily, I believe it is best not to bother Mr. Emerson with your poems. He is here as a guest. He has enough work to do with his lectures; he does not need to read your poems as well. I do not want him to receive the impression we asked him to stay here in order to thrust your work upon him."

"My poems are not a bother, Brother. They are my life's blood."

I busied myself with the coffee tray as if it were the most important task in the world. I hated when I was in the room and the family was in the middle of a disagreement. I never knew if I should stay or retreat.

"Of course they are," Miss Susan said, shooting an angry glance at her husband. "Austin knows this, and I think Mr. Emerson would do well to take a look at Emily's work."

Emily placed a hand to her cheek. "That's if I can work up the courage."

"You will, my dear," Miss Susan said. "And if you don't, I will do it for you."

Austin grunted and sipped his tea.

Miss Susan narrowed her eyes at him. "If you are not careful, Husband, you will be just like your father in a matter of days. Standoffish and cold."

Austin scowled at her in return.

I inched back toward the door that led into the next room. I didn't want them to notice that I was there. Clearly there was tension between the newly married couple already.

Emily frowned and looked out the window. The far-off expression had returned. She was no longer listening to her family's conversation. It was interesting, really, how servants could be standing only a few feet away from their employers but be practically invisible, for all intents and purposes. I knew to show no reaction, to keep my eyes averted, and to stay about my daily tasks, but sometimes it was hard. And really, if people wanted to maintain their privacy and the integrity of their affairs, perhaps they shouldn't talk about intimate things in front of servants. I wasn't one to gossip, but I knew others did. I started to slip out of the room to continue with my next task, when Miss Susan said, "Mr. Howard is quite an attractive man, is he not?"

"My dear," Austin said. "We have not been married a month, and you are already looking at another man."

She laughed, and some of the tension in the room floated away. "It was an observation, Austin dear. Nothing more. I don't believe I was the only one who noticed." She gave a pointed look at Miss Lavinia.

Miss Lavinia stood and walked toward the door. "I should go home and check on Mother. Emily, are you coming with me?"

Emily continued to gaze out the window.

"Emily," Miss Lavinia said a bit more sharply. "Let's go home."

Emily blinked at Miss Lavinia as if she were coming up from deep under the water. "Yes, let's go home. I have thoughts that must be put to paper."

The sisters left the Evergreens parlor, and Miss Susan and Austin were left alone except for Katie and me. Katie soundlessly left the room, and I slipped out behind her but stopped just on the other side of the door when I heard Miss Susan speak again.

"Mr. Emerson and Mr. Howard are settling into their rooms. I told them supper will be at seven. Your family will walk over. It will be a grand affair."

"In some ways, Susan, I feel like you are more excited about the arrival of Mr. Emerson than you were about our wedding." There was no hiding the bitterness in his voice.

"Austin, my dear, you must understand. This is our chance to set ourselves up as the home of scholars when they are visiting Amherst. We might not be Concord, but we can establish ourselves as another literary center of the commonwealth. The college is here. Why should we not be of import to learned men like Ralph Waldo Emerson?"

I couldn't hear Austin's reply, but Susan's words rang clear. "I am not doing this for Emily or myself. It is for your legacy and the legacy of the Dickinson name. I'm thinking of our future children."

"You and Emily are always so in tune with each other. If she were not my sister, I should be embarrassed by the friendship." Austin's voice was cold.

Their footsteps came down the hallway from the direction of the kitchen, and I slipped into Austin's library and leaned against a bookshelf. I didn't know what made me want to hide like that. The rest of the staff were aware I was in the house cleaning. Even so, I knew in my heart that the younger Dickinsons' conversation was not one they would have wanted anyone else to hear, especially not a servant.

I pushed myself away from the bookshelf to get on with my many tasks. I had a long list to finish before I could leave and return to the homestead to begin working on my duties there. I was much relieved this was my last day at the Evergreens. The house was as clean as it could be for Mr. Emerson's arrival. Now, it was up to the Evergreens's maid to keep everything up to snuff.

I was about to leave the library when Mr. Howard stepped in. I stumbled backward.

"I'm sorry if I gave you a start," Mr. Howard said. "I couldn't rest like Waldo, so I came to see what there was to read in this house. Books are my passion."

I wrinkled my brow. It surprised me that he would address his employer by his Christian name. Emily had given me permission more than a year ago to call her as such, but whenever I spoke of her to anyone else, I always called her Miss Dickinson. Mr. Emerson seemed an austere man. It was hard for me to believe he had given Mr. Howard permission to address him in such a familiar way.

I nodded. "This is Mr. Austin Dickinson's library. You will find plenty to read here. The homestead next door has an impressive library as well."

He smiled easily. "Have you been told this or can you read yourself?"

I bristled at his comment. He should know as well as anyone that it was becoming more and more common for servants and the lower classes to be able to read.

"I read, sir."

"Then you are too smart and lovely for a housemaid. I'm surprised that you still find yourself in service. I would think some handsome dairyman would have scooped you up to be his bride by now."

My stomach twisted. "I enjoy working for the Dickinson family, and I must continue on with my tasks now. With the two households, there is always much to do."

"I am sure there is," he mused. "What is your name?"

"Willa," I said.

He grinned. "And do you have a last name, Willa?"

I swallowed, not liking how close he was, but I didn't want to step away for fear of insulting him. "Noble."

"Willa Noble," he said, as if he were tasting the sound of my name. "It is a very fitting name for you. It suits you."

I could not stand to be so near him any longer, so I stepped around him and out the door.

"Before you go, Willa Noble, was I correct in hearing that Miss Dickinson is a writer?" He gave me a pleasant smile, but there was no kindness in his face from what I could see.

I said nothing.

"I would greatly appreciate if you could ask her to share her poems with me. I can be a good conduit to Waldo with her work. I could give her the recognition that she deserves." He paused. "Or even better, you could give me some of her poems before speaking to her about it. That way Waldo could read them without her knowledge. If he doesn't care for them, she doesn't have to be any the wiser. It would save her great embarrassment. We both know that there are many women who *think* they can write poetry, but in reality it is just romantic drivel. Waldo would be looking for something with more substance."

I said nothing and left the room, feeling much like Eve in the Garden of Eden must have when she first spoke to the serpent.

CHAPTER FOUR

THE NEXT AFTERNOON, I walked to the college with a large hamper of food for the family, Mr. Emerson, and Mr. Howard. Carlo, Emily's large brown dog, walked beside me. His broad tongue hung out of his mouth in his excitement. He was eager to see his mistress. It wasn't often that Emily left the house without her faithful pet, but Mr. Dickinson insisted Carlo stay home with Margaret and me because the bear-size canine would not be welcome in the college lecture hall. Why, I didn't know. Everyone in Amherst knew that Carlo was the best-behaved dog a person could ever meet. The only time he was aggressive was when his felt his mistress was in danger.

Outside of the grand lecture hall, I told Carlo to sit by the door. He sighed, flopped down in a heap, and looked like a carpet that someone had left piled up on the stone steps.

I carried the hamper into the building. I found myself in an entryway with a shining copper chandelier overhead. In front of me stood three sets of double doors. It reminded me of the entrance to the sanctuary of the Dickinsons' church. But this was a church of scholarship, and much larger and grander than I had ever seen.

Slowly I opened the door farthest to the right and slipped into the hall. I heard Mr. Emerson before my eyes adjusted to the dimness in the room.

"I have traveled to England twice now, and each time I have gone, I have returned in awe of the English power and taciturn resilience. That is why I wrote this work, *English Traits*, so that I could share my knowledge and observations with you. However, I believe—no, I insist—in America we pursue American ideas and thoughts separate from the English. England might be our base, but from that we can grow into our own identity. Our writers are the greatest source of this. If you write, I challenge you to write in a truly unique and American voice. Do not turn back to Europe to find your way. Find your own way. Imitation is nothing more than the less lethal cousin to plagiarism. Is there a greater sin in the literary world?"

I searched the audience and finally spotted Emily, who was sitting next to Miss Lavinia in the second row. Emily's face shone as she stared at Mr. Emerson. It was as if she were absorbing his every word and imprinting it on her mind.

To my surprise, Mr. Howard was sitting next to Miss Lavinia. He had his head bent toward the younger Dickinson sister and seemed to be whispering into her ear. My fingers tightened around the handle of the heavy hamper.

Mr. Dickinson, Austin, and Miss Susan sat in the very front row, and from what I could tell seemed to be completely unaware of what was going on between Mr. Howard and Miss Lavinia.

"I thank you for this opportunity, and look forward to more time together this week." Mr. Emerson stepped back from the podium.

An elderly man using a walnut cane shuffled toward the podium. Even though he appeared to be in poor health, his voice was clear and strong and filled the hall. "Thank you, Mr. Emerson. I know already that everyone here has been affected by your words. I certainly have. I have taught literature here at the college for thirty years, and I have never had a thrill as great as welcoming such an esteemed man to speak on the topic of literature. When the new term begins this fall, I will tell my students to write in an American voice. This concludes this morning's lecture. After the noon meal, we will continue."

The audience stood and started to make its way toward the exits. Still holding the heavy hamper, I moved to the side of the door. Emily, Miss Lavinia, and Mr. Howard rose as one. I noted that Mr. Howard put his hand on Miss Lavinia's back as they moved out of the row.

"Willa, there you are," Emily said when she came upon me at the door. "We're all so very hungry after Mr. Emerson's talk. I must tell you that it was riveting. Don't you agree, Vinnie?"

Miss Lavinia was looking up from under her eyelashes at Mr. Howard, and her face turned a bright shade of pink, as if she had been caught doing something wrong. "Yes, what is it, Sister?"

Emily frowned and studied her sister as if she was realizing something for the first time. Her dark eyes darted in the direction of Mr. Howard, and a scowl formed on her delicate face. Emily pressed her lips together. "I said that we all enjoyed the lecture, but now, I wonder if you remember what the topic was."

Miss Lavinia frowned this time. "Of course I do. Where is the food, Willa? I'm famished." She marched out of the lecture hall with Mr. Howard a few paces behind her.

"This is going to be an issue," Emily muttered under her breath.

Before I could ask her what she meant by that—although I could fairly guess—she also went out of the hall, and I followed. Outside, I blinked in the bright sunlight. Even being in the hall for a short while, my eyes had grown accustomed to the dark space.

"Willa, bring that over here," Emily called. She stood by a group of three picnic tables under an enormous elm tree. It provided plenty of shade. Carlo the dog seemed to agree, because he was sound asleep at the base of the tree.

As quickly as I could, I made up the tables for the picnic. I covered them all with white linen cloths and set out the dishes, food, and fresh lemonade to drink.

"Oh, this is just lovely," Mr. Howard said in my ear as I removed the roast beef sandwiches from the hamper. I jumped because I hadn't realized he was that close to me.

He chuckled. "There must be something about me that makes you hop, Miss Willa. I will take it as a compliment."

"Is there anything else you require, Mr. Howard?" I asked, hoping that he would say nothing.

He looked up into the tree's branches. "Not at this time, and I am quite happy that it is not spring."

I wrinkled my brow in confusion. Emily must have also wondered what he meant because she said, "What do you have against the spring?"

"Nothing. It is what it has against me. As I have said, I have terrible hay fever, and budding trees in spring are the very worst to be around. From the end of March to the end of May, I stay inside as much as possible."

"How awful," Emily said. "I would die for flowers. I do not think I would stay away from them even if it meant my own demise."

"Be grateful that you don't have to make that choice," he said.

"Emily!" a woman's voice called. "I thought I saw you in the audience." An attractive blond woman Emily's age hurried over to her. She wore a pink afternoon dress and had a matching pink ribbon in her hair. Her appearance was in deep contrast with that of Emily, whose dark red hair was held at the nape of her neck in a knot, and her lovely but much duller brown dress hung on her thin frame.

"Isadora Foote! I have not seen you since Mount Holyoke," Emily cried.

Isadora smiled prettily. "I know. It has been years. I was so sad when you left the college after just one year. Most of the girls left actually."

"It was time for me to expand my learning on my own, as my father said. You stayed?"

Isadora nodded. "You always did seem to be overtaken with your own projects, even if they weren't part of the curriculum. I remember you frustrating more than one professor that first year."

Emily said nothing in reply.

Isadora went on. "Yes, I finished my education there. Are you still writing? I used to love the letters you sent me. I was sorry we lost touch over time and your letters stopped coming."

"I write," Emily said a little more forcefully than necessary.

"I do, too, but I have never had the ability for verse like you have. However, I continue for my own enjoyment if for no other reason. As my aunt reminds me, it is time to start a family."

"Are you intended?" Emily asked.

I winced at the bluntness of her question. I hoped that since Isadora was an old friend of Emily's, she'd remember how Emily at times could be a tad forward.

Isadora frowned. "No, I am not." The way she said it made me think there might have been more to it. However, being a servant, I wasn't in the position to pry, and Emily was looking in a different direction.

"How did you enjoy the lecture?" Emily asked.

"It was wonderful. This is the third time I have heard Mr. Emerson speak. I have traveled to Concord twice with my father for his talks."

"Is your father here?"

A dark cloud fell over Isadora's face. "No, he passed away last year. It was very sudden."

"I'm so sorry."

Isadora nodded. "I'm living in Boston, in my family's brownstone. My dear aunt is appalled that I have the nerve to live there alone. However, there is nothing she can do or say about it. I am of age and was my father's sole heir. What my father left behind has afforded me the ability to do a little traveling, such as coming to Amherst this week for the symposium. I'm staying with friends."

"Oh, who?" Emily asked.

"Ruben and Cate Lynn Thayer. Cate Lynn is a good friend of mine I met in Boston."

"I know Cate Lynn from my Amherst school days. You all must come to our evening meal tonight at the Evergreens," Emily said. "Mr. Emerson is staying with my brother and his wife."

"I have never had the chance to speak to Mr. Emerson directly. I don't even know what I would say."

"You can always just sit and listen."

Isadora nodded. "Thank you. I will let Cate Lynn and her husband know my plans."

"Invite them to come with you. We always have more than enough food. They would be quite welcome."

"That is gracious of you. Yes, I will ask them." Isadora smiled.

"Join us now for the picnic. Margaret, our head maid, always packs much more than we can ever eat."

"I'm looking forward to the meal," Mr. Howard said from the far end of the table. "Sitting for such a time in a chair makes a man hungry. A person wasn't built to sit so long."

Mr. Howard stepped forward. "Miss Dickinson, can you introduce me to your lovely friend?" Before Emily could speak a word, he took Isadora's hand in his. "I'm Luther Howard, Mr. Emerson's secretary. I'm traveling with him as he tours, speaking on his new work, *English Traits*."

Isadora removed her hand from his. "Isadora Foote. It's very nice to meet you, Mr. Howard." Her tone was polite, if a little disinterested. "I have great admiration for your employer."

He nodded. "This is true for everyone I meet. As of yet, I have not met a learned man ..." He paused. "Or woman who has not admired Mr. Emerson." Mr. Howard stood up straighter. "It's very nice to make your acquaintance, Miss Foote. And did I overhear the two of you talking about your writing? Women writers are underestimated in my thinking."

"That's because men make the publishing decisions," Isadora said, looking him in the eye.

"Yes, well, that is how society works." He laughed uncomfortably. "Imagine if women made the choices."

Isadora and Emily scowled at him in turn. I would have guessed my expression looked much the same. I had been looking forward to Mr. Emerson's visit just as much as the rest of the family and staff. However, now, I could not wait for it to end because it meant Mr. Howard would crawl back under whatever rock he had slithered out from under.

Mr. Emerson, Mr. Dickinson, and Austin walked toward the picnic tables, and Mr. Howard stepped back.

"Your comments on the American writer were quite interesting," Mr. Dickinson said. "What do you mean when you say there should be a form of national identity?"

Mr. Emerson ran his hand down one long sideburn and then the other as he considered his response. "It's something that I have thought of for many years. All great nations have a distinct voice of the people. With all the immigrants and cultures that pour onto our shores, how can we achieve that as we do not have ethnicity as a common ground?"

Austin looked like he wanted to say something, but before he did, Mr. Emerson added, "And I do not see our lack of common ethnicity as a fault; in fact, in the end, it will be our greatest strength as a nation, as we will come together to make a new people here in America different from that of Europe."

Before the conversation could continue, a ruckus came from the direction of the road. A ramshackle wagon rolled onto the green. A man in a broad-brimmed felt hat sat on the wagon bench. He had a tambourine in his hand and a bugle at his lips. He shook the tambourine over his head and blew the bugle for all he was worth.

His gray mule flicked her ears as if in irritation at the sound, but also in acceptance, as if she knew nothing could be done to stop it. The wagon came to rest about fifty yards away from our picnic. Residents and guests who were on campus to listen to Mr. Emerson's lecture stared at the mule, wagon, and the man in the beige linen suit. He dropped his instruments on the seat and hopped from the wagon.

"Hello, Amherst! I'm here to change your life! I have the goods and wares you need to make every day fine and dandy! Ladies, do you want the doldrums of housework to improve? I can do that for you. Gents, are you interested in making money? I can show you how! Step right up and learn all about it!"

Mr. Dickinson stood up from the picnic table and addressed the man. "This is not the place for a lowly peddler. This is a place of learning."

The peddler looked in his direction. "Oh my, what a distinguished gathering I have stumbled upon! What great luck indeed! I know that I have something here in my wagon to spark your interest."

The mule *hee-hawed*, and Carlo jumped up from his shady spot under the tree and stood next to Emily. He was ready to protect his petite mistress if the need arose.

"Ladies, do you love your garden, but are devastated when your flowers are ravaged by pests? Are beetles after your roses, and aphids on your dahlias? I have the cure!" He walked over to his wagon and opened one of the dozen little doors on the side of it. He pulled out a yellow box. "This, my friends, is all you need to save your gardens. It is pyrethrin, and I can guarantee with just one treatment you will see a real difference."

"Do something about this," Mr. Dickinson said to anyone who might listen.

Austin started to get up from the picnic bench, too, but Mr. Howard was already on his way to face the peddler. "Do not worry, Mr. Dickinson. I'll rid us of this pest so that we can enjoy this lovely picnic."

The peddler put the yellow box back into the wagon, closed the compartment, and opened another. This time he pulled out a green box. "Ladies, are you tired of stains?" the peddler bellowed. "I have the solution. Don't throw away perfectly good clothing for a mere spot! Just like Lady Macbeth, get that spot out!"

"I'm sorry, sir," Mr. Howard said as he approached the peddler. "But you have stumbled upon a private society lecture. This is not the place for your kind of nonsense. I will have to ask you to move along."

"A lecture! I would love to hear it. As you can tell, I am quite an orator myself." He placed a hand to his chest. "I have been told my voice is so soothing that I should have been a stage performer. But who would want to be trapped inside a theater all day when I can be walking the streets of this great nation sharing and selling my discoveries to our fine ladies and gentlemen. Gentlemen like yourself!"

"That's all well and good," Mr. Howard said. "But this is not the place. You must go. Take your bobbles and potions somewhere else."

"My bobbles and potions? Do you mock me, sir?" the peddler asked. "Even the most learned man needs to know about my spices. If your meals are bland and tasteless, I have a solution all the way from the Far East!"

"What is your name?" Mr. Howard asked.

The peddler removed his hat, showing off the top of his bald head in the process. "I am so honored you asked. I am Paulo Vitali, traveling peddler and adventurer of our fair countryside. What is your name, sir? You are such a well-dressed gentleman, so I am sure I have heard it."

"I am Luther Howard."

Paulo shouted something in Italian and then pulled back his arm and punched Mr. Howard square in the nose. The young secretary stumbled back, fell to his knees, and covered his face as blood gushed through his fingers. Miss Lavinia screamed and ran to Mr. Howard's side.

CHAPTER FIVE

For a long moment, no one moved or spoke. Everyone was in such state of shock over Paulo's seemingly unwarranted attack on Mr. Howard.

Miss Lavinia removed her handkerchief from the sleeve of her dress and pressed it to Mr. Howard's face. "Luther, are you all right?"

He winced and smiled up at her. "You are too kind." Blood soaked the handkerchief. He was a mess.

I grabbed several dish towels from the picnic hamper and hurried over. Before I could give them to Mr. Howard, Miss Lavinia snatched them out of my hands. "Here, Luther," she said, handing him the cloths.

"Someone run to the police! That peddler needs to be arrested for assault," Mr. Dickinson said. "I have never seen such an outrageous display in my life."

"No, no!" Mr. Howard managed to stand up. With the

cloth pressed up against his face, his voice was muffled. "There is no need for that."

"That man hit you," Miss Lavinia said. "He needs to face the consequences. Your nose could be broken."

Paulo continued to rant in Italian, but I couldn't understand a word of it. I recognized the language because one of the baking assistants at Mrs. Cutter's Bakery uptown was Italian and constantly muttered in his own language. When I asked, Mrs. Cutter told me that was the language that he had been speaking.

"No, no, just let him go." Mr. Howard held one hand to his face with the other gripping Miss Lavinia's arm for balance. "This is Mr. Emerson's week of lectures, and I don't want to bring a black cloud over it with this little mishap. I will just return to the Evergreens and patch myself up. Lavinia, would you be so kind as to escort me across the road?"

Before anyone could protest, Miss Lavinia helped Mr. Howard to his feet and supported him as they walked in the direction of Main Street and the Dickinson property.

I stood by Isadora as they walked away, and she watched them with her arms folded.

Mr. Dickinson walked over to Paulo. "Mr. Howard might be too charitable a man to press charges in this case, but I can assure you I am not. Now, leave if you don't want to spend the night in jail. Amherst is an educated and civil town. We do not stand for such antics."

Paulo held his right fist in his left hand as if it pained him. He had hit Mr. Howard very hard. "You do not know what that man is capable of. He is a monster, but since you have been so unkind, you can make that discovery on your own. Don't tell

me that I didn't warn you when the time comes. You're going
to wish that you never met him. He will ruin all your lives as
he did so many others." Paulo climbed back into his wagon
and drove away.

"Well," Mr. Emerson said. "That was quite a display, now,
wasn't it? Shall we eat?"

"Mr. Emerson." Emily spoke. "Are you not concerned
about Mr. Howard's welfare?"

"I am," he said. "However, he is in much better hands with
your sister than he ever would be with me, and he would want
me to continue with the lectures. You heard him say that
yourself."

"Yes, but—"

"Emily," Mr. Dickinson snapped. "Do not question our
guest."

Emily looked at her father, and it appeared that there was
something she wanted to say to him. She stopped herself from
speaking, but I, for one, wished that I could hear what she was
thinking.

After everyone went back into the lecture hall and I re-
packed the considerably lighter hamper to return it to the
homestead kitchen, Carlo and I left the campus. I knew that I
should have gone straight home with the hamper, but I turned
in the opposite direction, toward downtown. Part of me was
terribly curious as to where Paulo the peddler had gone.

Peddlers were common visitors to the back laundry door of
the homestead. They stopped at the service entrances of
wealthy homes as they made their way through the county.
They tried to sell everything from books to cleaning solutions
to the latest gadgets. Knowing how frugal Mr. Dickinson was,

Margaret had the tendency to chase them away. I was always a little disappointed when she did. I was curious about the wares they sold from the heavy packs on their backs.

I had never seen a peddler in a wagon with as many compartments as Paulo Vitali's. Who knew what kinds of treasures he had inside of it?

When I made it to the downtown area, it took me no time at all to find him.

"Look at this! The stain is gone!" he cried from the middle of a crowd. I recognized him by his voice because I couldn't see him.

There were so many people standing in the street around him that I could barely see the wagon.

The crowd clapped at his proclamation about the stain.

Carlo whimpered at my side.

I looked down at the big dog. "I know, I know. We need to get home. I just want to see what he's selling."

With one hand tightly around the handle of the hamper and another at Carlo's collar, I squeezed into the crowd. Carlo had a way of encouraging people to step aside due to his sheer size.

A young couple stood next to me. The woman was beautiful with silky dark hair and wore a red-and-cream-striped dress. The man with her was just as attractive in his smart blue suit and perfectly combed hair.

"We should go home, dear," the man said.

"Oh, just a little while longer. Please? I find it all so fascinating."

"You want to buy something," he said. His tone turned churlish.

She looked up at him. "So what if I do. I have the money to do it, don't I?"

The man looked away. "As you wish."

Another man stepped in their place. "Is there something you need from the peddler, Willa?"

I looked up and found Officer Matthew Thomas looking down at me. My heart skipped a beat. It had been doing that a lot lately when I came across him. I told myself it was simply because I startled easily. He looked very smart this afternoon in his dark blue uniform and police cap. He held a wooden baton loosely at his side.

"Are you here in your official capacity, Matthew?"

He smiled. "I am. Several of the shopkeepers are nervous about the scene the peddler is making, and I am here to make sure that it doesn't get out of hand. As far as I can tell, he's only giving them competition to sell their wares. He's not doing anything illegal."

"Did you hear about the scene at the college?"

"I did," he said slowly. "How do you know about it?"

"I was there taking luncheon to the family. They were all at Mr. Emerson's lecture. He is staying with Austin and Susan Dickinson at the Evergreens."

He nodded.

"Will the peddler be in trouble for hitting Mr. Howard?"

"He could be if Mr. Howard wants to press charges. He hasn't yet."

I nodded.

"I have the finest cinnamon you can find in all the commonwealth!" Paulo cried.

"I'd like some." A woman raised her hand.

"Wonderful!" Paulo exclaimed.

The woman's decision seemed to break the ice, and more people came forward ready to buy from the wagon. Matthew watched it all with a wary eye as if he expected something to happen. What, I didn't know.

"Before you came here, there was a young couple standing next to me."

"I saw them," he said, not taking his eyes off Paulo and his customers.

"Do you know who they were?"

"It was Ruben and Cate Lynn Thayer. They have a large estate on the other side of town."

"Oh!" My eyes widened.

He glanced down at me for just a second before his gaze returned to the crowd. "Does that surprise you for some reason?"

"In a way. I had never heard their names before, and this is the second time that I heard them mentioned today. They have a houseguest, Isadora Foote, who is staying with them. She is an old friend of Miss Dickinson's. Miss Dickinson invited Isadora to dinner at the Evergreens tonight and asked her to bring the Thayers with her."

He glanced at me again. "And you find that odd?"

"It's not odd," I said, but even to my own ears I sounded unconvinced.

Carlo whimpered next to me.

I looked down at the big brown dog. He whimpered again.

"All right," I said. "You have been away from home long enough." To Matthew, I said, "I should return to the homestead. Margaret is making the meal for tonight and will want my help. I don't think she yet knows that three more people will be added to the party."

He grinned. "She will be thrilled to hear the news."

I chuckled. "Not likely."

His face fell. "I wish that I could walk you back, but I am assigned to stay here until the peddler moves along."

I heard Paulo shout out about his product that was guaranteed to kill beetles and aphids. I knew for a fact we could use some of that in the Dickinson garden and we had plenty on hand too.

"I will be fine. I have Carlo with me."

Matthew nodded. "Willa, I know I promised to be patient, and we have not spoken about it in many months. But have you thought about what I asked you last spring?"

My chest tightened. I knew that he spoke of his proposal of marriage. I had refused him once. The second time he asked, I said that I needed time to think on it. That had been well over a year ago. "Matthew," I said barely above a whisper.

He gave a crisp nod. "You need more time. All right. Be careful walking home." His tone wasn't angry, but I could hear the hurt in it.

I wished that I were brave enough to reach out and squeeze his hand to comfort him. Instead I said, "Goodbye."

CHAPTER SIX

Later that afternoon, I helped Margaret prepare the evening meal. The family would be eating at the Evergreens again, but Mr. Dickinson had asked Margaret to cook her lamb roast. He did not care much for Miss Susan's new cook at the Evergreens.

If the cook or Miss Susan was insulted by Mr. Dickinson's declaration, I never heard anything about it. I believed that everyone who lived or worked in either home just became accustomed to Mr. Dickinson's particular ways.

As I peeled the potatoes, I watched Horace hurry around the barn with his pruning shears. The gardener never seemed to stop moving. I'd known many hard workers throughout my life, but I didn't know any who worked as hard as Horace.

"How am I supposed to take this pot of stew over to the Evergreens and keep it warm?" Margaret complained. "The family never thinks of the practicality of things. I'm supposed to just find a way."

"We could carry it over and put it on the Evergreens stove top," I suggested.

"Do you have any idea how much that pot will weigh? I don't want to throw my back out over it."

Through the window, Cody stopped to speak to Horace. The two men seemed to be talking about something important.

"I'll carry it, and I'll ask Cody for help."

"Very well. If we're going, it should be soon. Go find Cody and bring him here."

I set my knife and the potato I was chopping down on the cutting board and wiped my hands on a tea towel. Before Margaret could come up with another solution, I slipped out the back kitchen door.

"It is none of our business," Horace told Cody as I approached. "Only when their actions spill over into what is right and wrong should we step in." Horace arched his brow when he saw me. "Willa, will you be helping in the garden again today?"

I shook my head. "I don't think I will be able to until Mr. Emerson leaves. There is much going on in the house."

"So I hear," Horace said, eyeing Cody as he spoke.

I wanted to ask them what they had been speaking about, but held back. If Emily had been with me, she would have asked, because she had the nerve and authority to. I had neither.

"Can we help you with something else?" Horace asked.

"Yes," I said. "I wanted to ask Cody if he'd help me carry Margaret's roast over to the Evergreens."

Horace clicked his tongue. "If Margaret was cooking dinner and the family is eating at the Evergreens, why did she not make the roast there? Am I the only one who makes practical decisions on these grounds?"

"You know she doesn't like to use anyone else's kitchen. No one puts things in the proper place like she does," I said with a smile.

Horace snorted.

In reality, Horace and Margaret were a lot alike. They both liked things done a certain way. I had thought many times that the pair of them would be a good match, but maybe not, because they were both too particular and would drive each other mad.

"I can help," Cody said. His Irish lilt was more pronounced, as it seemed to be when he was upset or excited about something. At the moment, he didn't look excited in the least.

I thanked him, and the two of us went to the kitchen while Horace went back to his first love—the Dickinsons' garden.

After receiving detailed instructions from Margaret about the right way to carry the roast and the heat to set it on when we reached the Evergreens kitchen, Cody and I walked out the laundry room door, around the back of the house, across the driveway, and to the wood chip–covered path that led to the Evergreens.

New trees planted by Austin lined either side of the path. He had a love for trees that rivaled Emily's love of flowers.

Our steps were quiet on the path as neither of us said a word. This was unusual. Cody was a talker.

"Cody, is something wrong?" I asked when we were half-way down the path. I knew we would not be overheard by anyone at the homestead or the Evergreens.

The sound of my voice made him jump, and the roast

sloshed in the pot. Thankfully, the lid remained intact, keeping the contents inside.

"Careful," I said. "Why are you so jumpy? It's not like you."

He swallowed hard and his Adam's apple bobbed up and down like it was in the water tub at the fall festival. "Horace said not to speak on it. He usually knows about these things and gives good advice."

I frowned. "If you're telling me, you're not speaking on it. I'm just another servant. What can I do? It seems to me that it will help you to get it out. You are quite tense. I have never seen you like this."

He seemed to consider this. "I saw that young man kiss Miss Lavinia!" It came out all in a rush.

I nearly dropped the pot this time. I thought he was going to say something like he had gotten into an argument with Jeremiah York, whom he shared his cabin with on the property. What he said about Miss Lavinia was the very last thing I would have expected.

"What young man?" I asked.

"The one staying at the Evergreens." He lowered his voice even though I was certain no one could overhear us.

"Mr. Howard?" I asked.

"Yes. He kissed her."

"And what did she do?" I asked.

"She said she had to tend to her mother and ran to the homestead."

"Was she upset?" I asked.

"I—I don't know. I think shocked—yes, shocked—is what she was. But when she ran by me, she was smiling."

My eyes widened. "Did she see you?"

"No, I was in the summerhouse tending to the small roses there. The beetles are frightful this time of year. I was treating them. When they are better, I will plant the roses with the others in the garden."

"When did this happen?" I asked.

"Just a half hour before you came out of the kitchen."

"Is this what you were speaking to Horace about when I walked up?"

He nodded. "He said for me to keep my mouth shut about it. He says the private affairs of the family are none of my concern."

"It is good advice. Of course, if Miss Lavinia was in any danger, you should say something, but it sounds like that wasn't the case."

"She may not have believed that she was in danger, but that doesn't mean that danger isn't nearby," he said.

I wanted to ask him what he meant by that, but by this time, we had reached the end of the path. There were two Evergreens yardmen trimming the lawn around the house. I said nothing more, due to the risk of being overheard.

Cody and I carried the pot to the back door that led into the Evergreens kitchen. The cook, who was a friendly Irish woman, stepped aside so that we could put it on the stove. Cody stepped back outside.

She smiled at me. "I suppose Margaret has detailed instructions telling me how to keep this warm."

"She does," I said with a smile, and I relayed those instructions to the cook.

The cook chuckled. "So keep it warm on the stove until

dinner. I think I can do that. I'm convinced that Margaret doesn't believe I know my way around a kitchen."

"Margaret doesn't trust anyone in the kitchen other than herself," I said.

The cook put her hands on her wide hips and laughed. I had expected that Cody would be outside waiting for me to walk back to the homestead when I left the kitchen, but he was gone.

CHAPTER SEVEN

AFTER DELIVERING THE roast to the Evergreens cook, I went upstairs to see where I could be of help to Katie as she feverishly prepared for the evening meal. I found her in the hallway. She yelped. She was holding a stack of freshly pressed bedsheets.

"Katie, are you quite all right?" I asked.

"Yes, yes." She looked around as if afraid that someone might catch her not working. "There is just so much to do. I have to finish setting the table and making the drinks for this evening, and now Mr. Howard wants fresh linens for his room. Apparently, he soiled the other ones after he was attacked on the campus. I do not have the time to change his bed linens now, and I don't understand why this can't wait until they are all seated for dinner."

I took the sheets from her hands. "Let me take care of the linens, and you go back to your normal tasks."

"Oh! You would do that?" She was breathless. "I need to learn the courses from the cook."

"Yes, I'm happy to." To prove my point, I turned toward the stairs and started walking upstairs.

"Thank you, Willa." She hurried toward the dining room.

On the second floor of the house, the wooden boards beneath my feet creaked with every step that I took. The Evergreens was still very much a new structure, and it was settling into its foundation. There was a faint smell of pine and wallpaper paste in the air that hadn't fully dissipated since construction.

Before I reached the room where Mr. Howard was staying, I heard angry voices. "I am telling you, sir, that I put the papers right here in this drawer just last evening. I would not lie to you."

Mr. Emerson's voice was calm but firm. "I'm beginning to believe that is a lie, Luther. You lie to me often. Now that I have discovered what you are up to, I cannot abide it. Is there a greater sin to commit against a writer than what you have done?"

"I tell you, I did not do it!" All of Mr. Howard's poise was gone. "You are accusing me of a crime that I did not commit."

"I can no longer trust you. I can't have a secretary whom I can't trust with my work. I have no choice but to dismiss you."

"But, sir, I did nothing wrong."

I pressed my back up against the new wallpaper in the hallway and held the linens to my chest.

"Don't lie to me," Mr. Emerson said. "I have been warned in the past about your reputation, and I foolishly felt like I knew your character better than these claims. Shame on me for being deceived, but it stops tonight."

"But, sir!" Mr. Howard cried.

"I have made my decision. You may stay through this week's lectures, but after, you will need to find new employment."

"You will be sorry that you did this." Mr. Howard's tone turned dark. "I know too much. You have too much at stake if I share what I know. I could ruin you."

"Do not threaten me," Mr. Emerson snapped. There was a pause, and then Mr. Emerson said, "I will see you at dinner. If you want a letter of reference from me to help you find a new position, you will say nothing about this to the Dickinsons or to anyone else while we are in Amherst. Understood?"

The hinges of the room's door creaked open, and I jumped through the closest doorway.

I examined my surroundings. I realized that I was in what must have been meant to be a nursery. There was little in the space other than a crib in the corner. I was surprised to see it. This was one of the few places in the house where I hadn't yet been during my week of cleaning. It had never occurred to me that Miss Susan would want to be a mother so soon after her marriage. I wondered if Emily knew. Did this mean Miss Susan was already with child, or was she just getting prepared for when the time came?

I shook these thoughts from my head as I heard the two men leave Mr. Howard's room. The sound of their footsteps receded down the hallway and then down the stairs. I waited a few more minutes before I left the nursery.

I stepped into Mr. Howard's room and found that his

bedclothes did have a bit of blood on them, likely from the bloody nose that Paulo the peddler had given him. As far as I could tell, that was all that was amiss. I changed the linens quickly and left the room, carrying the dirty bedclothes with me to take to the laundry.

For the next several hours, I helped Katie as best I could to prepare, as it was clear to me she was out of her depth. Just a few minutes before the dinner hour came, the Dickinsons from the homestead walked into the Evergreens parlor. At the moment, I was the only person in the parlor ready to greet them. Mrs. Dickinson slid into one of the chairs as if she were exhausted from the stroll between the two homes. Very possibly, she was. Her skin was pale, and she anxiously twisted her small white hands in her lap.

Mr. Dickinson strode around the room, stopping every few feet to look at one of the adornments Susan had selected for the space. He'd frown at it and move on to the next one.

Emily went to the window and looked out, and Miss Lavinia continually smoothed her hair as if she were trying to reassure herself that she wasn't going bald.

No one spoke to me.

"How wonderful that you are all here," Miss Susan said as she came into the room. She was followed by Austin. "We are just waiting for Isadora and the Thayers, whom Emily invited to dinner. I am looking forward to making their acquaintance." She glanced back at the doorway. "I'm sure Mr. Emerson and Mr. Howard will be down shortly as well." She glanced at me as if surprised to see me in the room. "That will be all, Willa."

I nodded, as I had been dismissed from the parlor. I tried

to catch Emily's eye as I went, but she stared out the window, lost in her own thoughts.

I went back to the Evergreens kitchen and was surprised to see Margaret there. It seemed that she felt the need to oversee her roast after all.

"Willa!" Margaret snapped. "Where have you been?"

"I—"

"I don't want to hear it. Get into the dining room. Katie needs help. Incompetent girl. I don't think she will last long here," she said.

By the time I made it to the dining room, the entire Dickinson family, Ruben and Cate Lynn Thayers, Mr. Howard, Mr. Emerson, and Isadora Foote were all seated at the table and starting their meal with a summer squash soup.

"Mrs. Thayer," Mr. Dickinson said. "I am quite grateful to have you and your husband at our party. Had I known that Myron and Beth Anne Mortimore's daughter was back living on their old estate, I would have invited you sooner. How is Pleasant Hill?"

"It is—" Mrs. Thayer was about to answer, when her husband interjected.

"We have renamed it Thayer Manor. We thought that was more fitting and would work better for the children we plan to have in the future."

Across the table from Mr. Thayer, Isadora Foote made a face in her soup course.

Mr. Dickinson turned to Mr. Emerson. "Myron and Beth Ann Mortimore were very passionate about the abolitionist movement from the start. Myron was in the railroad business and gave thousands of dollars to help the cause."

Mr. Emerson lifted his teacup, but he didn't take a sip. "I admire that very much."

Mrs. Thayer nodded. "Thank you, and I am continuing my parents' work by donating and raising money. I will not stop until slavery is gone forever."

Mr. Dickinson pressed his lips together. "Yes, quite." He changed the subject and looked to Mr. Howard. "Mr. Howard, how is your nose?" he asked. "Your under eyes are beginning to turn an impressive shade of purple."

Mr. Howard chuckled. "It's quite all right. That old peddler really gave me a wallop."

"Do you have any idea why that man hit you?" Mr. Thayer asked. "I still couldn't believe it when I heard the news. Things like this just don't happen in Amherst."

"Peddlers and travelers like him have to be a little bit off to do the work that they do," Mr. Howard said in a dismissive way. "They are alone on the road for days on end. The only time that they spend with society when they are is trying to convince others to buy products that they don't need, and then the peddler moves on before the person can realize that he has been fooled. He was deranged. It's the only explanation that can make any sense." He forced a laugh. "But then again, how do you make sense of a senseless act?"

"That is quite a harsh statement to make about a man that you don't know," Emily interjected. "I don't believe that it is right or fair to make that kind of judgment on the state of any person's mind, and that is all the more true about someone you do not know personally."

"Emily, there is no reason to raise your hackles," Austin said. "Mr. Howard is probably quite correct that this Paulo fellow isn't of sound mind. His behavior was that of a mad-man."

Emily looked as if she wanted to argue with her brother, but then Mrs. Thayer spoke. "Emily, Isadora tells me that you went to school together."

"We did. We attended Mount Holyoke together. I stayed only one year, at my father's command." She glanced at her father.

Mr. Dickinson scowled slightly as if he was attempting to determine whether his eldest daughter had slighted him in some way.

Mrs. Thayer shook her head. "What a small world it is."

"Where do you hail from, Ms. Foote?" Miss Lavinia asked.

"I live in Boston now in a home that was my parents'. They left me with a comfortable life, and I work here and there in offices in the city as a notetaker or correspondent when I need additional funds. However, that isn't often. My father was a very successful businessman and made good investments."

"Oh," Mr. Dickinson said, sounding intrigued. "What did he invest in?"

"The railroad mostly. He was one of the first investors in it and did quite well. However, I don't mind work when I need to take some on. I like to stay busy."

"This is true," Mrs. Thayer said. "Isadora sends me long let-ters of what she does during her week, and by the look of them, it appears that she never sits still. I suppose a lot of women living alone are like that as they try to fill their days."

"You live in the city alone?" Mr. Dickinson asked.

Isadora looked the patriarch in the eye. "I do."

"How do you get on?" Mr. Dickinson asked with shock in his voice.

She wrinkled her brow. "I have already told you that I have the funds to take care of myself."

"But surely, you want to marry for safety and protection. A young woman like yourself should not be living alone."

Isadora sipped her drink and then said, "There was a time that I thought I would marry, but when all of that fell apart, I realized marriage doesn't have any true advantages for me. The advantage would be to the man who by marriage has access to my position and wealth. The likelihood that I would marry a man in a higher position than I am is slim. Therefore, I see no need for it."

"That's exactly how Vinnie and I feel," Emily chimed in. "What are the advantages for a woman to marry when she is born into the status that we have?"

From my spot in the corner of the room, I saw Mr. Howard studying Miss Lavinia as if he were seeing her in a new light. Miss Lavinia stared down into her soup. It was impossible to believe that she did not sense his gaze, as she seemed to be so aware of his presence.

"It is a wonder how the young think today," Mr. Emerson said. "Is it not? It was my understanding that a young woman married because of the pursuit of caring for a husband and children. It seemed that I have been wrong in that assumption all this time."

"Times are changing," Mr. Thayer said. "However, I believe most women can be swayed into marriage. Isn't that right, my love?" He smiled at his pretty wife. "It did take me quite a while to convince my sweet Cate Lynn that I was the man for her."

Mrs. Thayer smiled at her husband. "You were very persistent, my dear."

Emily wrinkled her nose at the two of them as if she didn't like their conversation. However, she didn't comment on it, and went on to say, "I wish to get back to the peddler. I don't think he's mad. He had to have had a reason to strike you, Mr. Howard. He seemed fine and cheerful until you told him your name. Do you know him? Do you have any idea why he would have such a reaction to you?"

Mr. Howard laughed. "Those sorts of people don't have to have a reason for their behavior."

"And what sort of people are they?" Emily asked with an arched brow.

"Emily, please remember your manners," Mr. Dickinson said sternly. To Mr. Emerson and the rest of the guests, he said, "You will have to forgive my eldest daughter. She is quite opinionated."

Emily frowned at her father, but there must have been something in his expression that told her he was serious. She said nothing more, and the conversation moved on to more mundane topics. Mrs. Dickinson asked Mr. Emerson about his travels, and he shared some of his observations. Austin spoke of the construction of his home.

I noted that Mr. Howard was seated next to Miss Lavinia, and she had hardly touched her appetizer of onion tart. She smiled at every small comment he made. From across the table, Emily watched the pair of them with a frown on her face.

Mr. Dickinson also seemed to take note of their exchange, and appeared to be as happy about it as Emily was.

Mr. Howard sipped at his tea as he spoke to Miss Lavinia. He shifted in his seat and pulled at his collar. He took another long sip from the teacup.

"Mr. Howard, are you quite all right?" Mr. Emerson asked, apparently taking note of the young man's sudden discomfort.

"I am, sir." His voice was raspy. "I think I just need to step away for a few moments. I might have gotten overheated in the lecture hall today. It was such a warm day in an enclosed space."

Before anyone could argue, he got up from the table and went out the door.

Miss Lavinia started to move as if she planned to follow him.

"Lavinia, stay at the table," Mr. Dickinson said. His voice left no room for argument.

The youngest Dickinson settled back into her seat and stared at the doorway with a concerned expression on her face.

The meal went on, and Mr. Emerson resumed the story he was telling about a visit to Liverpool, England. His description of the city and the people was quite entertaining, and I found myself engrossed in the tale. It took me a little longer than normal to notice that Emily was waving me over to her chair.

I hurried to her side, and when she motioned me to move closer to her, I bent my ear to her mouth. "Can you please go check on Mr. Howard? He was looking a trifle green, and I'm concerned he might be ill. He's been gone nearly twenty minutes now."

I nodded and stepped back from Emily's chair. As I left the

room, I felt Mr. Emerson's eyes on my back. I couldn't help but go over the conversation I'd heard between him and Mr. Howard. Was it possible Mr. Howard was so upset from being dismissed that he could not bring himself to sit at the dinner party as if nothing were wrong? I couldn't say I blamed him. It would be very difficult to stay if I were in the same position.

I went up the back servants' stairs to the secretary's room. All the doors in the corridor were closed but for Mr. Howard's. I frowned. I distinctly remembered closing it when I changed the bed linens. Perhaps Mr. Howard was in the room.

An uneasy feeling fell over me. If he really was ill, I didn't think he would want me to intrude on his misery.

"Mr. Howard?" I called tentatively when I reached the door that was open a crack and knocked. The last thing I would want to do was startle a sick man.

There was no answer, and I knew I had to see if he was all right. I wished Emily hadn't sent me on this mission.

I stepped into the young man's room. There was no one inside. However, most surprising of all, the room was a mess. And not in the way many young men make a mess of their rooms. I had worked in a boardinghouse as a maid before coming to the Dickinson home, so I had seen how many young people kept their rooms and how disordered they could all be.

This untidiness was different. All the drawers were open in the bureau. Mr. Howard's clothes were strewn all over the floor, and the pockets turned out of every article of clothing. Papers were scattered across the desk as if they had been examined and discarded in great haste. At the top of the pile, there seemed to be a manuscript of sorts.

The bed linens had been ripped from the mattress, and the

mattress itself was off kilter. Mr. Howard's room had been thoroughly searched, and I guessed Mr. Howard himself hadn't been the one to do it.

From where I stood, I could see every inch of the room, and there was no sign of Emerson's assistant.

Where was he?

I walked over to the window. It was eight in the evening, but the sun was just beginning to fall toward the horizon. I saw a man staggering in the garden. By his clothing, it looked like it was Mr. Howard. If he was ill, what was he doing in the garden? Was he so disoriented?

I wasn't the only one who noticed him. Cody came into view and started to walk toward him. I could hear his voice as he called out, but I couldn't make out the words he said.

I left the window and hurried down the back stairs. When I was on the first floor again, I went out the back door. By the time I made it outside, I could no longer see Mr. Howard or Cody. However, since they were going toward the homestead, I decided to follow the path leading from the Evergreens.

Just as I reached the perennial garden at the homestead, Cody came running in my direction. He grabbed me by both my arms. "Willa, Willa, you have to help me."

"Cody, calm yourself! What on earth is wrong?"

"It's the young gentleman. The young gentleman who is here with Mr. Emerson."

"Yes, Mr. Howard. What about him?" I asked a tad impatiently.

"He's dead."

CHAPTER EIGHT

I FELT ALL the blood drain from my face. "Whatever do you mean?"

"He is dead in the patch of black-eyed Susans."

"Show me," I demanded. As much as I didn't want to see what Cody described, I had to make sure it was true before I ran back and told the Dickinson family. Perhaps Mr. Howard was just ill and in his delirium fell over into the flowers. He might be sick or hurt and just need to rest. Maybe something he ate hadn't agreed with him, but he couldn't be dead. Dead was unbelievable.

If he needed rest, why not go to his room for the night? Or had he, and then saw the state of the room and ran outside? But when he made the discovery, why didn't he come back to the dinner and alert the party? Surely, Austin and Miss Susan would want to know if there was some sort of intruder in their home, because who but an intruder would ransack Mr. Howard's room so horribly?

No amount of rationalization could change the facts. When I reached the perennial garden, I realized Cody had been right in his description. Mr. Howard's lifeless body lay in the patch of black-eyed Susans. His neck was turned to the side, and those bright blue eyes I thought had been so striking the first time I saw him were unseeing and dull. Their distinctive color seemed unearthly with no light of life within them.

I put a hand over my mouth to hold back a scream. Even though I had been prepared for the sight, it was still so much to take in. My brother had been killed the year before, but I never saw his body after he died. This sight reminded me of when I found our mother dead in her bed after a long illness. In her case, she was withered and eaten away by disease and heartbreak. Mr. Howard was young and strong but just as dead. The only piece of his pale skin with any color was the bruise that had formed around his eye after Paulo the Peddler had hit him.

Thoughts of Paulo made me wonder if he could have been the one responsible for Mr. Howard's demise. He and Mr. Howard clearly had a history, and not a good one. Could he have killed the other man? But how? Other than the black eye from being struck earlier in the day, I didn't see any wounds on Mr. Howard. He was just dead. Dead with no explanation at all.

Cody stood behind me, twisting his hands so forcefully I was afraid he might break his fingers. "Willa, what am I going to do? What am I going to do?" His Irish accent was as thick as I had ever heard it.

"Cody, you have to run to the Evergreens and tell the family. They will want to call the police."

"I can't do that. I'm not allowed into the house." He almost looked as pale as Mr. Howard when he said this. "You go, and I will stay here."

"I will stay here," I said firmly. As much as I didn't want to stand over a dead body, I couldn't trust Cody not to disturb the scene with his pacing and frantic movements. There was no evidence a crime had been committed, but even still, we needed to be careful. Matthew taught me about the importance of physical evidence at a crime scene. He said it was becoming increasingly essential as the police departments advanced. More important than witness accounts even, which he claimed were unreliable.

"I know Margaret has made a rule for all the servants that the outdoor workers aren't allowed anywhere in the home other than the servants' quarters and the kitchens, but, first of all, you aren't going into the homestead, and, second of all, this is an exception. A man is dead."

His eyes were wide. "But Miss O'Brien! I don't think she will care if it's the Evergreens or not. She will give me a tongue-lashing for going into either home in my muddy clothes."

I examined him, and he had a point. His boots and pant legs were encrusted with dirt. I still didn't believe that was enough reason for him to argue with me on the matter, but it was clear he was afraid of Margaret. I can't say I blamed him. When I'd first met her, I had been frightened of her as well.

"Very well. Run to the kitchens and tell one of the other servants to deliver the message to the dining room."

He hesitated a moment longer, as if he was trying to think of another excuse to stay behind with the body.

"Go!" I shouted.

"What about the police? I can't be here when the police come." He looked as if he might cry.

"Why not?" I asked. "They will want to talk to you. You were the last one to speak to Mr. Howard, and you found his b—him."

"I'm Irish," he said. "The police will take one look at me and blame me for this. They don't need any other reason to pin it on a dirty Irishman. I tell you, when they arrive, they will be looking right at me. You're here, too, but they will never suspect you, because you are not Irish, and you are a Yankee woman."

"Looking at you for what?" I asked, unsure what his point was. In the last few months I'd known Cody, I had become somewhat accustomed to his ability to talk in circles. His "gift of gab" as he called it could be confusing at times.

"For his murder."

"We don't know that he was murdered," I said a little more sternly than I intended to. It was not lost on me that if I really thought this, then why did I think it was mandatory that I guard what could be the crime scene? And why had I thought for a brief moment that Paulo Vitali could be to blame?

"But how else can a healthy young man drop dead in the middle of a garden?" Cody asked. "The only way I see it is if someone killed him."

"These are not ideas you want to share with the Dickinsons, their guests, or the police," I said sharply. "If you do, they *will* become suspicious of you jumping to conclusions."

He paled in the light of the setting sun, and the dusting of red freckles across his nose became more pronounced.

"There might be many reasons as to why Mr. Howard is dead," I said. "Perhaps he had an illness he didn't know about or was keeping a sickness secret. We don't know. Murder is just one of the possibilities, and I have to say it is the least likely."

Cody didn't exactly relax, but he at least stopped twisting his hands like he had them in some sort of vise.

"Now, run to the Evergreens and alert the kitchen staff like I asked, so that the Dickinsons and the police can be told. There is no time to waste."

"What are you going to do?" he asked, taking one more moment to stall.

"Don't worry about me." I gave him a little push. "Go!"

Cody stopped arguing with me and took off toward the Evergreens at a run. After he was gone, my eyes were drawn back to the body. Poor Mr. Howard. I couldn't say I liked the man, but I would not wish this fate on him. I could not help but believe from the agony contorting his face that he died in great pain. I had to look away.

There came the sound of movement on the path behind me. I looked behind me, expecting to see Cody returning with another argument as to why he couldn't be the one to tell the family what had occurred.

Instead, I saw a woman in white walking down the garden path in the gathering twilight. I placed a hand on my chest, and for the briefest of moments, I thought it might even be a spirit perhaps of my dead mother.

"Willa, did you find Mr. Howard?" Emily's breathy voice shook me from my momentary horror.

"Emily." Her name came out of my mouth like a prayer of thanksgiving, and I remembered she had chosen to wear her white lace frock to the dinner party that evening.

It was a summer dress with a broad collar and pointed sleeves. However, with the sun setting at her back, there was something ethereal about her. She seemed to float over the grass. I could very easily see why I thought of her as a ghost.

"Willa," she said in her soft tone that hovered in the humid evening air around us. "What has taken you so long? And why are you in my garden? I asked you to check on Mr. Howard."

"Did you pass Cody on the way from the Evergreens?" I asked, realizing by the way I stood I blocked her view of the perennial garden and Mr. Howard's body.

"I did. He wouldn't tell me why he was running, but said I would find you near the patch of black-eyed Susans. Why are you here? And why was Cody running? He was so pale. I thought his freckles were going to pop off his cheeks."

"It's Mr. Howard. He's dead." I said it as bluntly as she would. Perhaps there was something to just getting the words out without softening them in any way. Dead was dead.

Instead of reacting with shock or concern, as I would expect of anyone at such an announcement, Emily simply said, "Show me."

"It is a gruesome sight," I said. "He did not have a peaceful death."

"I conjure more gruesome images in my head than are possible. I assure you I can handle whatever it is."

I sighed and shifted aside so she could see the garden behind me.

She stepped around me, but she was nearly a foot shorter than I was, and I could see well over her head.

She looked down. "I heard a fly buzz when I died," she murmured.

As she said this, I noticed a large horsefly buzzing near Mr. Howard's unseeing eyes.

CHAPTER NINE

I WANTED TO shoo the fly away, but Emily stared at it so intently, I felt like I would be disturbing her if I moved.

Running footsteps came down the path, bringing Austin and Miss Susan. Miss Susan covered her mouth.

"It's true." She grabbed her husband's hand. "Oh, Austin, this is terrible. Terrible. The family's reputation . . ."

I turned. The family reputation? A man was dead, and the Dickinson reputation was the first thing that came to her mind. What about Mr. Howard? What about his family, the people who would mourn him?

Austin pulled his hand from his wife's grasp. "There is no reason this has to have an impact on the family at all. It's a tragedy, but it was clear at dinner that Mr. Howard was not well. It is not our fault if he took ill in our home."

Their conversation seemed to bring Emily back from wherever she had traveled in her thoughts. "He was a healthy man before dinner," Emily said.

Austin frowned at his sister. "That is your assumption. We can't possibly know the man's health."

Emily eyed him. "This is true, Brother, and for that reason, you cannot assume he was in poor health."

Austin's frown dissolved into a scowl, and Miss Susan furrowed her brow. I was certain that when they were on their wedding trip, they hadn't imagined something like this would occur so soon after their union, or ever in their lives, for that matter.

"What do we do now?" Miss Susan asked.

"We wait for the police to arrive. We sent Cody to the police station," Austin said to Emily. "He should be back soon with officers."

"So you don't think he was ill, Brother," Emily said.

"I *do* believe he was ill, but when a young man dies suddenly, it is only right to call the police. The doctor will take one look at him and be able to tell us what caused his illness."

At this point, I wondered if Austin continued to insist it was an illness in order to convince himself as well as Emily and Miss Susan.

I raised my brow at the mention of the yardman. Cody had been so worried about coming across the police. He must have been terrified to run into the station and tell of Mr. Howard's death. He could argue with me about going to tell the Dickinsons, but he could not have argued with Austin when given a direct order. I promised myself that I would check on Cody before the end of the night.

"Luther?" Miss Lavinia cried, and then covered her mouth as tears came to her eyes. She stood at the edge of the perennial garden.

Both Emily and Austin stared at her as if seeing their youngest sister for the first time.

Miss Lavinia turned without a word and ran toward the homestead.

"Vinnie is too sensitive for this sort of scene," Austin said.

"True, but it is also clear she had some special feelings for Mr. Howard," Miss Susan said.

Austin turned on his wife. "Don't be ridiculous. Vinnie doesn't have any aspirations like that."

Miss Susan gave her husband a look, as if she could not believe he was so naive.

Emily stared at the homestead with her mouth pressed into a thin line.

There was chatter along the garden path coming from the Evergreens. Cody, as white as ever, led four men down to the perennial garden. The first was in an evening suit, as if he had been taken away from a dinner party of his own. Three of the men following him were in police uniforms.

The man in the suit was tall and thin with a straight nose. I recognized him as Detective Durben immediately. My stomach turned at seeing him again. The last time I had spoken to the detective had been in January the year before, when my brother was killed. At the time, the detective believed Henry had been killed in a horse accident, an explanation I could not believe. He gave up on the case before it even started. If it hadn't been for Emily, I wouldn't know how my brother's life came to an end.

When the justice system had failed my brother, Emily and I had prevailed in discovering the truth.

I recognized the faces of two more of the officers, but I

didn't know their names. However, the fourth man in the group, I knew well, very well. Matthew still wore the smart police uniform I had seen him in earlier in the day.

He and I locked eyes, and I saw his shoulders relax. I could only imagine the fear that must have gripped him the moment he'd heard something had happened at the Dickinson home. I knew in my bones I was his first concern.

That knowledge made me uncomfortable and strangely pleased.

"I'm Detective James Durben of the Amherst Police Department," the detective said. "Can someone tell me what happened here, and how this dead man ended up in that patch of flowers?"

Austin puffed up his chest and stepped forward. "Mr. Howard, the deceased, was a guest of mine and my wife's and was staying here at the Evergreens."

Detective Durben peered over his glasses at Austin. "Where is Mr. Dickinson? I assume he would like to speak with me."

Austin's face turned slightly red. "My father is at my home, waiting to hear what we have found."

"I'd like to talk to him first, as he is the patriarch of the family."

"Of course," Austin said through clenched teeth. "I will take you to him."

Detective Durben nodded. "Officer Thomas, please review the scene." He turned to follow Austin back to the Evergreens, but then paused and asked, "Who came upon the body? That would be good to know."

I glanced around. Cody was nowhere to be found. As soon as he'd delivered the police to the gardens, he'd disappeared.

I stepped forward. "I did, Detective."

For the first time, Detective Durben looked directly at me. I was a blond, tall, and broad woman, but I was easily over-looked because of my maid's uniform.

A glimmer of recognition came into the detective's face. Did he remember me from the investigation into Henry's mur-der? The glimmer faded, and I was demoted to just a servant again. "Come with us."

"Sir," Matthew interjected. "Wouldn't it be better if Miss Noble explains what she found here at the scene?"

The detective's head snapped in Matthew's direction. "Who is Miss Noble?"

"I am," I said, trying to keep my voice calm.

"You're coming with me," the detective said.

Emily stepped forward. "Willa Noble is my maid. If you are going to question her, I am coming too. As her employer, I have the right to hear everything she has to say. When she speaks, it's a representation of the Dickinson family, and I must know that we are not disparaged."

Irritation flashed across his face. "Very well."

He started down the path again after Austin. Miss Susan stepped forward and joined her husband. She put her arm through his and, this time, he didn't shy away.

Emily took my hand. "Come, Willa, this time will be dif-ferent."

How did she know I was thinking about the last time I had been questioned by police? Then again, how could she not think of that? In any case, I truly hoped she was right.

CHAPTER TEN

"Austin, what is going on?" Mr. Dickinson rose up from his chair in the parlor as soon as we stepped into the room. His eyes fixed on the detective. "What has happened?"

Before Austin could speak, the detective stepped forward. "Mr. Dickinson, I am so sorry to disturb you this late in the evening, but it seems one of your guests has fallen ill and died."

I noted that he made no allusion to foul play.

"Died? Who?" Mr. Dickinson asked.

The detective frowned, as if he was having trouble remembering the victim's name.

"It was Mr. Howard," Austin said.

Mr. Emerson sat in one corner of the room. A book was in his lap. "What is this?"

The detective looked in his direction. "And who are you?"

Mr. Emerson studied the other man, who was young enough to be his son. "I am Ralph Waldo Emerson of Concord. I'm here this week to give lectures at the Amherst Literary Society symposium. Luther Howard was my secretary."

Detective Durben removed a stub of a pencil and a small leather notebook from his inside coat pocket, turned to a clean page, and wrote a note. "And what is it that you do, Mr. Emerson?"

"Detective, Mr. Emerson is one of the foremost thinkers and writers of our time," Miss Susan said. "Surely, you have heard of him."

The detective eyed her. "I don't have much time for pleasure reading, being the only detective in the department."

"She did not mean that comment as an insult, Durben," Mr. Thayer said as he stepped into the room.

"I did not know you were in attendance at this party, Thayer," the detective said.

"Yes, it seems my wife's houseguest is old friends with Miss Dickinson, and that led to our invitation. We are pleased to be here but, like everyone else, wish the evening had ended on a brighter note. I would like to ask that I take my wife and her friend Miss Foote home. They are waiting to leave in the library. You know how these sorts of things can be so upsetting to women."

It was clear Mr. Thayer and the detective knew each other. Was it just because they were both citizens of Amherst, or something else? Neither Mr. Dickinson nor Austin seemed to be as familiar with Detective Durben as Mr. Ruben Thayer was.

The detective nodded, as if he knew this to be true, and I noticed that Emily's shoulders tensed up.

"We won't keep you, Mr. Thayer. Would it be all right if I

stopped by your home tomorrow morning for a statement should the need arise for one?"

The gentleman arched his brow. "Is there more to this than a man dying of illness?"

"We have not determined that yet, sir. It is only a precaution."

"Susan, why don't you and Emily leave the room so we can talk to the detective alone?" Austin suggested. "Some of the points we will be discussing about Mr. Howard's death might be difficult for the two of you to hear."

Susan scowled at her husband, but it was Emily who spoke up. "Austin, Susan and I are perfectly able to digest any of the information that is about to be shared. This is our home, too, and we have a right to know what has transpired when a young, seemingly healthy man drops dead in the middle of our garden."

Austin scrunched up his face as if he wanted to argue with his sister but didn't know how to go about it.

"I would like to speak to Miss Noble first. Alone," the detective said.

"Not alone. With me," Emily said.

The detective looked in her direction again. "That is quite irregular."

"I don't believe it's irregular at all." Emily folded her arms over her white dress. "She is a servant, and you need my permission to speak to her."

"She is *my* servant," Mr. Dickinson said. "You do not pay her wages, Emily."

Detective Durben turned to Mr. Dickinson. "May I speak to Miss Noble?"

"Yes, but since my daughter so adamantly wishes it, I would like her to be there." He stood. "And if you wish to speak to me, you can do so tomorrow. I have already sent my wife home with our maid, Margaret. It is quite a long night for her. I should go home and check on her and make sure my youngest daughter made it home safely as well."

The detective's eyes widened, as if he didn't expect this response from Mr. Dickinson. But rather than argue with him, he said, "Very well."

"Miss Noble, Miss Dickinson," he said to us each in turn. "Let us go into the dining room to chat."

We did as he asked. To my surprise, everything on the table down to the silverware was still there from the meal. Why hadn't the servants cleared it away? I doubted anyone would have much of an appetite after hearing about Mr. Howard's death.

Emily sat on one of the dining room chairs. "May Willa sit?"

Detective Durben nodded. "Yes, but I will stand. I find it helps me think."

Now that he mentioned it, I realized I had never seen the detective sitting in a chair. When he'd come to the Dickinson home to interview me after Henry's death, he had stood the whole time as well. No wonder he was so painfully thin. He never allowed himself off his feet.

I thought about continuing to stand myself just so I was on even footing with the policeman, but working for two households over the last week, as well as the day's and evening's events, fell over my shoulders like a leaden blanket. I perched on the chair next to Emily.

"Let us begin at the beginning," the detective said. "How did you discover the body?"

My stomach twisted from the lie that'd come out of my mouth not so long ago. I had claimed I was the one who came upon the body, which was true, but I hadn't been the first one to see it. Cody Carey had. Why had I been so quick to lie?

In actuality, I knew why. It was because of what Cody had said about being blamed for the crime because he was Irish. And because of Henry. I was still looking to protect my younger brother—or whatever facsimile I saw of him—more than a year after his death. If Henry had been in the same position as Cody, I would have wished someone had stepped in for him too.

"Miss Noble," the detective said when I didn't immediately answer.

"I'm sorry, sir. As you can imagine, this has been a great shock. Mr. Howard seemed to have fallen ill at dinner. He was behaving strangely and got up abruptly, leaving the party. After a few minutes, Miss Dickinson"—I nodded at my mistress—"asked me to go see if he was all right."

"And what were you doing at the Evergreens for this meal?"

My mouth fell open. So Detective Durben did remember me.

I cleared my throat and regained my composure. "I was asked to help. The dinner party was larger than normal, and everyone who works for the family can be asked to work at either home at any time."

Emily spoke up then. "Detective, my brother and Susan do have their own household to run, but as a family we share everything, including servants. If there is help needed at the Evergreens, we send over our servants, and the reverse is true. We may be two households, but we are one family."

He made a note in his little book. "And who was in attendance tonight?"

Emily answered this time. "Everyone you saw sitting in the parlor when we arrived except for my mother, and sister Lavinia. As my father said, he sent my mother home with our head maid, Miss O'Brien, because of Mother's headaches. A man dying in the family garden is sure to cause her distress. Also, Cate Lynn Thayer and Isadora Foote were not in the parlor when you arrived. It seems the men were taking care of sheltering the ladies in the house from any unpleasant news. Had I still been here, I would have refused to leave. It is far better to receive a shock straightaway than to have it concealed and discovered later. Do you not agree?"

The detective didn't answer her question. Instead, he asked, "What do you think of Mr. Emerson's relationship with his secretary?"

I felt my body tense as I vividly remembered the argument I'd overheard between Mr. Emerson and Mr. Howard just minutes before the dinner. The secretary had been dismissed, but Mr. Emerson had given permission for him to stay for the remainder of the week in order for Mr. Howard to resign gracefully and salvage his reputation.

Thankfully, Emily answered for me. "They seemed to be fine as far as we can tell. Mr. Howard was always at Mr. Emerson's side and appeared to be well versed in his employer's work. There is no reason at all for us to believe anything was amiss. Do you have a reason to suspect something more sinister?"

He did not answer. "Is there anything else you remember, Miss Noble?"

I nodded. "When I went to look for Mr. Howard, I began in his room, as I assumed that would be the first place an ill man would go to rest. He was not there. Instead, I found the place was a mess, as if someone had searched it."

The detective took a step toward the door. "Take me to his room."

I stood up, and Emily did as well.

As I expected her to, Emily led the way to Mr. Howard's room. When we reached the hallway, Detective Durben stepped in front of her. "Do not go inside of the room," he ordered. "I need to take a look at it first."

He went inside and examined the tousled bedclothes, carpet-bag, and papers on the floor. Emily and I stood in the doorway and watched.

He put his hands on his hips. "This changes the way we look at this case entirely."

That's what I'd been afraid he was going to say.

"Is anything missing?" he asked.

"I do not know," Emily answered. "My brother and Susan would be the ones to ask as far as their belongings that might have been in this room. However, we have no way of knowing what Mr. Howard had brought with him when he arrived."

"I need to speak with my officers. We need a thorough search of this space." He stepped out of the room and made his way down the hallway.

When Emily and I didn't immediately follow him, he turned. "You're both coming downstairs with me. No one goes into that room without my permission. No one."

Back on the main floor, the detective sent a young servant

from the Evergreens to tell the officers at the scene to come into the house, and then he dismissed Emily and me.

When Emily and I returned to the parlor, we found it empty except for Austin and Miss Susan. The newlyweds sat on opposite sides of the room, as far away from each other as could be.

Miss Susan stood when we walked into the room. "What has happened? We saw three officers go upstairs."

"It seems someone has ransacked Mr. Howard's room," Emily said. "We do not know if it was before or after he fell ill. The police are searching it for clues."

"It had to have been after," Austin said. "He could not have sat through dinner if he knew his room was in disrepair."

Miss Susan sat back down. "Or it could have happened during the meal."

I, for one, knew it must have happened during the dinner, since I had changed Mr. Howard's bedclothes before the meal began and the room had not been touched. However, I said nothing. Who could have gotten up to his room during the meal other than a servant? But I wasn't ready to place the blame on another member of my class just yet.

"By whom?" Austin challenged his wife.

"I don't know. Who would have done it after he fell ill?" she snapped back.

Emily watched them with a knit brow. "I see everyone else has left."

"Yes, they have all gone home." Miss Susan pressed a handkerchief to her forehead. "I hope all of this does not affect the society meetings tomorrow."

"Will there be society meetings tomorrow?" Austin asked.

"Why should it be canceled?" Miss Susan said. "Mr. Howard wasn't speaking."

Austin scowled as if seeing something in his new wife that he didn't care for.

"We should return to the homestead. I wish to check on Vinnie," Emily said.

"Yes, maybe I should go with you," Miss Susan said, half rising from her seat.

"You would leave your new husband alone with police officers in the house?" Austin stood and walked toward the window.

Miss Susan stared at his back as if she was considering something. "I will stay here. I will be over in the morning to check on all of you."

"Of course," Emily said, and kissed both her new sister and her brother on the cheek in goodbye.

As we left the house, I saw Katie begin to clear away the dishes on the long dining table. However, Mr. Howard's place was not touched. Matthew sat in his chair packing Mr. Howard's dishes and leftover food into a wooden box.

I wanted to tell Emily what I had seen Matthew doing in the dining room, but as soon as we stepped out of the Evergreens, she grabbed me. "Come, Willa, run!"

She pulled me along behind her until my legs cooperated and I was running beside her.

"Why are we running?" I asked, out of breath.

"With all the police inside of the house looking at Mr. Howard's room, this might be our only chance to see the crime scene and look for evidence of our own! Come. Let's hurry."

However, as we came upon the perennial garden, we were stopped from searching the scene. Detective Durben was there with another man, and two more officers who must have been called in to assist as well.

"I won't know for sure until I take him to my lab, but I would say it was asphyxiation from swelling in the back of the throat. You gathered everything he ate, so I can test it?" the man in a black coat asked.

"Yes," Detective Durben said.

"Good. I don't know if the poison was ingested or absorbed through the skin. He does have that suspicious rash on his arm."

Emily gripped my hand when we heard the word "poison," and then she guided me away from the perennial garden and detoured behind the barn. We walked around the large building and went inside the house through the back washroom leading into the kitchen.

In the empty kitchen, Emily grabbed my right hand in both of hers. "Willa, Mr. Luther Howard was murdered."

It was exactly what I thought she was going to say.

CHAPTER ELEVEN

THE NEXT MORNING, I awoke before dawn as always. As second housemaid in the Dickinson homestead, I was required to be the first one up to start the fires in the kitchen and the living spaces. Thankfully, in summertime, the only fires I had to start were in the ovens. Even so, there was much to do. I needed to walk through the house and make sure all the windows were open in order to let in what little breeze could be found in central Massachusetts at the tail end of summer.

It was still dark when I opened the windows in the second parlor. I rubbed my eyes to remove the sleep left in them. Usually, I was quick to wake up, but the events of the last evening kept me awake late into the night. I was torn over whether I should tell Detective Durben or Matthew about Cody. I did not believe for one second that the young Irishman killed Mr. Howard. He had no reason to. But if it came

out later that I lied to police even if that was not my intention, it could lead to trouble for me and for the Dickinson
family.

I knew Margaret would be just waking up and in the
kitchen soon to begin the morning meal. Emily would be in
the kitchen shortly to make her three loaves of brown bread
for the day.

Even so, I had a few free minutes and, on a whim, I went
outside and hurried to the workmen's cabin. The small cabin
was on the edge of the woods, and the stable hands and yardmen lived there as well. Horace Church, the head gardener,
lived in a little cottage of his own across Main Street by the
Dickinsons' church. He walked to the Dickinsons each morning to tend to what he believed were *his* beloved gardens, no
matter the weather.

Because Horace didn't live in the cabin, it was occupied by
the yardman, Cody Carey, and the stable hand, Jeremiah York,
with a revolving door of seasonal or temporary laborers who
moved in and out.

Even though Cody was like a young brother to me, and Jeremiah was my friend, I was still hesitant to knock on their
door so early in the morning. It was nothing close to proper for
a young woman like me to be calling on young men before the
sun rose.

I knocked on the door. A moment later it opened. Jeremiah
blinked at me from behind his glasses. "Willa, what are you
doing here? Is something wrong?"

He was already fully dressed for the day. In fact, there was
fresh mud on his boots, which was a clear sign he'd already

been to the barn to check on Terror and the other horses. Terror was a horse Mr. Dickinson had purchased from Jeremiah's former employer when the man threatened to put the retired racehorse down. Emily convinced her father to take the horse in. As stern as he was, Mr. Dickinson had a soft spot when it came to his eldest daughter.

"Did Cody tell you what happened last night in the garden?" I asked.

Jeremiah looked over his shoulder. "No. What has happened?"

"One of Mr. Austin Dickinson's guests was found dead."

"What?" Jeremiah cried.

I nodded. "It was quite a scene. I'm surprised you didn't hear all the commotion. The police were here for what seemed like hours."

"I wasn't here. I was out . . ." He trailed off.

I knew what had kept Jeremiah away. It was the same thing that had ultimately led to my brother's death. I said nothing about it.

"Is Cody here?" I asked. Not knowing who else might be in the cabin and listening, I did not want to mention Jeremiah's nocturnal activities.

"He was just a moment ago. Let me see." He stepped back into the cabin.

I peered inside. The small room was neat and clean, something never guaranteed with young men living alone in close quarters. There was a potbellied stove in one corner, and I could feel heat coming off it from where I stood. On the stove top, a coffeepot bubbled. Even with all the windows opened wide, it was quite warm.

Jeremiah was back a moment later. "I'm sorry, Willa. Cody was just here, but now it seems he's gone. That's unusual. He is a cheerful champ, and always says when he's heading out into the gardens. At times, it's infuriating because he will even do it when I'm in a dead sleep."

I bit the inside of my lip and thanked Jeremiah. "I will speak to him later, then. I should return to the house and help Margaret with breakfast."

He nodded with a look of concern on his face.

As I hurried back to the servants' entrance of the homestead, I could not help but wonder if Cody had left the cabin when he heard me knock on the door, and if so, why?

When I entered the kitchen, both Margaret and Emily were there. Emily was kneading the dough for her breads. She looked up from the table. "I'm making three loaves of brown bread and a honey-nut loaf as well. I thought we all deserved something special to get through the day. It promises to be a complicated one."

I removed my kitchen apron from the peg by the door and put it on. "Complicated" was one way to describe how the day was sure to go. "Will you be leaving for the lectures with your brother and his wife?"

"No, I plan to go a bit later. I have promised Vinnie that I would go on a walk with her."

"Is she all right?" I asked. "She seemed quite upset last night."

"That is what I will determine. I hate to see my sister in such a state. Of the Dickinson women, she is the steadfast one. We can't have her falling apart like Mother and me. There needs to be one Dickinson woman with a level head."

"Willa," Margaret interrupted. "Take the eggs and sausage to the breakfast table."

I set the items on a silver tray. The eggs were scrambled and displayed in a blue-and-white tureen, while a matching blue-and-white plate held the links of sausage. Slowly, I lifted the tray so the sausage would not roll off the plate onto the tray, or even worse, onto the floor.

"When you are through with that, take up the coffee and juice," Margaret said.

Emily put her breads in the oven. "I will help you carry it, Willa. I can take up the juice and coffee."

Margaret wrinkled her nose. Helping set the table was not something Emily did often. I knew she simply wanted to speak to me without Margaret's constant disapproval.

In the dining room, I set the tureen and plate on the sideboard and then began setting out the breakfast dishes stored inside of it.

Emily placed the juice and coffee next to the glasses and cups I laid out. "I want you to come to the lectures again today."

I looked up from the silverware. "But I was there yesterday."

"Yes, but only to bring us lunch. I would like you to be there for the lectures. I think you will learn much."

I looked down at the spread and felt satisfied. All that was needed was Emily's sliced brown bread and the family would be well fed. "I don't think Margaret would like it if I was gone a full day again. She is still upset I wasn't here last week since I was working at the Evergreens."

"It won't be *all* day. As I have said, I plan to go on a walk with my sister after breakfast."

I opened my mouth to protest again, but she spoke first. "You let me worry about Margaret. Just be ready to leave at ten sharp." She grabbed a sausage off the plate and walked out of the room.

CHAPTER TWELVE

Margaret was not happy to hear I would be accompanying Emily to the lecture hall, and she wasn't the only one. As we made our way through the yard to the road, I spotted Miss Lavinia standing in Emily's bedroom window. It surprised me, as Emily didn't like anyone going into her room; it was her safe haven. Even when it was time for me to do the weekly dusting, she put up a fuss about it.

As we walked to the lecture hall on the college campus, I wanted to ask Emily how her morning walk with Miss Lavinia had gone, but I held my questions back. I'd never had a sister, but I could imagine such conversations between them were sacred and should not allow others in.

Much had happened since the day before, when I carried the heavy lunch hamper into the hall, and that was apparent as soon as we entered the lecture hall and the room chatter stopped. Everyone turned to look at us.

"Yes," Emily said. "You continue to gossip about us and Mr. Howard's death. Carry on like we aren't here."

"Emily," Mr. Dickinson said as he stepped into the aisle to meet his daughter. "Do not make a scene."

"Am I making a scene, Father?" She raised her voice slightly. "Or is it the rumormongers?"

Mr. Dickinson clenched his jaw, but he didn't reprimand his daughter for a second time. Near the front of the room, Isadora Foote stood up and waved her hand.

"Aah," Emily said. "One friendly face at least."

She hurried off in that direction.

Mr. Dickinson had yet to comment on the fact that Emily had brought me to the lectures; however, he was stopped by a gentleman I didn't know, and I didn't want to hover, so I followed after Emily.

Isadora gave Emily a big hug. "Oh, my friend, how are you holding up? I could not believe it when Ruben told Cate Lynn and me what happened. How horrible. And what a terrible thing to happen to your family!"

I glanced around and could not help but notice some of the attendees had their ears tilted in our direction as if straining to overhear Emily and Isadora's conversation.

I couldn't tell whether Emily didn't notice this or didn't care. I thought either scenario was possible when it came to my mistress. At times, she could notice the minute details of a butterfly's wings. Other times, I had to yank her back from the road so she wasn't run over by a passing wagon.

"We will get through it," Emily said.

"Did the police arrest that yardman?" Isadora asked.

I tripped over my own two feet when I heard her say this, and grabbed on to the arm of an elderly woman in a fur coat.

"Pardon me!" the woman cried, and pulled her arm away from me like I was a hot stove that had burned her.

Why she was wearing fur in the warmest part of summer, I didn't know, but at least it had been soft to land on.

Emily and Isadora turned to look at me just as I righted myself and apologized to the woman.

"You brought your maid?" Isadora asked, as if she could not think of a more absurd guest to bring to a literary lecture.

"Yes, Willa is quite a reader. I think she's read through half of the books in our family library. Haven't you, Willa?"

I cleared my throat and willed my skin not to turn red. Although I thought it was a little too late, if the searing heat on my cheeks was any indication. "I don't know if it's half the library, but at least a third."

"See," Emily said to her friend, as if my comment proved her right.

Isadora shook her head. "You have always made your own rules, Emily. I remember you were like that in school too. I always thought you left Mount Holyoke for that reason. You couldn't abide the rigid structure. While for me, places with rules and structure are where I do best. I have many more challenges outside of academics than I did within it."

Emily took her seat and shook her head. "No, that is not why I left." She turned her attention to the podium in front of us and didn't say another word.

Isadora settled in the seat next to her old friend with a pinched expression on her face, as if she realized she had said something wrong but wasn't certain what.

I didn't know either. It seemed to me that Emily often re-treated into herself much more now than when I had first met her. I tried not to worry about it too much.

"Is this seat taken?" a man's voice said behind me.

An older man answered, "No." He stood and let the first speaker into the row. I looked over my shoulder at the familiar voice and locked eyes with Matthew. As if I had been stung, I snapped my head back around to face the podium just as Matthew took the seat directly behind me.

Throughout the first lecture given by a literature professor at the college, I felt Matthew's eyes boring into the back of my neck, but every time I happened to look over my shoulder, he was staring straight ahead at the person speaking. I was acutely aware of Matthew sitting there. I reminded myself he wasn't there for me. He was working. I knew the police investigation into Luther Howard's death had to be the reason for his presence. I also noted he was out of uniform. I did not know if he did so to blend in while on the job, or because he had come to the lecture of his own volition. The last time I had known Matthew to investigate a crime in civilian clothes, the former of those two options had been true.

Finally, the professor's lecture ended, and I almost felt the collective sigh of relief. The next speaker was Mr. Emerson, and it was no secret to anyone that hearing him speak was the reason why there were so many people in the audience.

I had overhead Miss Susan say that typically the literary society symposium had twenty to thirty members who came to listen to poetry, essays, and lectures by learned men. The lecture hall could hold two hundred souls, and from what I could see, every seat was filled.

After he was introduced, Mr. Emerson stood at the podium and opened his leather-bound folder. "I am very happy to be with you on this second day of the symposium. You in the town of Amherst are some of the lucky ones due to the college and its generosity of including the community in its activities. You are able to have a high-quality, lifelong education. I applaud how you and the college work together. I also want to thank the literary society, which believes everyone should have a chance to write and express themselves with the pen."

As he spoke, I watched Emily out of the corner of my eye. She leaned forward in her seat and was taking in every word.

"Before I continue my lectures on *English Traits*, I wanted to address what I have a feeling is the main topic of conversation on this day." He paused. "Yes, it is true that my young secretary, Mr. Luther Howard, died suddenly last night during dinner. No, I will not go into the details of his death, but I will say that he is greatly missed."

Greatly missed? I didn't believe for a second that Mr. Howard was to be missed by Mr. Emerson.

I realized that I had yet to tell anyone about the last conversation I had overheard between Mr. Howard and Mr. Emerson. The conversation in which Mr. Emerson had fired the younger man and yet promised that he could stay this last week of lectures within hours of Mr. Howard being found dead. And then there was what I knew about Cody.

Mr. Emerson and Mr. Howard's argument might have been the last direct conversation the secretary had with anyone. How awful to argue with a person just before they died. When that happened, you didn't have an opportunity to apologize or make it right. I wondered if that was how Mr. Emerson felt at the moment. I doubted it by the way he stood tall and regal at the front of the lecture hall.

"Luther was my secretary, but he was also a gifted writer himself. I have discovered many of his writings in his things, and I have to say I was moved by the emotion and thought he poured into each and every piece. It has inspired me to ask my publisher to publish Luther's work posthumously. I know it was what he most wanted, and his talent deserves to be shared, even after his death. I cannot think of a better way to honor my secretary and friend."

Isadora leaned over and whispered something into Emily's ear that I couldn't hear, and Emily shifted uncomfortably back and forth in her seat like there was a pin in her skirts.

"Now, let us continue with my observations from my trips to England."

An hour later, the audience clapped as Mr. Emerson gave a half bow and stepped back from the podium.

The boring literature professor returned to the podium. "We will take a short break before our next lecture."

As a collective, the audience stood. Isadora took Emily's arm and led her out a side door. Not knowing what else to do, I followed them.

"That must have been so difficult to hear Mr. Emerson speak of Mr. Howard's death when you know everyone will be looking at your family," Isadora said.

Emily removed her arm from Isadora's. "I don't see why. It was very sad, but clearly Mr. Howard wasn't well. I don't know why anyone would be looking poorly at our family because of that."

Isadora stepped back and covered her mouth. "You don't know."

Emily's dark eyes bore into her. "Know what?" she asked harshly.

If Emily looked or spoke to me in that way, I would have withdrawn into myself, but Isadora didn't seem to mind. She appeared to be too intent on sharing her news. "I cannot believe you haven't been told."

"Told what?" Emily asked through gritted teeth.

"Mr. Luther Howard didn't die of an illness. He was murdered."

CHAPTER THIRTEEN

I GASPED, AND Isadora's neck snapped in my direction. It was clear to me she had forgotten I was even there, which is a rather common thing to happen to servants.

Emily remained calm. "How do you know this?"

"Detective Durben came to the Thayers' home this morning to interview us about last evening. When he was there, I overheard him tell Ruben, Mr. Thayer, that the coroner found evidence Mr. Howard had been killed. There was a chemical burn on his right forearm and residue of some sort of powder on his sleeve. The coroner knew what it was right away." She paused as if she enjoyed holding us in suspense.

"Please continue," Emily said a little less harshly. "What was the powder?"

"Pyrethrin, the detective said. It is used to rid gardens of pests. It affects those who are prone to hay fever, to the point they cannot breathe. It appears Mr. Howard was one of those people."

"I know this about pests," Emily said. "I have used it in the garden to remove aphids and beetles from roses."

"So you have some on your property."

"Everyone with a garden is likely to have some of that powder in their shed or barn," Emily said.

"Where is it kept? Perhaps the killer got it from your family." She tapped her cheek. "But then, the police might look at your family even more closely. Lavinia was distraught over the news of Mr. Howard's death. The police might take that into consideration."

Emily smoothed the sleeves of her dress. The irritation she seemed to have felt just a moment ago appeared to have gone away. She was back in control of her emotions.

"This is unfortunate news, but I doubt the police will be looking at our family so closely. We have an impeccable reputation in Amherst. Half of the improvements to this town are to the credit of my father. There would not even be a train station in Amherst without him. I believe the detective will think twice before causing any trouble for our family."

"I don't know," Isadora said. "Based on the timing of Mr. Howard's death, and the incriminating substance, the detective might want to take a harder look at everyone."

"Perhaps Mr. Howard got it on his arm when he was walking through the garden," I suggested. "None of us know where he went when he left the table. He could have very well been wandering about and rubbed up against a plant with the powder on it."

Isadora glanced at me. "Maybe your maid has a better idea. She did leave the dining room right after Mr. Howard."

My eyes went wide. Was Isadora implying I might know something about Mr. Howard's death?

"I asked her to go look for him, and she did as I bade. She found him. Unfortunately, he was already dead when she did," Emily said as if I weren't standing just a few feet away. "Besides," Emily went on, "if Mr. Howard was killed with this substance, how did the killer know he would have such a bad reaction to it? Only someone who knew him well could have possessed the knowledge that he might become ill or even die."

Someone like Mr. Emerson, I realized.

"Furthermore, if Mr. Howard had such terrible hay fever, then why would he choose to go into the garden?" Emily asked.

"Perhaps it wasn't his choice." Isadora looked back at the hall. "I should go inside; Cate Lynn will wonder what has become of me. She and I had planned to return home after Mr. Emerson's lecture. We aren't staying for the rest of the speeches today. I think we all need a little rest after the evening before."

"Indeed," Emily said.

Isadora smiled at her and held her thin shawl over her shoulders. "Do not worry, Emily. This will all blow over. I'll be sure to tell everyone who might ask me that your family could not have had anything to do with this." She paused. "It would probably help if Lavinia came out into society within the day. If she stays home, it may give the wrong impression."

Emily arched her brow. "And what impression is that?"

"Oh, you know." Isadora waved her hand. "People talk."

She went back into the lecture hall, and Emily walked in the opposite direction. Unsure what else to do, I followed my mistress.

Emily strode across the college green toward Main Street. Without even stopping to look right or left for a passing carriage, she marched across the street. Her chin was held high, and her arms hung loosely at her sides.

She did not go into the family home like I expected her to. Instead, she stepped around it and walked with purpose to the garden shed. The doors to the shed stood wide because I could see Horace a few yards away digging up a rose of Sharon bush that Emily wanted moved closer to the house so she could enjoy its blooms from the first floor.

August was not a good time for such work, and Horace would be the first one to say so. The weather was hot and humid, and the stress of being uprooted and moved under those conditions was hard on a plant, even a hardy rose of Sharon. Horace would have to water it well for the next week until it recovered from being pulled from the earth. I noted that he already had the new hole dug, so the shrub would not have to be out of the ground for very long, assuming he could get it out of the ground in the first place.

Emily stepped into the shed and stared at the crowded shelves at the back of the building.

She pointed up. "There. Can you get it down, Willa?"

She had been so set in her mission to reach the gardener's shed quickly; I hadn't even realized she knew I had been following her all this time.

I easily reached the box she pointed out. I pulled it down. A skull and crossbones was emblazoned across the middle of the box, and below that, the words "Pyrethrin Toxic" were stamped.

Emily took the box from my hand and walked over to the corner of the shed with a worktable. She opened the box, and we were hit with the scent of chrysanthemum. I sneezed.

"Do you have hay fever too?" Emily asked, holding the box away from me.

"No, not usually. I think the smell just tickled my nose."

"Good. Because you could not be around this if you did. I believe that it killed Mr. Howard due to his hay fever. Do you not remember how he rejected my flowers when he and Mr. Emerson first arrived, because he said they would make him sneeze and cough? If those flowers would make him uncomfortable, inhaling pyrethrin would make it almost impossible for him to breathe."

"Then maybe it was an accident. Maybe he inhaled the pyrethrin by mistake," I suggested.

Emily shook her head. "Unlikely. Mr. Howard knew that he would become ill from the scent of plants. He would have avoided the exposure. He would be aware if there was something that would cause him discomfort nearby."

"If that is true, why did he go into the garden in the first place? That seems like the worst place for him to be."

Emily seemed to consider this. "Could it be that someone lured him out into the garden, then?"

"You mean like a trap?" I asked.

"Precisely," she said.

"Then we have to rule out the members of the dinner party," I said.

"Why's that?" Emily cocked her head and closed the box.

"Because you were all at the table when Mr. Howard was killed. No one at the party lured him out into the garden," I said.

"We can't rule out all the guests completely. No one can be ruled out at this point."

No one can be ruled out. The peddler who arrived at the lectures the day before. He seemed to have a turbulent history with Mr. Howard, but I didn't know what that history might be. However, what stood out to me the most was what he said when he first arrived. "Ladies, do you love your garden, but are devastated when your flowers are ravaged by pests? Are beetles after your roses, and aphids on your dahlias? I have the cure!"

Emily handed the box back to me. "If it was someone at the dinner party who killed Mr. Howard, the person must have had help."

"Emily," I said, ready to tell her what I remembered of the peddler and the argument between Mr. Emerson and Mr. Howard, but before I could even start, there was a knock at the shed door.

"Miss Dickinson," Cody said. "There are policemen here. They want to speak to Mr. Dickinson or Mr. Austin, but I told them they are both away. Should I fetch Mrs. Dickinson?"

"No," Emily said a bit too sharply, and marched to the house. "I will speak to them."

I followed her with the box of pyrethrin still in my hand. That was my first mistake of the day.

I blinked in the bright sunlight and found Matthew and Detective Durben standing on the edge of the rose garden. There were just a few blossoms left at the end of summer. The roses reached their height of brilliance at the end of June. This time of year, beetles ate tiny holes into their leaves, and it was a constant battle to keep them healthy until the next year. Cody shook the rosebushes every morning to knock any beetles off them, and at times he sprinkled the leaves with the chemical in my hand.

My heart constricted. Could I have been wrong about Cody all this time?

"Miss Dickinson, I am so sorry to disturb you," the detective said. "But we're here to speak to your father. I am disappointed to learn that he is away."

"He's not far away. He is at the symposium for Mr. Emerson at the college."

"And I assume that is where the young Mr. Dickinson is too."

"Quite right." Emily nodded.

"We won't keep you." He turned to go. "We'll talk to your father at the end of the symposium."

"What do you wish to talk to him about?" Emily asked.

The detective turned back around to face her. "I don't think I'm at liberty to share that with you. It's something your father should hear first."

Emily cocked her eyebrow. "If that is the case, why did you already tell the Thayers? Shouldn't my father have heard your news before they did since it affects his family the most?"

"I'm unsure what you mean." Sweat gathered on Detective Durben's upper lip.

"What I mean is you told the Thayers that Luther Howard was murdered in our garden, and now, it is afternoon and you are just getting around to telling my father. What was the reason for your delay?"

The detective's face turned a bright shade of red, made even brighter because of his pale skin. Even though it was the middle of summer, Detective Durben didn't have any color in his cheeks. Perhaps because of the wide-brimmed hat he wore. The only time I'd ever seen him take it off was inside.

"I need to discuss this with your father," the detective said with a clipped voice. Clearly, he wasn't happy that Emily had already been tipped off.

Detective Durben went on. "This is not a matter to discuss with a lady." He glanced at me. "And her maid."

Behind the police detective, I saw Matthew shift back and forth uncomfortably on his feet.

Detective Durben narrowed his eyes at me. "What is that in your hand?"

I looked down to the box of pyrethrin that I was holding. I should have put it back on the shelf the moment Emily handed it to me.

"It's pyrethrin," Emily said. "I was informed this is the substance that killed Mr. Howard."

"Who told you that?" he asked.

Emily arched her brow. "Did you not think if you told the Thayers that Mr. Howard had been murdered that it would get out before luncheon? Cate Lynn Thayer has been a notorious gossip since she was in pigtails. I'm sure everyone from the baker to the chancellor of the college knows the story by now."

Detective Durben grimaced. "And when you heard this, you did what? You rushed home to dispose of the rest of it before we had a chance to collect it?"

"No," Emily replied, unruffled by his tone. "I just wanted to see it was where I expected it to be in the garden shed, and it was."

The detective pressed his lips together. "Officer Thomas, please take the box from the maid," he ordered.

"Her name is Willa Noble, as you well know," Emily said.

"I would prefer that you refer to her as Miss Noble out of respect to me."

He gritted his teeth. "Please take the box from Miss Noble."

Matthew gave me an apologetic look as he took the box from my hand.

"Show me where you found it," Detective Durben said.

"Willa, can you show him? I have no desire to go inside of that hot shed again. It was terribly uncomfortable the first time, and now I know that there is nothing of interest to be found there. I see no reason to cause myself further discomfort."

I nodded and walked back to the shed. The door stood open. I might have thought that would have reduced the temperature inside, but with no breeze to speak of, there was little chance of that. Inside the shed, the detective removed his hat, but this time I didn't think it was to preserve his reputation. He did it because it was just so warm inside the building.

"I took the box from the highest shelf there." I pointed.

"Who has access to this shed?" he asked.

"What do you mean?" I asked.

"Is it kept locked when it's not in use? Who can go in and out of here?"

"It's not locked, sir. It's just a simple garden shed to store tools and supplies for the garden. There is no reason to lock it."

"In my opinion, there is always a good reason to lock things up tight. The citizens of Amherst are too trusting, but bad things can happen here. I assure you that they can and do happen."

It wasn't something that he had to convince me of, because I knew it far too well. Last year, Emily and I became very familiar with the corrupt and criminal side of Amherst.

I pulled on the collar of my dress. The inside of the shed was so stuffy, and the detective stood too close to me in the cramped space. He seemed to realize it, too, and thankfully backed out of the building. I gratefully followed him out.

Emily and Matthew were waiting when we reappeared.

"Are my family and guests in the clear, Detective?" Emily asked.

I was surprised she asked that, since she herself still suspected everyone at the dinner party. Except she couldn't be including her family in her number of suspects, could she? What reason would any of the Dickinsons have to hurt Mr. Howard? However, just as I thought that, Miss Lavinia and the kiss that Cody had witnessed came to mind. Could Mr. Dickinson or Austin have learned about it and decided to remove Mr. Howard as a threat to break up the family? I shook the thought away. It was too extreme, wasn't it?

"Who is cleared and who is not is none of your concern."

"You are wrong there," Emily said. "It's a great deal of my concern, and I can assure you that it will be my father's concern as well. It seems to me that you are bound to have an uncomfortable conversation with him."

The detective twisted his mouth as if he wasn't looking forward to it. Despite the way Detective Durben had treated me in the past, I felt a little bit of sympathy for him if he was about to face Mr. Dickinson with unwelcome news. But only a *little*.

CHAPTER FOURTEEN

For the rest of the day, I didn't find an opportunity to tell Emily what I knew about the peddler and the conversation that I heard between Mr. Emerson and Mr. Howard just before dinner on the night Mr. Howard was killed. As soon as the police left, she headed to the Evergreens to consult with Miss Susan on the matter. Since I was not invited to join her, I went back into the house to assist Margaret.

The head maid put me through my paces. She had me up on ladders dusting chandeliers and cleaning the top of every cupboard and picture frame in the house. I knew it was her form of punishment, but in some ways, I appreciated the work.

Just like everyone who must earn a wage to survive, I did not always want to work. However, I did find satisfaction in a sparkling window or a pristine fireplace. I could clean and let my mind wander to many other things simultaneously. Most times, I thought of the latest book I had borrowed from the family's library, or what I wished to do in the afternoon on

Sunday, my one day off for the week. At other times, I thought of a new recipe that I would like to try or something funny I'd witnessed about the house that I wished to tell Henry to make him laugh. He would have gotten so much amusement out of my tales about the Dickinson family and the people who visited. One of my greatest regrets in life was that I could no longer hear his laughter.

During my dusting that afternoon, my mind didn't wander to any of those topics. Instead, I thought about the murder and what I hadn't told Emily. I wasn't just thinking about the peddler and the argument that Mr. Emerson and Mr. Howard had. I still had not told Emily that Cody had been the one to find the body. It was something I needed to remedy soon.

"Margaret," I said as I walked into the kitchen. "I have finished the list of tasks. Would you be terribly upset if I went into the garden and weeded for a bit?" I paused. "I would like to visit the perennial garden just to make certain there is nothing left that might be upsetting to Mrs. Dickinson's eyes."

Margaret frowned but then relented. "Yes, do that. We don't want Mrs. Dickinson to stumble upon anything that would upset her when she makes her evening walk through the garden."

It was the answer that I expected, as Margaret had a softness for Emily's mother. I thought it was because her own mother was ill. Margaret spent all of her money on her mother's care, and her Sunday afternoons were spent more and more frequently at her mother's bedside.

Mrs. Dickinson's illness was different, of course. She had headaches and needed to be alone quite often. I had yet to hear what was wrong. I didn't think the doctor even knew. He guessed and prescribed medicine that made her sleep for what seemed days at time. There were whispers of her being delicate and having a disorder of her nerves. I knew very little as Margaret and the Dickinson sisters had taken it upon themselves to care for Mrs. Dickinson, and it was something that Emily rarely spoke about when we worked together in the kitchen or the garden.

Outside of the house, I let out a breath. It was the first time that I had truly been alone all day. Most of the time Margaret and I worked in separate parts of the homestead to complete tasks more quickly. It was a division of work that I most enjoyed because Margaret wasn't peering over my shoulder the whole time to make sure I was cleaning the "right way." However, that afternoon it seemed that she was following me from room to room. Perhaps it was because she was afraid that I would leave again.

I walked around the garden looking for any signs of what may have occurred the night before and anything at all that might aggravate Mrs. Dickinson's nerves if she came upon it. I found nothing. I didn't even find anything of interest in the black-eyed Susan patch where the body had been discovered. The only indication anything might have happened there was an impression in the ground and a row of broken blossoms.

I wondered if I should clean up the blossoms.

"The detective told Horace to leave the garden as it is," I heard Cody say from behind me.

I turned and the young Irishman kicked at the tuft of grass at his feet.

"How did you know I was thinking of tidying it up?" I asked.

"Because everyone who has been by here today had to think the same thing. None of us want fragile Mrs. Dickinson to see anything that might upset her on her evening walk."

I nodded.

He swallowed, and his Adam's apple bobbed up and down. "I wanted to thank you for saying you were the one who found the body, Willa. You don't know what it means to me. Before I left home to come to this country, my father told me never to tangle with the American police. He said it never ended well for Irishmen who did that. I've been here two years, and I have been able to avoid it up until now. Even when I was in New York City those first few months, I kept my nose clean. Amherst was the last place I thought I would run into any kind of trouble that might want to catch up with me. I moved out of the city to escape it. All I want to do is make an honest living and send money back home to feed what family I may have left."

I nodded. "Can you tell me what you saw last night?"

He picked up his shovel. "I don't even want to talk about it."

"I understand, but the police have said that they believe Mr. Howard was murdered and the Dickinson family might be in trouble. If you know something, you have to share it for the family's sake."

His eyes went wide. "I don't want anything bad to happen to the family. They've been good to me."

"None of us want any trouble for them. It might help to know what you saw, so that we can really get to the truth." I pressed my lips together and prayed that he would tell me more.

"Will you tell the police that I was the one who found the body?" His green eyes bored into me.

I sighed as I realized that this was the situation that I had put myself in by lying to the police in the first place. "I will try my very best not to."

His shoulders sagged. "I can't ask for anything more than that. You have been so kind to me, Willa. I really see you as a big sister."

My heart constricted, and I thought about Henry, like I did a thousand times a day. They never tell you grief is a mantle you wear for the rest of your life. It changes and softens, but it was a constant companion I felt would always be there. It was lighter on some days, heavier on others. I had learned this with my mother's death, and with Henry it was that much worse. Perhaps because my mother was ill and had a slow decline, I'd had time to prepare and time to say goodbye. I saw the end draw near.

Henry was just *gone*. One night he climbed out of my bedroom window after stopping by to say hello and then he was gone . . . forever.

"Thank you, Cody. That is kind of you to say. I will protect you as best I can. Although, I do need to tell Miss Dickinson you were there that night. She at least should know."

"Why?" His eyes were round.

"Because she deserves to know, and it is important she trusts me. Now, please tell me everything that happened until you found Mr. Howard."

He sighed. "I was behind the house doing the evening survey of the gardens like I do every night. Making sure everything is watered, and deadheading any flowers that had wilted during the heat of the day."

I nodded.

"I walked behind the Evergreens. Mrs. Susan Dickinson's cook has a kitchen garden there, and I like to keep an eye on it too. That's when I heard a bang like a window closing very suddenly. I looked up and spotted a person in the window."

"Who was it?" I asked.

"I don't know. I only saw the ruffle of the curtain and a hand." His eyes grew wide as if the memory haunted him in some way.

"Can you show me which window it was?" I asked.

He nodded, and I followed him down the path toward the Evergreens. When we were behind Austin Dickinson's house, he pointed up. "It was that window right there."

I looked up. If my recollection was correct, the room he pointed to was where Mr. Howard had been staying.

"Was it Mr. Howard in the window?" I asked.

"I don't know. Like I said, I only saw the hand. The sun was beginning to set, and the back side of the house had grown dark."

Cody took a deep breath before he went on. "A few minutes later, I saw Mr. Howard straightaway. He stumbled out the back door of the Evergreens. When I first spotted him I was convinced that he'd had too much to drink. I kept my distance. I didn't want to get tangled up in whatever mess he was in. Even so, instead of going to my cabin for the night, I stayed nearby so I could keep an eye on him. He didn't look quite right to me. He was staggering and gagging like he might be ill. To be honest, it sounded like he was sobbing."

"Sobbing?" I asked.

"Yes, like I said, I didn't walk up to him for fear of embarrassing him or myself."

"Then what happened?"

"He grabbed at his throat and began to run. It seemed to me he wasn't running in any particular direction. He was just running. Finally, panting, he toppled over into the black-eyed Susans. By the time I reached him, he was dead. That was that."

That was that. A life ended.

However, the reason Mr. Howard collapsed was still unknown.

"Can I go now? Horace has asked me to trim the front lawn while the family is at dinner at the Evergreens."

I arched my brow. "The whole family is eating at the Evergreens again tonight?" I didn't expect Emily to think to inform me of such details, and I was still on Margaret's bad side for working at the Evergreens so much over the last week.

He shrugged. "I don't pay much attention to their comings and goings, but that is what Horace said. We always try to trim the lawn when the family is away. They don't like us walking back and forth in front of their windows."

I nodded. Many times, servants were meant to be neither seen nor heard. I supposed that was why I found my friendship with Emily so startling. She had noticed me from the moment I stepped through the Dickinsons' door when they'd all lived in the white clapboard house on North Pleasant Street.

"I should go then," I said. "In case I am needed to help."

He nodded and started back in the direction of the barn.

"Cody," I called after him.

He stopped and turned. "Over the short time that Mr. Howard was here in Amherst, did you see him speaking to anyone?"

"He spoke to Miss Lavinia outside in the garden the first night he was here."

It did not surprise me that he spoke to Miss Lavinia, but why would he choose the garden? He had expressed that he had severe hay fever. The garden was the last place he should be for his health.

"Anyone else?"

"Just Horace," he said.

Horace was a complete surprise.

CHAPTER FIFTEEN

As I expected, Margaret had not heard the family was to eat at the Evergreens again tonight. She shook her wooden spoon at me after I shared the news. "You know who is behind it. It's that cook! Because she is a Yankee and I'm Irish, she thinks she has more clout in the family than I do. Well, I will show her how wrong she actually is!"

"What are you going to do?" I asked, even though I knew Margaret hated it when I questioned her, but I could not help it. I was so curious to see how far Margaret would take this feud, a feud I wasn't even certain the Evergreens' amiable cook knew anything about.

Margaret turned back to the stove. "Never you mind about that. Instead, please go ask Mrs. Dickinson if this is true about dinner. Cody is not the most reliable source."

Thinking of everything Cody had just told me in the garden, I found this revelation alarming. "Why do you say that?" I asked.

"Is any young man reliable?" she asked over her shoulder.

I left the kitchen in search of Mrs. Dickinson. I hated the thought of bothering her. In the last year, her health had worsened.

As I expected, I found her in her room on the second floor of the house. She was seated at her dressing table. She was dressed for dinner even though she would not have to leave for the Evergreens for another hour. She appeared to be frozen on the seat, looking out the window. For a moment, I thought I was looking at Emily in twenty years' time. She was in her own little world, one only she could truly understand. It was the first time I saw a real resemblance between mother and daughter.

Most of the time, I viewed Mrs. Dickinson with her quiet ways and failing health as the polar opposite of Emily, who always seemed so alive. Even when she was deep in her own thoughts where no one could reach her, she thrummed with life.

I cleared my throat. "Mrs. Dickinson."

She did not turn around, just continued to stare out the window.

"Mrs. Dickinson, Miss O'Brien would like to know if you and the family plan to dine at the Evergreens tonight."

She looked over her shoulder then. "Yes. I am sorry. I forgot to tell Margaret. There has been much plaguing my mind these last few days."

"It's all right," I said. "I know Miss O'Brien will understand."

"Susan is going to be much better at this than I ever was. Maybe I was too sheltered as a child or there were so many people in my family that I always knew someone else would take care of things. Since I married Edward, I have tried to be the perfect wife and mother, but I can never be that. Susan can. She is already in more control of her home as mistress than I have ever been or ever will be."

I didn't know what to say.

She smiled at me. I thought it might be the very first time I had ever seen Mrs. Dickinson smile. "I don't think I have done much to equip my daughters for marriage and family life, either, with my example. It is no wonder Emily wants nothing to do with it and Vinnie could become so taken with the first man to show her affection." She sighed. "At least we won't have to worry about Mr. Howard any longer. That is an answer to a prayer." She turned back toward the window.

I backed out of the room. As I made my way down to the kitchen to tell Margaret about dinner, I could not get the last bit of what Mrs. Dickinson said out of my head: *At least we won't have to worry about Mr. Howard any longer. That is an answer to a prayer.* My chest tightened. Could someone in the Dickinson family have had something to do with Mr. Howard's death after all?

As it turned out, Margaret's meal did not go to waste. Mr. and Mrs. Dickinson went to the Evergreens to dine with the younger Dickinsons and Mr. Emerson again, but the two sisters stayed home.

Miss Lavinia ate in her room, but Emily ate in the kitchen with Margaret and me.

Emily dipped her bread in the simple potato soup Margaret had made when she thought she was cooking only for the staff that night.

"This is my favorite kind of food," Emily said. "It's more real than the jelly and platters that circulate at parties, and it's more comforting than a giant Sunday roast."

"Thank you for saying so, Miss Dickinson," Margaret said. "But if I had known you were to eat with us, I would have made something more elaborate."

"No, this is just the thing. It has been a difficult few days, and it promises to become more difficult as time goes on. My sister is unhappy, and I struggle to comfort her when she usually is the one who comforts me."

"I know you staying in the house with her tonight will be a great comfort," I said.

"I hope that's true."

"Is she ill?" Margaret asked. "Should I call the doctor for her?"

Emily shook her head. "She is sick in her heart, and the only cure for that is time." She finished her soup and stood up. "I will go check on her."

Margaret stood, too, even though she had barely touched her own soup. "Let me cut her a piece of chocolate cake. I made it when I thought the family was to eat here tonight, and then I got word of the Evergreens, and my cake was not welcome." She said the last part with a sniff and then pulled herself together. "It seems it was meant to be, as I cannot think of a better remedy for a broken heart than chocolate cake."

"I agree," Emily said. "Had I had more foresight as to what my sister needed, I would have made my black cake, but it is a great deal of work. Your cake is most welcome."

If Margaret was offended as to how Emily compared her chocolate cake to Emily's black cake, she didn't show it. She merely cut a large slice for Miss Lavinia and put it on a white plate for Emily to take with her upstairs.

After Emily left, Margaret and I made quick work of cleaning the kitchen for the night and setting things out for tomorrow morning's breakfast. We worked in silence, and all the while, I kept thinking of how much I wanted to speak to Emily and tell her what Cody had said, but I certainly wasn't going to barge in on her and Miss Lavinia to have that conversation. I was on thin ice as far as Miss Lavinia was concerned already.

Margaret wiped her hands on a plain white tea towel and draped it over the edge of the sink. "I must say, one advantage to the Dickinsons dining at the Evergreens is we are done for the night so much earlier. I think I will go to my room and put my feet up."

I smiled. "You deserve that, Margaret. You work very hard." As I spoke, I hoped she caught the sincerity in my voice. In truth, Margaret O'Brien was one of the hardest-working women I had ever met.

She nodded, and there was the hint of a pleased smile on her face as she left the room.

I, too, should have taken advantage of the unexpected free time and gone to my room for the night with a book from the Dickinson library, but instead, I went out into the gardens in search of Horace.

There was no one in the gardens, but I heard voices on the other side of the barn. I walked around the large barn to the barnyard. Jeremiah York was in the yard walking Terror in a circle with a lead rope. I watched the two of them for several minutes.

The horse was completely in tune with even the slightest

movement of Jeremiah's feet or wrist. Terror almost looked like he was floating through air as he galloped around in the circle.

Finally, Jeremiah gave a tug on the lead rope, and Terror came to a stop. The horse blew hot air from his nostrils. Jeremiah waved at me, and he and Terror walked over to meet me where I stood by the fence.

"He looks good," I said.

Jeremiah flashed his teeth and adjusted his glasses. "He's still a racehorse at heart. With the family walking over to the college every day for the symposium, Terror hasn't gotten much exercise lately. I'm not needed this evening, so I thought it would be a good time to work him out."

I nodded, knowing he meant he wasn't needed for the Underground Railroad that night. Jeremiah constantly risked his life to move runaways through Amherst toward Canada. Emily knew this about him, but none of the other members of the family did. The three of us had agreed it should stay that way just in case an official ever came knocking on the door asking uncomfortable questions.

"I'm glad both you and Terror are here."

"We have you to thank for that, Willa."

"No, you have Miss Dickinson to thank."

He gave me a look as if he didn't believe so.

I decided to change the subject. "I'm looking for Horace."

"Horace? He's already gone home for the night. He said he had some moonflowers set to bloom by the church after dark. He's been talking about it for days. Honestly, I have never met a man who loved plants as much as he does."

"Neither have I, and I love plants too."

"Then you are in good company with Horace around. He's a thoughtful man. We've had many conversations. His family has hidden runaways, you know. I have great respect for him. I wish a man like Horace could be making the decisions in this country instead of who we have now."

I nodded.

Jeremiah sighed. "I should brush Terror down and get him in the barn for the night. I still have to warm up that potato soup Miss O'Brien gave Cody and me for supper." He tugged on Terror's lead, ready to go back to the barn.

"Before you go, what can you tell me about the night Mr. Howard died?"

He stopped and looked at me. "I have already told you I was away."

I nodded. "You did, but did you see anyone with Mr. Howard before you left? Anything odd throughout the day?"

"Not that I can think of. I only saw him once in the garden in the late afternoon, and he was speaking to Horace."

My stomach twisted. Another person who saw Mr. Howard with Horace. It seemed that Horace Church was the next person I needed to speak to.

The Congregational church the Dickinsons had both started and attended—and where Horace lived and served as sexton—was across the street from the homestead. Also, if what Jeremiah said was true, and I had no reason not to believe him, Horace would be outside in the churchyard waiting for his moonflowers to bloom. I wouldn't even need to knock on his door to speak to him.

"Willa, there you are," Emily said as I walked back around the barn. "I went down into the kitchen and could not find you."

"I'm sorry, miss, I had some free time, and I was visiting Terror."

She nodded in an understanding way. She knew the horse was important to me because he'd been with my brother when Henry passed. In some ways, keeping Terror near was a way to keep Henry alive and close.

"How is Miss Lavinia?" I asked.

Emily glanced in the direction of the house. "She is upset. It seems Mr. Howard made her some promises. I feel torn, Willa, and that is the truth. Vinnie wanted to marry that man. How she knew after one day, I will never know, but it seems he felt the same."

"Why are you torn?"

"Because I am quite relieved. I don't want my sister to marry. I want things to stop changing." She wrapped her purple shawl close around her body.

I suppressed a shiver. Mrs. Dickinson had said much the same in her way, but she had said Mr. Howard's death was an answer to a prayer. The longer I worked for the Dickinsons, the longer I realized what an intertwined family they were. Austin wanted to head west to find his fortune, but Mr. Dickinson trapped him in Amherst in a crystal snare with a beautiful house and a partnership in his law firm. The girls had suitors who came and went. Nothing was serious in the ways of marriage or attachment. Could it be that their parents discouraged it? Could it be they knew when either girl married, she would have to go wherever her husband led? No house, no job, would keep her in the fold.

"Now, tell me about your day since I have last seen you. Have you found anything new?" Emily asked.

I blinked at her. There seemed to be so much to say. "I will tell you on the way to the church," I said. "It's a short walk, so I will talk fast."

"Why are we going to the church? You know I have no use for it."

It was true. Even though the family were prominent members of the church, Emily did not attend Sunday services, nor did she ever join the church. She said she found worship elsewhere. How someone found worship outside of a church, I did not know.

"We need to speak to Horace."

"What about?"

"The murder."

CHAPTER SIXTEEN

As we walked through the garden and across the street to the church, I filled Emily in on all I had learned. I told her everything, from the argument between Mr. Emerson and Mr. Howard not long before the latter was killed, to Cody being the first to see the body—not me, like the police thought. Carlo came with us, of course, and kept pace with his mistress. I was happy for his company, as was Emily. I wasn't sure I would be comfortable out walking at night without the large dog nearby, and as the light dimmed, he looked more and more like a bear, which was sure to scare off anyone who might want to give us trouble.

"My, Willa, you have been quite a busy bee while I have been comforting my lovelorn sister." Her eyes sparkled with interest as she considered all that I'd learned.

I blushed and stopped in front of the church. The church itself was a large stone building with a slate roof. Its most impressive feature was the steeple that rose high in the air. Inside, the bell waited to ring on Sunday morning. I stared up at it. The church was a far cry from the country Baptist church I had attended until coming to work for the Dickinsons. At times, I missed the feeling of family there. However, Mr. Dickinson required everyone under his roof to attend services at the First Congregational Church. The rule applied to everyone but his eldest daughter.

The sun was setting, and the steeple was awash in pink and purple.

She looked up at it. "The steeples swam in Amethyst."

I did not ask her to explain her observation. I rarely did when she had that tone of voice, as if she were speaking just to herself. When she did that, I felt like an intruder in her thoughts.

She shook her head as if forcing herself to return to the present from whatever faraway place she had traveled.

She studied me. "So Cody was the first one to find Mr. Howard. Why did you say you were? You put yourself under suspicion."

"I knew how afraid he was," I said. "I see a lot of Henry in him . . ." I trailed off.

Emily's face softened.

"I told him I wouldn't tell the police if I didn't have to."

"That is quite a big promise to keep."

"I know," I admitted. "But I have an urge to protect him."

"Because you cannot protect your brother any longer," Emily said in her blunt way.

I stared at her, surprised she stated how I was feeling so succinctly.

As if she did not expect me to respond to her last comment,

she went on to say, "I don't see why Cody would have any reason to hurt Mr. Howard. He did not know about the situation with Vinnie, and to be honest, Vinnie has never been particularly nice to him or any of the outside help."

I bit the inside of my lip. I had neglected to tell her about the kiss that Cody had witnessed between Mr. Howard and Miss Lavinia. I remained silent on the subject. Miss Lavinia might not care for me, but she deserved her privacy.

"I can't see him killing someone for her," Emily went on. "If it can be proven pyrethrin in our garden shed had been used, maybe I will think differently because he would have very easy access to it. No one pays any attention to how many times a yardman goes in and out of the gardening shed."

I let out a sigh of relief. "Thank you."

"However, I am glad you told me. I would not be happy if I found it out later. Lying is not something I abide."

I knew this. Loyalty was one of the greatest tenets of the Dickinson family.

"You said Horace was waiting for his moonflowers to bloom. I know just where he will be."

She headed toward the church, but instead of walking up to the front doors, she skirted around it and walked into the courtyard in the back.

Horace's little cottage was on the Amherst College campus. From that spot, he could walk in every direction of his responsibilities in mere minutes. The college was behind him, the Dickinson homes were across Main Street, and the church was just in front of him.

Emily and I found Horace sitting on a stool in front of a trellis covered with bright green vines, heart-shaped leaves, and curled up, three-inch buds waiting for the perfect moment to unfurl.

"Miss Dickinson," Horace said. "Is it not a little late for a stroll through the churchyard?"

Emily patted the top of Carlo's head. "There is nothing to fear when Carlo is near." She chuckled at her rhyme.

The gardener nodded. "This is true, and he is a good dog too. Getting him was one of the better decisions your father made."

I thought Emily might ask him what he meant by that, but she didn't.

"We came here to speak with you," Emily said.

Horace's eyes slid to me. "About Mr. Howard I would think."

"Why do you say that?" Emily asked, genuinely curious.

"I've seen Willa walking around the Dickinson grounds talking to Cody and Jeremiah. She might not have seen me, but I heard Mr. Howard mentioned in more than one of those conversations."

I blushed. So much for collecting information without being noticed. And if he knew that, did he know it was actually Cody who found the body, not me? If he did, he didn't say so. Not yet, anyway.

"Willa and I will both work on being a little less obvious when we are asking questions, then," Emily said. "And yes, we are here to speak to you about Mr. Howard. Cody revealed to Willa that you spoke to him before he died."

"I gathered as much." He shifted on his stool but didn't offer us a place to sit.

That didn't stop Emily from sitting on the grass in front of the trellis of moonflowers. Unsure what to do, I sat next to her, taking care not to get grass stains on my skirt. Emily moved about until she was comfortable. I supposed she didn't care about grass stains, as she would not be the one to contend with them.

Carlo lay next to her with a mighty sigh and placed his massive head in her lap. She petted his head over and over again. "What did he talk to you about?"

"It wasn't anything about Mr. Emerson or Miss Lavinia, if that's what you are wondering. He was asking my advice about gardening."

"Why would he want to know about the garden if it makes him ill?" Emily asked.

"I was surprised too." Horace nodded. "He was asking me if there was something to help with his hay fever. He has a terrible case of it. He claimed to be made ill by everything that grows."

"A person can't be made ill by everything," Emily said, looking up from Carlo.

"Maybe not. He came to me for help because he bumped into the bee balm with his bare arm, and red welts showed up almost immediately."

I raised my brow. This could explain the mark on his arm. However, if the garden was so dangerous to him, wouldn't that be the last place he would go if he was feeling ill? Unless he was delirious or so shaken up by finding his room ransacked that he hadn't been thinking clearly.

"That is when he told me about his many ailments when in contact with plants," Horace went on. "All I could tell him was to wash his arm with soap and water and stay out of the garden. If he was affected by pollen, this was the worst place for him, especially at the end of the summer. You can practically see the pollen floating in the air."

"But he died in the garden. Why was he there?" Emily asked.

"I don't know this. By that time, I was here at the churchyard waiting for my moonflowers to bloom. They didn't bloom that night, but they will tonight. I can feel it." There was wistfulness in his voice.

"I feel like this is a dead end," Emily said. "Luther made no secret of his aversion to plants. It was one of the first things he said to all of us when he got out of Mr. Emerson's carriage."

I tensed. That meant the Dickinson family wasn't free from suspicion. Could they have killed Mr. Howard? But for what purpose? So he would not court Miss Lavinia? It seemed like a stretch. Less of a stretch was Mr. Dickinson as a suspect. He was a controlling father. He would not let Austin leave the fold, and I already wondered if he felt the same way when it came to Emily and Miss Lavinia. But murder? It seemed like a lot of trouble to go to when all he had to do was refuse to give his blessing to Miss Lavinia and Mr. Howard. Miss Lavinia, from what I knew, was an obedient daughter and was even afraid of her father at times. She would not defy him.

As all these thoughts went through my mind, Emily whispered, "It's happening."

I looked up and watched as the moonflowers bloomed. The flowers unwound into large trumpet-shaped white blossoms close to the size of my hand.

Even Carlo was captivated by the blossoms, and there were many. At least thirty opened up within minutes.

"They are so beautiful," I whispered.

"And like anything glorious, so fleeting," Emily murmured in a voice just above a whisper.

"Yes," Horace said. "They will close up at first light."

"Why plant moonflowers?" I asked. "The church is a place of activity in the morning and during the day. That is when the blossoms are gone. The parishioners can't enjoy them."

He looked me straight in the eye. "Because we must see beauty in the darkness to make our way through. The good Lord gave us this beauty to sustain us, without it we have nothing."

I examined the large white trumpet-shaped flower and saw he was right. It was beauty in darkness. Its white petals glowed in the light of the moon for which they were named.

"We grow accustomed to the Dark," Emily whispered. "When Light is put away."

I did not know if Emily was speaking of the moonflower. When she said this, I thought of the flower, but also of losing Henry, or losing my mother, and those facing the very sudden loss of Mr. Howard.

CHAPTER SEVENTEEN

I SAT ON the edge of my bed that night and rubbed my feet. It had been a long day, made even longer by investigating Mr. Howard's death. Now, I worried the Dickinson family might have something to do with it. It pained me to realize I couldn't completely rule them out, not yet, and I wondered if Emily had come to the same conclusion.

There was a knock at my door.

I dropped my feet to the floor. It could only be Margaret. It wasn't often, but at times, she knocked on my door and told me if there were some special directions for the next day.

"Yes?" I asked.

"Willa, it's me! Can I come in?" Emily asked.

I hopped off my bed and went to the door to let her inside. "Emily, what are you doing here at this time of night?"

"I felt like it was imperative that we begin formulating a plan." She paced the floor.

I quickly shut the door, for fear of waking Margaret. "A plan."

"Yes, what we have learned today does not look good for the family. Even if the detective doesn't wish to investigate us, once he hears everything we have discovered, the police will be looking at us as criminals. Do you know what kind of harm even just the scrutiny will do to our reputation? It will destroy my father. Reputation is everything to him. He had to fight once before to put the family name in good standing after his father lost all the family money. He can't be put through that again."

"Why do you think the police will want to look at your family?" I had my own reasons for believing that, but I wanted to hear if they aligned with Emily's.

"Isn't it obvious?" She threw up her hands and began to pace faster. "Mr. Howard was trying to trick Vinnie into falling in love with him. The only reason he would do so would be for her money."

I winced when I heard this. Miss Lavinia didn't care much for me, and I was well aware of it. However, I hated that Emily could think a man would want to marry her sister only for her money.

"He also wanted the prestige of being attached to our family," Emily added.

"How do you know this?" I asked.

She stopped in the middle of the room. "Can you think of any other reason he would profess his love to Vinnie within one day's time of meeting her?"

"He said that he loved her?"

"Not in so many words, but he told Vinnie he wanted for them to elope."

I gasped. "He did? After one day?"

She nodded. "The police will suspect my brother or father for the murder because they will want to protect Vinnie. They would not want her to run off and marry anyone. It would ruin her reputation and that of the family's."

"Emily, I must ask a difficult question."

"I know what you are going to ask, and no, I can't believe my father or brother would have killed a man. All Father would have to do is tell Lavinia not to marry Mr. Howard, and that would be the end of it. My sister always does what is expected of her."

"What about a woman in the family? Throwing pyrethrin on him would not require a great deal of strength."

She looked at me. "Are you wondering if I killed him, Willa?"

"No." I shook my head. "I mean, I know you would not want your sister to be hurt, but I don't believe you would go to those lengths. There were many ways you could have convinced Miss Lavinia he wasn't the right suitor. She wouldn't do anything that might harm you."

"Whatever do you mean?" she wanted to know.

I placed a hand on my cheek and perched on the edge of my bed. "The day Mr. Howard first arrived, he asked me if I could retrieve copies of your work, and he promised to show them to Mr. Emerson. He claimed Mr. Emerson would review it and see if they could be published."

The color drained from Emily's face. "What? You would never do that."

I let out a breath that she trusted me so well. "I wouldn't, but I thought of it again in light of the conversation I overheard when Mr. Emerson dismissed Mr. Howard for stealing his work."

"What did you say when Mr. Howard asked this?"

"Nothing. I simply walked away when he asked. To be honest, he made me uncomfortable. He would not have been a good match for Miss Lavinia. I know that as a fact."

She nodded, and color returned to her face. "We are in agreement. The question remains. Will the police think the family was so against the match that we would take drastic measures?"

"I don't think so," I said. "You are a prominent family. They would need much more to accuse a Dickinson."

"Have you told the police what you overheard between Mr. Emerson and Mr. Howard?" she asked.

I shook my head. "You are the only one I have told."

"Good. Because we have to speak to him before they do, and we will do that at first opportunity tomorrow." She went to the door. "Sleep well, Willa, because tomorrow we catch a killer." She went out the door with a flourish.

THE NEXT MORNING, I woke up at three, an hour earlier than I usually rose from my bed. It was pitch black outside, and I was dead tired. It took me twice as long to get ready for the day as I fumbled about, but I was still forty minutes ahead of my normal time.

I had arisen early because Emily wanted me to go with her to the college again that day, and I knew it would not sit well with Margaret. In all honesty, if I were in Margaret's shoes, I, too, would have been upset to be left at the homestead with all the work.

To soften the blow, I hurried through many of the morning tasks in the house, setting the table for breakfast, starting the fire in the stove, opening the windows, and fluffing the pillows in the parlors.

By the time Margaret came into the kitchen, I had porridge bubbling on the stove top, and a mug of coffee was waiting for her with fresh cream from the homestead's dairy cow, just how she liked it.

She stared at the blue speckled coffee mug. "Is that for me?"

I stirred the porridge. "Yes, I thought with everything going on, you could use a cup right away."

She picked it up, took a sip, and closed her eyes as she allowed the hot liquid to warm her. When she opened them again, she was looking at me. "What is it that you want, Willa?"

I kept stirring. I had to or the porridge would burn. "I did all the morning chores, and the table is ready for breakfast. I have a tray ready to take up to Mrs. Dickinson's room as well, in case she does not feel like coming down this morning."

She set her mug down and folded her arms. "Willa."

There was a warning tone in her voice.

"Miss Dickinson would like me to go with her to the lectures again this morning," I said in a rush. "She is more comfortable if I am with her."

Margaret's face flushed red. "Is it going to be like this every day until the week is over?"

"I hope not," I said honestly, because I was very tired, and the thought of getting up at three in the morning the next day almost brought me to tears.

Emily came in the kitchen then. "I'm here to make the morning bread," she said with a smile. "I'm a bit early, but

Willa and I will be heading to the lectures early. I trust she told you."

"She just did," Margaret said with a sniff. "Isn't taking Carlo with you enough support?"

"Carlo cannot come into the lecture hall with me. As much as I would love to take him, he would be much happier napping in the gardens with Horace and Cody than he would be sitting outside a lecture hall on campus wondering when I will reappear." She began measuring flour into a bowl.

"Very well," Margaret said with a sigh. "I suppose this is something I must get used to, like so many other things in this house."

If Emily was offended by this comment, she didn't show it. Instead, she hummed under her breath while she made the day's brown bread.

Emily and I left the house before the rest of the family even made it down to the dining room for the morning meal. Carlo was not happy when she said he had to stay back with Horace. He flopped on his side in the middle of the rose garden path like he didn't have the spirit to go on.

Emily shook her head as we made our way down Main Street. "Carlo can be so dramatic at times. I don't know where he gets it."

"No idea," I murmured. Then I cleared my throat. "Why are we leaving the house so early? It was my understanding that the lectures don't begin until eight thirty."

She grinned at me. "Well, it is very nice to know something before you do, Willa. It seems like during this whole investigation you have been one step ahead of me. Yesterday when I went to the Evergreens, Susan mentioned to me that Mr.

Emerson planned to go to the lecture hall very early this morning in order to meet with some of the college literature professors. It was the only time that he could squeeze in the meeting."

"So we are barging in on their meeting?" I asked.

"I wouldn't call it 'barging in.'" She slipped her arm around mine. "We're out for a morning walk and just happened to stumble upon it."

That sounded a whole lot like barging to me.

It was a fine morning but already hot. There was a mist in the air, and dew dripped off the corn in the Dickinsons' fields across from the homestead. It wasn't until I lived at the homestead that I realized how much land the family owned. There were the two homes, gardens, barn, barnyard, and acres of farmland across the street just in front of the college.

The field was far too wet with dew for us to cross through it, so Emily and I made our way to the sidewalk that led into campus.

In the fall, the campus would be bustling with students and professors rushing to and fro to make their next lecture or appointment. But in summer it was quiet. Like the quiet before a storm.

"How are we going to speak to Mr. Emerson when he is in a meeting?" I asked nervously. "We don't want to give him the wrong impression."

"Do not worry, Willa. I am Edward Dickinson's daughter, I know politics."

I wrinkled my brow, unsure what politics had to do with this.

The front door to the lecture hall opened, and three men in

brown tweed suits stepped outside. They spoke excitedly to one another, but Emily and I were too far away to hear what they were saying.

"I recognize Dr. Arnold. He is one of the literature professors," she said. "You know what this means, don't you? It means we are in luck. The meeting must be over. This is our chance to speak to Mr. Emerson."

The three men stood at the foot of the lecture hall steps as another exited the building. I recognized him right away by his impressive sideburns.

"There is Mr. Emerson now!" Emily released my arm and hurried toward the lecture hall.

It took me three strides to catch up with Emily, even though my legs were longer than hers.

One of the professors shook Mr. Emerson's hand. "Thank you again for being here this week to speak to our community and students. So many of our literature students came back to campus a month early just for the opportunity to hear you speak."

"It is quite an honor when both young and old find value in your work," Mr. Emerson replied. "I believe I will walk back to my rooms at the Evergreens and review my notes before my lecture starts. I don't want to disappoint any of your students by not knowing the content of my talk."

The men laughed, as if this were some sort of impossibility.

They said their goodbyes, and Mr. Emerson began walking in our direction. He nodded at Emily. If he recognized her, he gave no indication. I found this odd since he had met her on at least three occasions over the last few days, and at least two of those times had been over a meal. At her family home!

Emily turned as he walked by. "Mr. Emerson, may I speak with you for a moment?"

Mr. Emerson turned around with something akin to weariness in his eyes. Then his expression cleared. "Oh, Miss Dickinson, I'm so very sorry I didn't greet you." He smiled. "I suppose I was just too caught up in my own thoughts."

"I very much understand how that happens," Emily replied.

"Aah, yes, I believe your brother Austin mentioned you are a writer too. Is that what you wish to discuss? I suppose you want me to review your work. You must understand I'm a very busy man and cannot possibly read everything that everyone sends me, and still create my own essays and lectures."

"I understand that. The creative process cannot be interrupted."

"Quite," he agreed, as if he was surprised she didn't shove a manuscript into his hand and run away.

"I more wanted to speak with you about Mr. Howard."

Color rushed to Mr. Emerson's face.

"We are all very sorry about what happened."

"Yes, well, it is a very bad thing, but I don't blame anyone in your family. I have told the police this. I'm sure they will find the culprit soon enough. However, I for one don't have any idea as to why someone would want to kill such a young and gifted man. He had the makings of a great writer, which is why I took him under my wing in the first place." He shook his head. "It is a loss."

"Is it not true that you dismissed him right before dinner?" Emily asked.

Mr. Emerson sucked in a strangled breath. "Excuse me?"

"Is it not true that you dismissed him just before dinner the night he died because he was passing your work off as his own?" Emily asked, looking him straight in the eye.

"What?" he sputtered. "Where did you hear such an outrageous claim?"

She pointed at me. "Willa told me."

I blinked.

Mr. Emerson's eyes bored into me. "And you are?"

"Oh, this is my maid Willa," Emily said, speaking for me. "I like company on my walks. Sometimes I take my dog, Carlo, with me, and sometimes I take Willa."

I frowned at being compared to a dog, even though I knew Emily revered Carlo more than she did most people.

Emily's demeanor speaking to Mr. Emerson was so different from how she'd acted when she'd first met him. I could only attribute that to the fact she was now on a mission to find a killer and clear her family name. The mission had removed her shy persona.

"I see," he replied. "And why would you make such an accusation?"

He addressed this question to me.

Everything in me wanted to run as fast as I could to the homestead and hide in the safety of the kitchen, where I belonged. I shouldn't have come on this errand with Emily. This wasn't my place.

But even though that was how I felt, I straightened my spine in challenge, not unlike Henry would have done under the same circumstances. "Because it is the truth. I was working in the Evergreens that day and was outside of Mr. Howard's room when I heard the two of you fighting. You were arguing about something missing. It seemed as though you thought he had stolen your work, and dismissed him. You then said he could stay for the rest of the symposium, but after, he would have to find work elsewhere."

Mr. Emerson studied me. "I do not abide falsehoods." He deflated slightly. "And that goes for my own falsehoods too. I regret you overheard the conversation. I thought it would be buried with Luther. However, what you have said is true. I will not deny it."

My brow went up in surprise. I had fully expected Mr. Emerson to call me a liar. I was a servant, a lesser person to a man like him, or so I assumed he believed. However, he had admitted right away I was telling the truth.

"Well," Emily said, also sounding a bit taken aback herself. "Don't you believe you should share this with the police?"

"Why should I? It has no bearing on Luther's death."

"You don't know that," Emily said.

He scowled at her. "When I first met you, I took you to be a timid girl."

"First impressions can be deceiving," Emily said.

"Quite," he agreed.

"Mr. Emerson," I began, finally feeling brave enough to pose a question of my own, "how did you know Mr. Howard was stealing your work?"

He looked at me for a long moment as if he was considering whether he should answer. Finally, he said, "Because my editor sent me a letter. I received it just before leaving for Amherst."

"What did the letter say?" Emily asked breathlessly.

He sighed. "It said a junior editor at the publishing house had received work from one Mr. Luther Howard. This junior editor was so impressed that he passed it to my editor for final approval for publication. The junior editor didn't know Luther was my secretary; however, my editor did. As he read the work, he became suspicious. It sounded too much like a copy of my voice and tone. He alerted me to the fact that he believed Luther might be stealing my writings yet to be published or trying to imitate my voice as a writer. These sins are unforgivable in my literary world. The editor sent me the manuscript Luther was attempting to have published, and even though it was not in my hand, I immediately recognized it as an unfinished work of mine I had abandoned when I started writing *English Traits*."

Emily folded her arms and seemed to consider this revelation. "Didn't he know he would be caught just as soon as the work was published? You would know it was yours right away."

"I don't have an answer for that, and it's not something we can learn from Luther either."

That was certainly true.

"Apparently, this was not the only work Luther had submitted to the junior editor," Mr. Emerson added. "He also submitted a collection of essays the junior editor hoped to publish, but when it was found out he had stolen my work, the publisher and editors broke all contact with Luther."

"Have you read the other work?" Emily asked.

"Yes, it's quite good. I would say the style was lyrical even. It's a shame Luther tried to steal my work, because I believe he would have gotten there on his own. It is most upsetting, as he was a good writer. He wasn't yet at the point where he would have great success, but he was just on the cusp of it. It seemed he didn't want to put in the work to improve. He wanted the easy way out, and so he cheated."

"You, of course, knew Mr. Howard had hay fever," Emily asked.

Mr. Emerson blinked. "He made no secret of it. He complained constantly when we were outside, and often felt ill in the spring and the fall." He cleared his throat. "I don't know what this has to do with anything." He looked in the direction of the Evergreens. "I really must return to my room if I want to look over my notes before my lecture."

"He died from a hay fever reaction. There was evidence on his face and clothing that he came in contact with pyrethrin, an insect repellent used in gardens."

"That's unfortunate," Mr. Emerson said. "Your family has a very large garden, perhaps he rubbed up against it there. There were a great many things that would trigger his hay fever."

"If you knew such a substance would make him ill . . ." Emily trailed off.

Mr. Emerson frowned. "You do know by posing these questions to me, you are harming yourself as a writer. I have great power in the literary world. If you ever want to be published, I would recommend you don't accuse me of a crime."

"I'm not accusing you. Just asking some questions. Let us not forget a young man in his prime is dead. I'm just trying to find out who would most benefit from his passing, and clear my family's name."

"Are you asking if I killed my secretary?" Mr. Emerson asked.

"I am," Emily said.

"Then you have lost your mind," Mr. Emerson replied.

"Mr. Howard said that he could ruin you. What did he know?"

"He was my secretary. He knew everything about my business, but I can assure you that was an empty threat thrown out by a desperate man. I have nothing to hide."

Before Emily could respond, there were shouts and the pounding of hooves on the road beside us.

"Police! Stop! Police!"

We turned to the road as one and saw Paulo the peddler cracking a black whip over the head of his mule, who was pulling the wagon down Main Street. He looked over his shoulder at Matthew and another officer who chased him on foot. They stood no chance of catching him and the terrified mule.

"Stop!"

One of the officers blew a shrill whistle, but it was no use. Paulo, the wagon, and mule disappeared from sight.

CHAPTER EIGHTEEN

MATTHEW WAS IN the middle of Main Street, bent at the waist and holding on to his knees. His chest heaved up and down. I didn't know how far or for how long he had been chasing Paulo and his mule, but it had seemingly been long enough to completely exhaust him. A strong urge came upon me to run over to him and make sure he was all right, and I even took a step in that direction before Emily's voice stopped me.

"It seems they found the killer before we did. Now, they just have to catch him."

My head snapped back in her direction. She stood alone by a low stone wall. It seemed Mr. Emerson had taken advantage of the commotion to slip away. I could see him halfway down the walk on the way to the Evergreens.

"What do you mean 'they found the killer'?" I asked.

Emily looked at me. "Is it not obvious, Willa? The police think Paulo is the killer. Why else would they be chasing him?"

My brother was chased by the police on more than one occasion for good reason too. Henry always had the best of intentions, but sometimes those intentions had broken the law. Because of this I could think of many reasons why the police might be chasing the peddler.

The other police officer walked over to Matthew and patted him on the back. Matthew straightened up, and he seemed to recover from losing his breath. I gave a sigh of relief.

"There is only one way to find out for sure," Emily said, and marched in the officers' direction.

"Emily!" I called after her, but it was no use.

Emily stepped onto the street. "Good morning, Officers."

Matthew and the other officer looked at us.

"Are you all right? My maid and I were just out for a walk, and we saw you chase that peddler on the road. You would have been much better off on horseback."

The other officer turned red. "We didn't know he would run, ma'am."

"Ma'am?" Emily asked with an arched brow. "I am quite a bit younger than you, I would dare say, Officer . . ."

"Phillips, miss. I apologize."

Emily nodded. "And, Officer Thomas, I am surprised a strong young man like you wasn't able to catch him."

"He cracked the whip on that poor mule quite hard, Miss Dickinson; I can never run as fast as a frightened animal."

"Few of us can," she agreed. "What did he do?"

"We aren't at liberty to say, miss," Officer Phillips said.

"You are if it has anything to do with my family." Emily sniffed. "You know the death of Mr. Howard in our gardens has been quite upsetting for all of us and for our guest, Mr. Emerson. Perhaps he is the most upset because he was the closest to Mr. Howard. If the peddler has anything to do with it, we deserve to know. If you don't tell me, you will surely have to speak to my father on the matter."

Officer Phillips went pale at the idea of speaking to Mr. Dickinson. I could not say I blamed him. The patriarch of the Dickinson family was a stern and critical man.

Matthew looked at me then, and his face softened. I wished I knew what he was thinking. Did he feel the same way about me as he claimed to last year? Had I stalled too long in giving him an answer and missed my chance? My chance for what? I asked myself. I was happy at my post in the Dickinson home. Yes, with Miss Susan and Austin's marriage, the arrival of Mr. Emerson, and Mr. Howard's murder, it had been a difficult few weeks, but overall this was the life I wanted, wasn't it? I never doubted it until I looked into Matthew's eyes.

"Did you not hear my question, Officer Thomas?" Emily asked.

Both Matthew and I broke eye contact.

"I'm sorry, Miss Dickinson, what was your question?" Matthew asked.

"Did Paulo Vitali kill Luther Howard?"

He looked at her. "Yes, we believe he did."

"But why?" I blurted out.

Officer Phillips frowned at me. He might be willing to answer Emily's questions, but mine were not given the same weight.

Matthew glanced at me. "Mr. Vitali and Mr. Howard have

a history. Mr. Vitali admitted as much before he ran. He was selling the murder weapon, pyrethrin, from his wagon, so he had access to the substance."

"What is their history?" Emily asked.

"I can't tell you that," Matthew said.

Emily folded her arms. "Well, it doesn't look like you will have much luck catching him now. It's clear he was leaving Amherst. He's going to get away."

Officer Phillips frowned. "We will notify other police departments throughout the commonwealth to look for him. Unless he dumps the mule and wagon, he won't be too hard to eventually find. He tends to stand out."

That was true.

Emily nodded as if she was satisfied with this answer. "And my family won't receive any more scrutiny?"

"No. We're confident we've found the identity of the killer. We just have to catch him now," Officer Phillips said. He turned to Matthew. "Let's get back to the station to alert the other departments."

Matthew nodded. "Please don't tell anyone what you have heard here today. We know it will all be out before long, but we can't rest until the murderer is caught."

I promised I wouldn't, but Emily said nothing.

After Matthew and Officer Phillips left, Emily slipped her arm through mine again. "I don't believe it, Willa."

I looked at her out of the corner of my eye. "You don't believe what?"

"That this Paulo person is the killer. He wasn't at the dinner party that night. When could he have killed Mr. Howard with the pyrethrin?"

"Maybe it didn't happen that night. We don't know how long it takes for a person to react to it."

She stopped in the middle of the sidewalk. "Willa, you are a genius, and yes, you are right. We need to find out what pyrethrin really does to narrow down our suspects."

"Or broaden them," I muttered under my breath.

AT THE NOON meal, Carlo and I walked to campus again. I carried another heavy hamper of food, and he pranced happily with the prospect of seeing his mistress, who had been in the lecture hall most of the morning listening to Mr. Emerson and other scholarly speakers.

I knew the large dog was also excited at the idea he might get one of the sandwiches in the hamper for his own lunch. Margaret had made egg salad that day, and it was the giant pup's favorite.

He kept trying to stick his nose in the hamper, and I had to move it from arm to arm in order to keep him from stealing a bite.

By the time Carlo and I reached the lecture hall, Emily and the rest of the Dickinson family were at the picnic tables under the elm tree just outside.

It seemed to me there was a bigger crowd for this lecture, and it took me some time to reach the Dickinsons.

Two men stood in my path.

"Well, it is no wonder an immigrant would be the killer. They want to take everything that is rightfully ours. They come here wanting to take, take, take, if you ask me," a portly man in a brown suit said.

"Yes," his companion agreed. "And I hope the police catch him soon. My wife is frantic. I don't like the idea of a foreigner running around the town when my wife and children are home alone. What am I to do though? I have to give my lectures here at the college. I can't have my wife and children come with me. That would be inappropriate."

"I'm sure," the portly man said, "that the women in Amherst are beside themselves. I tell you a hysterical woman is almost as bad as a murderous foreigner."

I gripped the hamper's handle so tightly that the wood bit into my palm. Next to me Carlo growled. I relaxed and patted his head. "I don't like them either," I whispered. The large dog had always been a good judge of character.

"Willa!" Emily waved at me.

I skirted around the men—who didn't even step aside to let me pass—and finally reached the picnic tables. Emily scratched Carlo's ear and praised him while I quickly set the tables so the Dickinson family could eat.

"Willa." Miss Susan came up to me as I set out the silverware. "Did you bring three extra place settings? Mr. and Mrs. Thayer and Isadora Foote will be joining us for the meal too."

"I—I didn't realize, I'm sorry. I can hurry home and get more."

"There is no time for that. The lecture will begin in an hour. There should be enough as Mr. and Mrs. Dickinson did not attend today, and Mr. Emerson said he preferred to go on a walk rather than eat with us." She pressed her lips in a thin line. "I do hope this mess with Mr. Howard does not give him a bad impression about our hospitality."

I didn't know how it could give him a good one seeing as how his secretary had been murdered, but I kept those thoughts to myself.

"If those three are not here, then yes, there is enough."

"Good. Next time, I hope you will pack extra just in case. We need to be nimble when it comes to these things."

I nodded and returned to my work.

Isadora Foote and Cate Lynn Thayer walked arm in arm over to the picnic.

"Isn't this lovely," Mrs. Thayer said. "It looks like a painting."

"Yes," Isadora agreed. "It is a splendid meal for a splendid day. I have learned so much from Mr. Emerson's lectures."

Mrs. Thayer smiled. "And I admire Mr. Emerson, as he is able to so easily speak when he suffered the loss of his secretary just days ago. It's just a sign of what a good orator he really is."

"I'm sure it helps," Isadora said, "to know the police have identified who the killer is."

"Yes, but if I were Mr. Emerson, I would be on edge until I knew he was caught," Mrs. Thayer said. "I have to admit, I am on edge as it is, and I have no reason to believe Paulo the peddler would have any interest in me."

I removed the tea towels from the plate of sandwiches. It seemed Matthew's goal to keep the killer's identity a secret had been unsuccessful.

"The police will catch him, and that will put this all to rest," Isadora said.

I wanted to hear more, but the table was set, and if I

hovered much longer, it would just appear strange. Reluctantly, I stepped back from the table.

I retreated to wait by the elm tree while the family and their guests ate.

"I, for one, am not surprised in the least that a foreigner is the killer," Mr. Thayer said as he selected a sandwich from the platter being handed around.

"Because he is foreign?" Emily challenged.

Mr. Thayer looked in her direction. "Not entirely, but that is part of it. People from other places have different sets of rules. They aren't like us."

"Aren't we all descendants of foreigners at this table?" Emily asked. "Not a single one of us is an Indian, correct?"

"You are missing the point. He came straight here from another country, a hot one to boot. Italians are known to be hotheads. All Mr. Howard had to do was look at him sideways and he would be furious."

"I would think poisoning someone would take a bit more thought than a crime of passion. If he was stabbed with a knife or shot with a rifle, then yes, perhaps you could say they had some sort of argument. But that is not the case. He died of a reaction."

"I'm not saying the Italian is not clever in the way he killed him. Surely, he did that so someone more learned would be blamed. Such as someone from your own family, Miss Dickinson. I assume you're relieved your family is no longer under suspicion?"

"I'm never relieved when the truth is buried for convenience," Emily replied.

"And what do you plan to do about it?" Mrs. Thayer asked.

Emily looked at her. "I will find my own answers."

Austin forced a laugh. "Please don't listen to my sister on this account. She has an inflated belief in her own intelligence. It is clear the police know who their man is. They will find him soon, and that will be the end of that. A man can't run forever."

Mrs. Thayer tapped her glass with her knife. "I believe this is the perfect time to make our announcement. Ruben, would you like to do the honors?"

Mr. Thayer scowled as if he was still miffed that Emily dared challenge him. "No, Cate Lynn. Why don't you do it? It was your idea."

Hurt flashed across Mrs. Thayer's face, but she soon recovered. "As Friday is Mr. Emerson's final day here in Amherst, Mr. Thayer and I have decided to host a ball at our home in his honor. We hope that all of you can attend."

"A ball," Miss Susan said. "That sounds wonderful. Austin, don't you think so?"

Austin nodded. "I think it will be just the thing to raise all of our spirits after the week we had."

"I don't believe a ball will erase the fact that Mr. Howard is dead," Miss Lavinia said, speaking for the first time. "If you will excuse me."

She stood up from the table and hurried away.

Emily rose, too, and followed her sister. I very much wanted to go after them to hear what Miss Lavinia had to say, but I couldn't see a way to do that without adding to the scene.

Austin's cheeks were a slight shade of pink. "You will have

to forgive my youngest sister. She has not been feeling too well over the last several days."

"Oh, Austin," Mr. Thayer said. "We are all friends here. We know Lavinia had her sights on Mr. Howard as a potential husband. It must be a great disappointment for her and knowing she's not getting any younger either."

It wasn't often I felt bad for Miss Lavinia. However, in this moment, I did feel for her. It must have been so humiliating to realize everyone knew how she felt about Mr. Howard.

"The lectures will begin again in five minutes. Five minutes," a young college student said as he made his way through the green.

Austin stood. "I suppose that is our cue to go back inside. Mr. Emerson will be speaking again this afternoon. I'm looking forward to it."

The Thayers, Miss Susan, Austin, and Isadora all left the picnic table and went into the lecture hall. That left Carlo and me to clean the mess left behind. Me, actually, but Carlo was there for moral support.

By the time I finished packing everything back into the hamper, I was alone on the lawn except for Carlo.

I picked up the much lighter hamper from the picnic table and whistled for Carlo to follow me as I made my way back to the homestead.

As I entered the gate in front of the Dickinson estate, I heard voices.

"I don't want the life you do. As my sister, you have to accept that."

"You will never find a place that fits you better than here. Why did you even consider giving that up?"

I saw the two sisters sitting on a bench together outside of the conservatory where it attached to the dining room of the house.

Unless I walked around to the other side of the house—which would take twice as long—I would have to walk right past them, and I knew Miss Lavinia would not appreciate that in the least.

However, Carlo took away my choice. He woofed and ran to his mistress.

The two sisters spotted me behind him.

I straightened my back and carried the hamper over to them.

"Willa, thank goodness you are here. Will you tell my sister it is not worth giving up her independence to marry? Willa is a perfect example of this. She said no to a man's offer of marriage."

Heat rushed to my face. I had told Emily that Matthew had proposed to me, but I assumed she wouldn't share it with anyone else.

"You were proposed to and said no?" Miss Lavinia asked in a disbelieving voice. "Was he homely? Poor? Why would you say no?"

I thought of the first time Matthew asked for my hand. I didn't want to end up like my mother, whom my father left with two small children to raise on her own, and who was so protective of Henry and me that I would not let love in, so I could not love Matthew. Then. Confusion filled my mind. But now? What about now?

"I didn't want to marry without love," I said finally, because it had been the truth when I refused him. I had bottled up any feelings about Matthew that I might have had at the time in a sort of armor around myself and around Henry. Was my armor cracking? And if it was, was I willing to risk my position in the Dickinson home to find out?

Miss Lavinia stood up. "Then you are a greater fool than I thought." She marched away.

CHAPTER NINETEEN

EMILY RAN TO catch up with her sister and put her arm around Miss Lavinia's shoulders. At first Miss Lavinia tried to push her sister away, but then she stopped fighting and leaned into Emily. It was one of the few times I witnessed Emily caring for her younger sister and not the other way around. Emily was a little more than two years older than Miss Lavinia.

I walked a few paces behind the sisters. Their heads were bent together. Even though it was clear Miss Lavinia was still upset with her sister over not wanting her to marry, I knew they had a bond that could not be broken.

I could not help but wonder what it would have been like if I'd had a sister to lean on like that. Henry had been a good brother. Not good in the way he constantly found himself in trouble. But I knew if I ever needed help, he would have been the first person there. It was difficult to realize I didn't have a person like that in my life any longer.

Matthew came to mind again. He wanted to be that for me.

Matthew had said he would wait as long as it took for me to decide if I wanted to marry him or not. But was that really fair? He needed to move on and start a life and family. It was wrong for me to string him along like this. I needed to tell him I could never marry him, even if I did not know how I truly felt.

The sisters went into the house through the front door, and I walked around to the entrance through the laundry shed like I always did. Before I reached the shed, Jeremiah came running from the barn. "Willa! Willa!"

I almost dropped the hamper. "Jeremiah, what is wrong?"

"It's Cody. The police detective is questioning him."

Fear spread through me.

"Why?" I asked.

"I don't know. I can't go over there."

I knew what he meant. Because of his work with the Underground Railroad, Jeremiah avoided the police as much as possible. The less they knew about him, the better.

"Where are they?" I asked.

"I saw them in the orchard."

I nodded and glanced at the house. I felt torn between running inside to tell Emily and running to Cody's side to make sure he was all right. "Can you take this into the kitchen to Margaret? If she asks, tell her I will just be a moment."

He pushed his glasses up the bridge of his nose. "Margaret hates me."

I thrust the hamper at him. "She does not. She's just prickly in nature."

He accepted the hamper but gave me a look that told me I was naive. Perhaps it was true.

"If you see Miss Dickinson, can you tell her what you told me?"

He nodded, and I ran toward the orchard.

The orchard was a stand of young apple and cherry trees in the middle of the Dickinsons' large garden. It was Horace Church's pride and joy. Most of the apple varieties he had created himself through selective breeding. He was on a constant quest to make the perfect apple. The last time he'd spoken of it to me, he'd said he wasn't quite there yet, but he was close. To Horace, a quality apple must be firm and sweet, yet tart enough to make you pucker your mouth just a little.

I spotted Cody standing in front of one of Horace's apple trees. He was facing me, and I could see Detective Durben's back. Cody was up against the tree as if he had no place to run.

Matthew stood a few feet away from them as if he was poised to chase after Cody if the young yardman decided to take off.

"What is your relationship with Paulo Vitali?" Detective Durben asked.

"I don't know the man," Cody said. His voice was high and pinched.

"Then why were you speaking to him the afternoon before Mr. Howard died?"

"I—I wanted to buy a gift for my sweetheart and send it back home to Dublin. He said he had nice trinkets."

"As a man who makes your meager wages and needs to send money home to feed your family, I wonder why you would spend on such a frivolity."

"Even though I am poor and my family is poor doesn't mean we don't deserve nice things."

The detective said something else I couldn't hear.

"If you don't believe that's what I bought, ask the peddler. I am sure he would remember." A bead of sweat ran down the side of his face.

"I would love to ask him a whole host of questions, but I cannot because he's on the run," the detective replied.

"If you are talking to me, you should be talking to others as well. I wasn't the only one who bought items from the peddler. He had a long line. There were ladies and gentlemen there too. It is not fair you come to me just because I am a poor Irishman."

"Where you are from has nothing to do with it," the detective snapped. "The reason I came to you is because Mr. Howard died in this garden."

A hand touched my back and I jumped. "Willa, it's just me," Emily whispered.

I placed my palm on my chest as if to slow my rapid heartbeat.

"What is going on here?" Emily asked.

Whispering, I told her what I'd heard between the two men in the orchard.

"Hmm," Emily said, and before I could stop her, she marched over to Cody and the detective. "I'll just have to find out."

I sighed. I was both inspired and infuriated by Emily's forthrightness at times. However, in this case, I thought if we were hidden for just a little while longer, we might have learned more.

Cody's eyes went wide as Emily approached. Detective Durben looked over his shoulder to see what had caught Cody's gaze. The detective seemed to suppress a groan when he saw Emily.

"Miss Dickinson," the detective said. "If you will excuse me, I'm having a private conversation with your yardman."

Emily cocked her head. "And is this conversation something you spoke with my father about? He would not like the police speaking to his servants without his knowledge."

Detective Durben scowled. "I believe Mr. Dickinson would agree there is no time to waste in finding Paulo Vitali. He is a murderer, and as long as he is on the loose, the people of Amherst should be on guard."

"I don't understand what that has to do with Cody." Emily wrapped the end of her shawl over her arm.

"Who else is with you?" the detective asked.

"Willa is here," Emily replied.

I grumbled to myself as I walked over to join them. I glanced at Matthew, and he shook his head.

I didn't know if the headshake was telling me not to say anything or just showing his general disapproval of Emily and me both being there. However, I didn't know why he or the detective would be surprised that Emily or I were in the garden. We lived here.

"A source informed the police that he witnessed Cody speaking to Paulo just hours before Mr. Howard was killed. I came here to find out how the two men are connected," the detective said.

"Who is this source?" Emily asked.

"Miss Dickinson, I cannot answer that. In order to uphold the integrity of this investigation, I can't share too much information with the public."

Emily folded her arms. "I'm not the public. I am a Dickinson."

A pained expression crossed Detective Durben's face. "Very well. If Cody would just show me this trinket he supposedly bought for his sweetheart as proof of why he was speaking to the peddler, I will be on my way."

"It's in my cabin," Cody said.

Detective Durben gestured for the yardman to lead the way.

The cabin was tucked in the woods behind the farmyard. As we walked by, the cows and sheep in the yard lifted their heads. Terror hung his head over the rail and stared at me. I wished I could walk over and give his forehead a scratch, but I was afraid to do anything that might remind the detective I was there. He may allow Emily to come along with him and Cody, but a lowly maid was quite a different thing.

Cody opened the cabin door, and Jeremiah—who was sitting at the small table in the corner of the room with his suspenders hanging loose at his sides—jumped up. He wasn't wearing any shoes.

"Miss Dickinson," Jeremiah said. "I'm sorry." He struggled to pull up his suspenders. "I just came in for my noontime meal. Did you need something?" He grabbed his work boots as if he was prepared to throw them on his feet.

"Have a seat, Jeremiah; there is no reason to be all worked up. This is your home. You should be able to take your shoes off in such a place," Emily said. "Cody just needs to show the detective something, and I am here to make sure everything is done properly."

The detective grunted when she said that. Matthew stood just outside the door. I was aware that he was blocking it so no one ran out.

Jeremiah relaxed just a little and made eye contact with me.

"Cody, may I see this trinket?" the detective asked.

Cody's Adam's apple bobbed up and down, and he walked across the room to the two single rope beds that were just like my bed in the house. Cody lifted his straw mattress and pulled out a wad of cloth. Slowly, he unwrapped it. Inside was a clay ornament of an American goldfinch.

"My sweetheart loves birds, and there are no birds like this in Ireland. I wanted her to have it so she would recognize one of the many birds she will get to see when I have enough money to bring her here. It is my promise to her that she will see it in person one day."

The detective held out his hand. "It looks expensive. Would not the money have been better spent on your girl's passage here?"

Cody's cheeks flashed so red that his freckles disappeared for a moment. "It will be many years before I will be able to save that kind of money. I want to give her a bit of hope to hold on to."

"Hope is a thing with feathers," Emily murmured.

The detective's head turned in her direction. "What was that?"

Emily's face cleared. "I think it was a loving gesture, Cody. Your sweetheart will be touched."

Detective Durben rewrapped the bird in the cloth and tucked it into the pocket of his uniform.

"Wait, you can't have that," Cody exclaimed.

"Yes, I can. May I remind you that we are in the middle of a murder investigation and anything pertaining to it should come to me." He paused. "You can have it back when this is all over."

Cody's shoulders sagged.

"I thank you for your cooperation." The detective turned to Matthew. "Search the cabin. You know what to look for." He strode out of the cabin with Cody's little clay bird in his pocket.

"Yes, sir," Matthew said, and then he looked at me.

CHAPTER TWENTY

"YOU ARE NOT going to search this cabin without my father's permission," Emily said to Matthew. She folded her arms and stood in front of Matthew. If the situation weren't so serious, it would be comical, as Matthew was at least a foot and a half taller than her.

"Miss Dickinson," Matthew began. "The detective . . ."

"What are you looking for?" Emily asked, still not moving an inch.

"Evidence of the crime."

"I won't allow it."

Jeremiah stood up. "Miss Dickinson, Cody and I are grateful that you want to protect us, but we have nothing to hide. Let Officer Thomas search the room so that we can be done with it. It won't take very long. It's not a big space."

Emily opened and closed her mouth like she wanted to argue.

Jeremiah walked over to Cody and put his arm around the

yardman's shoulders. "Come with me, Cody. We will wait outside."

Looking beaten, Cody let Jeremiah guide him out of the cabin.

Emily, Matthew, and I were alone.

Emily stepped aside. "All right, search if you must."

"You two shouldn't be in here while I'm doing this," he said.

"Why not? So we won't see you stick something in your pocket you won't tell us you took?" Emily challenged.

"Emily," I said, aghast. "Matthew would not do that."

"Thank you for your confidence, Willa," he said with a smile. "I wouldn't do it, but Miss Dickinson is not wrong. It does happen."

Emily nodded at me with a smug look. I rolled my eyes in return. It wasn't something I would ever do in front of anyone else in the family and certainly not in front of Margaret. The head maid would be horrified.

Matthew began searching the room. The first thing he did was walk the entire perimeter. He ran his hand along the top of all the windowsills and looked behind all the curtains. He flipped over chairs, and opened drawers. He picked up the mattress and peered underneath. He went through the pockets of Jeremiah's and Cody's clothes that hung from pegs on the walls, and he checked the pants' cuffs.

"Find anything yet?" Emily asked as he checked the first set of clothes for a second time.

He hung the shirt he was holding back on the peg on the wall. "Not yet, but if something is here, I will find it." He moved on to looking underneath the small kitchen table.

"Are you looking for the murder weapon?" Emily asked.

He was bent at the waist looking under the table. He glanced up at her. "No, we already know what the murder weapon is."

"The pyrethrin," Emily said.

He frowned. "Yes." He went back to searching.

"I know pyrethrin is not good for people with hay fever like Luther," Emily said.

Matthew straightened up and looked a bit disappointed that he hadn't found anything yet. I wondered what Detective Durben would say if he returned to the station empty-handed. I guessed that Matthew was wondering the same thing. "It's not good for anyone to inhale. It enters the nose and lungs and causes a reaction that makes it difficult to breathe. However, for someone with Mr. Howard's condition, it is deadly, as it caused his throat to swell closed."

Emily frowned. "How did Luther get this affliction? Was he born with it? Was it acquired?"

"The doctors are still not sure how hay fever works. They don't know exactly what causes it. However, it can be very challenging, especially in the summer months. Many things can cause a reaction."

Emily seemed to consider this. "If the doctors don't really know what would cause such an attack, how do you know that Luther was murdered in the first place? He might have just come across something in the garden that triggered a reaction."

"We know it was intentional because his face was covered with it. Short of Luther deciding to rub his own face in a huge pile of pyrethrin, we don't know how it could have gotten on him like that."

"You think someone threw it on him?" I asked.

Matthew looked at me. "Yes, or blew it on him. In any case, it was done with purpose to cause him harm. What we aren't sure of is if the culprit had intended to kill Luther or if he just wanted to make him very uncomfortable."

"How long would it take him to react to the pyrethrin if it was thrown at him?" Emily asked.

"From what the doctor said, everyone with hay fever reacts a little bit differently, but he said if there was going to be any reaction, it would happen within a half hour. The most common reaction is sneezing, coughing, and trouble breathing."

"The poor man," I said. "It was a terrible thing to do."

Matthew nodded his agreement and went back to the search. He opened the doors to an old pie safe where the young men kept their few dishes. They had only one pot, and a few plates and cups. Thankfully, it wasn't often that they had to cook for themselves as Margaret, if begrudgingly, fed them on a daily basis.

A memory hit me of the night that Mr. Howard died. That night Matthew had packed up Mr. Howard's dishes.

"What about Mr. Howard's dishes?" I blurted out.

Emily frowned at me. "Willa, I doubt that Mr. Howard brought any of his own dishes to the Evergreens."

"I know that," I said. "What I mean is when I left the Evergreens the night that Mr. Howard was killed"—I turned to Matthew—"you were packing up his dishes. Why?"

Matthew closed the doors to the pie safe. "Because all of his dishes had to be tested."

"For poison." Emily clasped her hands together as if she had just made a great discovery.

I felt excitement rising in me too. "What did they find?"

"Nothing," Matthew said. He was now standing at the door. It seemed that the search had come to an end, and he came up empty-handed.

"What do you mean nothing?" Emily asked.

"There was nothing on his dishes or in his dishes that was poisonous, and from what we could tell, it didn't look like Mr. Howard even had a chance to eat before he ran from the room."

"That is true," Emily said. "He seemed to fall ill just after we had all sat down. He said that he needed fresh air."

Matthew nodded. "Because he had trouble breathing."

"Poor man," I said for the second time.

"Willa," Emily said. "Luther Howard wasn't a poor man. He was devious and a thief. He was constantly looking for a way to improve his life and didn't care whom he stepped on in the process."

"Why do you say that?" Matthew asked.

"Because he stole Mr. Emerson's writing and asked Willa to steal mine as well. He had no loyalty."

Matthew's brow furrowed as if he was realizing something for the very first time.

"But still, what a terrible way to die. When I brought luncheon to you on the first day of the lectures, he mentioned his hay fever. It seemed to be something that he worried about constantly. It must have been a nightmare for him that that was the way he died. I can't help thinking that the person who did this knew that about him, too, how upset his condition made him."

Emily clicked her tongue. "You are a better woman than I,

Willa, but I would wager that everyone in this room already knows that."

I started to protest Emily's last comment, when Matthew said, "Willa, never lose your gift of compassion for everyone, even the most difficult of men. It's what I admire most about you," and then he left the cabin.

I refused to look at Emily, but I was certain that she was staring at me now as I walked out of the small room.

CHAPTER TWENTY-ONE

AFTER MATTHEW LEFT, Cody returned and sat on his bed. "I know I will never see that bird again."

As Cody spoke, Jeremiah also came back into the cabin.

"You will," Emily said. "I will make sure of it. You said you weren't the only one to buy something from the peddler that day. Who else was there?"

"I can't tell you all of their names, miss. There were so many of them. There were gentlemen, ladies, and servants all together. The peddler was doing a good business. If he knew what was going to happen, I am sure he would have left Amherst that afternoon, because he made quite a bit of money. But then again, perhaps he stayed because he thought he could make more money the next day as well."

What he said was true, as I remembered what I had seen when I'd been standing next to Matthew outside the peddler's wagon that afternoon. He had many customers. It seemed like every housewife and servant in Amherst wanted to buy one of his bobbles or remedies.

Jeremiah sat back down at the kitchen table, but I noted his boots were on.

"Did you see what they were buying?" Emily asked.

"A little bit of everything, miss. The peddler had so many things. Most were household products. I noticed the wives and maids bought many of them," Cody said.

"What were they?"

"I'm sorry. I don't know, not exactly. It just seemed they bought lots of powders and creams."

"If we knew who—if anyone—bought pyrethrin from Paulo, then we might be able to dwindle the suspect list," Emily mused.

"But the only one who would know that is Paulo," I said.

"Exactly," Emily said. "That is just the reason why we need to find him."

She left the cabin, and I followed her.

Emily and I walked around the barn and were almost to the house when I heard running feet behind us. "Miss Dickinson!"

Emily turned around. "What is it, Jeremiah?"

"I might know where the peddler is hiding."

"Where?" she asked excitedly.

"There is a camping spot in the woods. At times, it's a place where I meet run—people who are traveling through Amherst."

He didn't need to specify who the people were that he met. Emily knew his secret.

"Where is it?" she asked breathlessly.

"It's by the clearing behind the Suffolk farm."

Emily nodded. "I know it well. Carlo and I walk there often on our rambles." She looked to me. "We go tonight." She marched off toward the house.

The rest of the day my stomach was in knots. I knew it was a terrible idea to go into the woods at night to look for Paulo, but Emily would not be swayed on the matter. She was determined to go. If I didn't go with her, she'd go alone. She'd take Carlo I was sure, but I couldn't let her go alone. If something happened to her, I would never forgive myself.

Emily said we would leave in search of Paulo after everyone else in the house had gone to bed. Knowing her family would not approve of her searching the woods for a possible killer, she wanted to make sure no one would see her leave the homestead.

I stood in the kitchen and wiped the counter down for the fourth time. Margaret removed her apron and watched me. "You are going to rub a hole in the butcher board if you keep that up. It's clean already."

I blinked and looked down at my rag. "I'm sorry. I just have much on my mind."

Margaret sniffed. "We all do. The best cure for it is a good night's sleep. Good night, Willa." She left the room and didn't hear my returned good night.

I waited ten whole minutes before I went in search of Emily for this foolhardy plan. Before I left the kitchen, I removed two large carrots from the larder, and tucked them into the pocket of my skirt.

I found her in her conservatory off the library. Carlo lay on the floor, and in the dim light, I might have mistaken the large brown dog for a carpet. Carlo lifted his head from his massive paws, saw it was me, and let his head fall back down. Even when exhausted, he was vigilant about keeping his mistress safe.

Emily studied an oleander blossom so closely I wondered if she was counting the veins in the petals. I was uncertain she even knew I was there. There was a private air in the humid space. Perhaps it would be better to come back after a few more minutes had passed. I took one step backward.

Emily spoke. "Fame is a bee. It has a song. It has a sting. Ah, too, it has a wing." She looked at me.

I didn't speak. She seemed to be deep in that part of her mind again where no one else could reach her.

In front of her on the worktable, a book lay open. It was Emily's herbarium, her collection of pressed flowers that she started when she was a child and continued into her teenage years. She had shown it to me many times.

Emily said in a clear voice, "There is a bumblebee sleeping in this flower. I am trying to decide if I should leave him here for the night or put him outside so that he can rejoin his colony."

"I would release him outside," I said. "You know how your mother is about insects of any kind in the house. If Margaret sees it, she might kill it."

"People always kill what they do not understand. It makes them feel powerful. Usually, the crime is a slow death."

I twisted my hands over my skirt. Was she talking about Mr. Howard? About the bee? Or about something else entirely?

"The bumble deserves this flower because he gave me much inspiration tonight. Anyone who can inspire a poem deserves a flower to have and keep." She opened the closest window.

Using the pruning scissors from the potting table, she snipped the oleander blossom from the plant and set the blossom and bumble bee outside of the window on a rhododendron bush. She then closed the window again. "The blossom will be withered in the morning, but for this night he will sleep in bliss."

"That was very kind of you."

She looked at me. "I strive to be kind to all the world's creatures. I admit it is not always easy when one comes face-to-face with a hairy spider."

I smiled.

She pointed down at the book in front of her. "The *Nerium oleander* blossom that I pressed on this page more than fifteen years ago is from this very plant. With careful tending the plant is as strong and healthy as it was then. Plants are much like people in that way."

I rocked back on my feet. During the night was when Emily was most thoughtful. Perhaps it wasn't the time to go in search of Paulo Vitali. I needed my mistress to be aware of her surroundings if we were to go on this adventure.

She dusted pollen off her hands. "Are you ready to leave, Willa?" She looked out the window at the clear sky and stars. "It is late enough. The others will be asleep."

"Are you sure you want to do this? It sounds like you're thinking of a poem."

"No." She shook her head. "The muse has floated out the window behind the bumble. I am here now." She clapped her hands at Carlo, who jumped to his feet like he had been prodded with a hot poker. "Let me gather my cloak."

"Your cloak? Won't you be too warm?"

"If I am to go on this clandestine trip, I will need a cloak to look the part."

I nodded and wondered if Emily viewed finding Mr. Howard's killer as a game. Except there were real people and real lives involved. Paulo may be guilty. I didn't know if he killed the secretary or not, but if he was innocent, he may go to prison for the rest of his life for something he didn't do merely because he was a stranger who'd arrived in the town at the wrong time.

However, I couldn't discount that Paulo clearly knew Mr. Howard. I remembered how he shouted at him and hit the secretary the first day of the symposium. And by sunset on the same day, Mr. Howard was dead. The police had good reason to suspect him.

Emily reappeared in the doorway of the greenhouse in her cloak. "It's time. Do not worry so. We are in no danger when Carlo is with us."

As if to reaffirm her statement, the large dog leaned against her leg, and she patted his broad head in approval.

Emily, Carlo, and I went out the back servants' entrance to the house, walking to the right and into the garden. It was a balmy night, and I didn't think Emily needed her cloak. However, she was so much smaller than I. She tended to be cold.

Just minutes ago, Carlo had been half-asleep on the rug in the conservatory. Now, he was wide awake, looking in every direction and ready to pounce if anyone dared even look at his mistress the wrong way.

"I will lead," Emily said. "I know a quicker path to the spot. Carlo and I both do."

We walked beyond the garden, the barn, and the grazing

area for the animals. All the livestock were in the barn for the night. Beyond the farmyard, there was a path leading into the dark wood. Fallen leaves and pine needles cushioned our steps as we ventured deeper into the trees. We moved silently through the forest, but we were the only things that were silent.

The woods thrummed with activity. An owl hooted above our heads, and I could hear little creatures scurry away in the underbrush as we drew near. Like Carlo, I looked in every direction. I wondered what the dog could see, hear, or smell that we could not.

I jumped with every rustle of the leaves around us and wondered how long we would have to follow this path. It felt as if we'd been walking through the woods for more than an hour, but it was impossible to know for sure. It was as if we were outside the constraints of time in the deep woods.

As if she sensed the questions bouncing around in my head, Emily said to me, "It's not that much farther. If he is not there, we can go home and see if we can track him down tomorrow. He can't hide forever."

She was assuming Paulo didn't just up and leave Amherst altogether. It was what I would have done in his position.

My feet hurt from being on them all day, and I could feel the weight of extreme tiredness settling into my limbs. I prayed the peddler had camped somewhere else for the night. However, that hope was short-lived as we saw light break through the trees. Emily held up her hand, motioning for me to stop.

I froze in the middle of the path, uncertain what to do. Apparently, Emily didn't have the same problem, as she pulled her hood up over her head and purposely walked forward with Carlo at her side.

Paulo sat by a small fire with a frying pan on the hot coals. I could smell the bacon as it sizzled in the pan. When he saw Emily, he picked up a pot and wooden spoon. "Back, spirit! Back! I do not welcome you." He hit the pot with the wooden spoon. "I banish you back to the underworld. Go, you fiend. Go!"

Carlo didn't like the tone Paulo was using with his mistress, so he raised his hackles and growled softly as a warning.

The peddler yelped and jumped back behind his mule. "Get that beast away from me. You can't tell me you aren't an evil spirit, and you have Cerberus at your side! Call him off."

Emily snapped her fingers. Carlo stopped growling and fell to her feet.

"I do not mind being thought of as a spirit, but an evil spirit?" Emily said, pushing her hood back to reveal her face and hair. In the firelight, her pale skin shone and her hair seemed redder than ever. I could see why Paulo would find her appearance frightening. "Why can I not be a good spirit?"

Paulo's jaw went slack. "You can speak." He banged on the pot again with the spoon, and in the light of the campfire, the whites of his eyes glowed orange. If anyone was an evil spirit, it wasn't Emily.

"Why aren't you leaving?" he demanded. "Loud noises are sure to chase you away. That's what the Romani woman told me."

"When did you talk to a Romani woman?" Emily asked, as if it were the most natural question in the world to ask.

"When I was at home in Milano. I should have never come to this country. Yes, I was poor there, but at least no one shunned me because I was foreign. I was with my own people. I was understood there."

"I'm sure she told you the truth about loud noises and spirits," Emily said. "But the reason I have not run away is because I'm not a spirit at all."

He lowered the pot and spoon. "Then who are you?"

"I'm Emily Dickinson, and I am here to ask if you murdered Luther Howard."

Paulo gasped.

And I stopped short of covering my eyes. At times, Emily was just too blunt.

Paulo raised his wooden spoon and sputtered. "Do you work for the police? Are you here to arrest me?"

Emily chuckled. "Sir, I'm a lawyer's daughter and this is my maid. We aren't here to arrest you. We don't wield that kind of power."

He lowered his spoon. "Then why do you want to speak to me about the awful man?"

"'Awful man'?" Emily asked.

"Luther. I won't pretend I'm not happy he is dead. It's justice served. He received what he deserved."

"What did he do?" Emily asked.

"He killed my Gabriella," Paulo said, and burst into tears.

CHAPTER TWENTY-TWO

EMILY LOOKED BACK at me as Paulo cried. "What do we do?"

I shrugged my shoulders. I wanted to comfort the man, but he was still holding the wooden spoon, and I didn't doubt he would use it if provoked.

Paulo's shoulders heaved up and down as he cried, and he sat back down on the log. He covered his face with his hands.

Emily and I might not know what to do at a time like this, but the same could not be said for Carlo. The large dog stood up, walked over to the peddler, and laid his giant head over Paulo's lap. Paulo cried into his fur.

After a few minutes, Paulo wiped his eyes. "I am sorry. I am so sorry. It's just anytime I think of Gabriella, I am overcome with emotion. She was the light of my life and my lifeline after coming to America."

Emily walked toward the fire and sat on a log opposite

from Paulo. I remained standing. One of us needed to be able to run for help in case something went wrong.

"Who is Gabriella?"

"She was my niece, the only child of my beloved sister. My sister died the year before I came to America, but she knew I planned to come here and make my fortune in the world. She made me promise to take Gabriella with me so she could have a good life in America too." He gave a bitter laugh. "It is so funny to me how everyone back in the Old Country believes America is the promised land of opportunity. It's not, not for everyone at least. Maybe if you are a white Yankee, but if your skin is dark or you have an accent, your life is difficult, very difficult. I was lucky to save up for my wagon and mule. It took me a decade to do that. A full decade, but when I had my business, I thought Gabriella and I would finally be all right, until she met him." His tone was bitter.

"How did she meet Mr. Howard?" Emily asked.

"She lived in Concord when I was starting my business. Being on the road as a peddler was not the place for a young woman. She was seventeen at the time. The back roads of this country aren't as safe as the government would like us to believe. I have been jumped and hit over the head so many times. I constantly have to be on my guard. I can take care of myself. I am aware of the dangers, but I didn't want to expose Gabriella to them.

"Concord seemed like a nice little town where she could stay. I found her a room above the seamstress's shop. Gabriella was a talented seamstress like her mother. My sister Arabella made lace and taught everything she knew about the textile arts to Gabriella. By the time she was seven, Gabriella was making her own dresses," he said proudly. "And they were the most beautiful dresses you have ever seen."

"Did she work as a seamstress?" I asked, speaking for the first time since we arrived in the woods.

Paulo looked at me over the fire. "Yes, in exchange for room and board, she worked for the seamstress. She became so good at it, Viola, the seamstress, who was a very old woman, began to send Gabriella out for measurements and fittings of the wealthy customers. One family Gabriella visited often was the Emersons."

Emily stared into the fire as she listened to his story. I thought she might be in her own world again, but she proved me wrong when she said, "And that is where she met Mr. Howard."

Paulo poked at the bacon in the frying pan with his wooden spoon. "Yes. Gabriella was taken with him immediately. From the letters I received from her, it seemed he felt the same way about her. He promised her they would marry. I was happy for this. Luther was attached to an important family in the commonwealth. It appeared he had a bright future in front of him. He was a Yankee and could help Gabriella blend into American life. That was all I wanted for her. She would be the safest that way. As she came here as a child, she had little or no accent to speak of. She could appear as if she was a Yankee. She could have a good life that way."

"But," Emily said.

His eyes narrowed when he stared into the fire. "But he broke every promise he made to her. He said that his father told him to marry in his class or above, never below. She was heartbroken. She told me this in a letter." A tear ran down his cheek. "It was not until I returned to Concord after a long trip selling my wares in Philadelphia that I learned how extreme her pain really was."

Emily and I were silent, and even Carlo, whose head was still on Paulo's lap, scarcely breathed.

"She had been with child, his child. When she told Luther this, he said the child was her problem. She saw no way out and one night filled her pockets with rocks and drowned herself in the lake there in Concord."

Emily and I didn't say a word. Above our heads a dove cooed in the trees. It was an eerie sound so late at night.

"I'm so sorry," I breathed.

"If I had been there, I would have tried to stop her. I know it would be difficult to care for the baby, but we would have made it work. Gabriella was a daughter to me, and this baby would have been my grandchild. I would have taken care of them. I would."

"Were you in Concord when she died?"

Paulo swallowed. "No. I was still traveling. I was trying to reach her as quickly as I could because I knew she was distraught, but I never for a moment thought she would take her own life. I found out what happened in a letter she left with Viola." He dropped his head. "I failed her and my sister. I failed at everything."

"Did Luther know you were Gabriella's uncle when you saw him the first day of the symposium?" Emily asked.

Paulo shook his head. "I do not know, but I knew who he was. I would have killed him right there if I had the nerve."

"Did you kill him later?"

"No," Paulo said. "But I am glad someone else did. I am not ashamed to say that."

Behind Paulo, his mule was tied to a tree. I reached in my pocket and pulled out the two large carrots. "May I give this to your mule?"

Paulo frowned. "You brought him a gift?"

"Yes, I saw you today in town, and he seemed to be exhausted."

He nodded. "I had to push Rocco like never before. It will take quite a long time to make it up to him."

"You named your mule Rocco?" I asked.

"Yes, it is a fitting name," he said.

I supposed it was. I walked over to the animal with my two carrots stretched out in front of me. The mule bared his teeth to me and gently took one carrot and then the other into his mouth. I rubbed his forehead, and he gave a happy sigh.

"Do you have pyrethrin for sale in your wagon?" Emily asked.

I glanced over my shoulder. Emily wasn't yet giving up the idea that Paulo might be the killer. She was going to ask every question until she proved to herself that he was innocent.

"I have many home remedies for sale. That is why people buy from me. I have the real thing from the source. Each one has a special purpose."

"And what is pyrethrin for?" I asked.

"It is to ward off pests in the summer months."

"Do you know this is what killed Mr. Howard?"

"What? That I don't believe. It might make you sneeze or cough if you use too much of it, but it will not kill you."

"Did you know about Mr. Howard's ailments?" Emily asked.

"What ailments? To me he looked like a healthy young man."

"He had severe hay fever. He didn't like to be outside or around plants more than he had to. With this in mind, the coroner believes pyrethrin killed him."

"You mean he ate it?" Paulo asked in disbelief.

"No," Emily said. "He inhaled it and it made him unable to breathe."

"He drowned in it," Paulo said. "This is right, that he would die in such a horrible way after what happened to my Gabriella."

"Do you know anything about that?" I asked.

"No, nothing. This is why the police are looking for me? They think I killed him? No, no, no. I did not do it. If I were to kill him, I would not take such a risk of the weapon not working. I would shoot him in the middle of the day, and everyone would know I did it. Before I shot him, I would tell him why too. I never got a chance to tell him what he did to her."

I shivered.

"Gabriella can't be the only woman Luther did this to. I heard rumors there were others," he said.

"Other women who died?" I asked, shocked.

"No, but he was a flirt. There were other women he led on, and he discarded them one by one when he found someone more affluent to attach himself to."

On the other side of the fire, I saw Emily stiffen. She had to be thinking of Miss Lavinia and the promises Mr. Howard made to her.

"All I have left of Gabriella is a letter I have never read."

"What?" Emily asked. "She left you a letter and you haven't read it?"

"It wasn't for me. The instructions on it said I was to give it to Luther, but I never did. This was two years ago." He patted the breast pocket of his coat. "I carry it with me always but cannot read it, nor could I bring myself to find Luther and give it to him. He did not deserve to be the last one to hear from her."

"Can you read the note now?" Emily asked. "They are both gone. There is no reason to hold on to it any longer."

Paulo's eyes were red, as if he was on the verge of crying. "I can't. I don't think I could survive seeing her words."

It was something I could understand. After Henry died, his journal had been left to me. It'd been so difficult for me to read. I hadn't wanted to touch it, but at the same time, it held information he had wanted me to know.

"I will read it for you," Emily said.

At first I thought Paulo would never agree, but then he gave a slight nod and removed a crumpled and yellowing envelope from the inside pocket of his coat. With a shaky hand, he held it out to Emily.

She stood up, walked around the fire, and accepted the letter.

"Do you want me to read it to myself or aloud?" she asked before opening it.

"Aloud," Paulo said barely above a whisper.

She returned to the log and sat. She opened the letter and began to read. "'My Dearest Luther,'"

I don't know how you could turn your back on me like you have. You made promises we were to marry and have a family. You told me that was what you wanted. When I told you about the baby, you were happy and said we would elope right away. What happened in a day's time? What caused you to change your mind so quickly? Did you change your mind about the baby? I would have given the baby up if that is what you wanted, if that was how we could be together.

From his seat across the fire, Paulo gasped, but he said nothing. Emily read on.

I know your father did not believe I was the right match for you, but you said it didn't matter. You said our love was enough. Why did you lie about this? If I had money, would things have been different? Would you have been able to find it in your heart to love me as much as I love you?

Your career has always been your focus, and I have always taken care to stay out of the way of your work. When she could help you with your writing, I didn't say a word. I knew that she was much better suited for that. I am no help to you with the pursuit of your dream. Even so, I never knew your admiration for her would become love. I truly thought your love was for me and me alone. I was a fool.

All I know is I will never love anyone else. I told you that. Since you have rejected me, I can't go on.

If you are reading this, I have left this note with my zio Paulo, and I am no more. Ending it all is better than

enduring this pain. It is better than bringing another fa-
therless child like me into the world.
My love forever,
Gabriella

Emily let the letter fall to her lap, and we all remained in silence for a long moment. The only sound was the forest at night and the crackle of the dying fire. The bacon was forgotten and charred in the frying pan, and the acrid scent of burnt fat filled the air.

Emily spoke first. "I can understand how she feels. Loving someone with your whole heart and not being able to be with that person is one of life's greatest pains. I have felt that in my own life."

I glanced at Emily in surprise. I had never heard her speak of a lost love. I had never heard her speak of wanting to marry at all. In fact, the opposite was true. Emily often spoke about marriage as if it would be a great cost to her. It was what she told Miss Lavinia. She felt her sister should share the same opinion and have no desire to marry. But she still loved someone? Then why not marry that person? No one would turn a Dickinson away.

She folded up the letter and tried to give it back to Paulo. He waved his hands as if to ward it off. "No, keep it. Now that it is open, I may read it in my weakest moments, and I don't want to. I would rather remember Gabriella as I knew her, not as this woman with a heart so broken she would take her own life."

Emily nodded and slipped the envelope into the pocket of her cloak. "Who was the girl Luther left Gabriella for, the one who could help him as a writer?" Emily asked.

"I don't know. This is the first I've heard of it. I knew there were other women, from what Viola had said, but she said nothing about anyone in particular."

"Police!" someone shouted in the forest. "Paulo Vitali, you are under arrest for the murder of Luther Howard."

Paulo jumped up from his log with his wooden spoon ready to strike, but it was no use when he was surrounded by policemen with pistols raised.

CHAPTER TWENTY-THREE

Matthew, Detective Durben, and three other officers stepped out of the trees.

"Miss Dickinson, thank you for leading us to Paulo," the detective said.

"You betrayed me!" Paulo shook his finger at Emily.

Emily stumbled to her feet. "I did not. We didn't tell the police where you were. We would never."

"She's telling the truth," the detective said, still aiming his gun at Paulo. "But I had the foresight to keep my eyes on the Dickinson home. When one of my officers alerted me that Miss Dickinson and her maid went into the woods in the middle of the night, I knew nothing good would come of it."

"You were spying on my family?" Emily asked, aghast.

"I was keeping your family safe at the request of your father. If you don't believe me, ask him."

"I will," Emily snapped.

Matthew handcuffed Paulo's wrists behind his back. Two of the other officers searched Paulo's wagon.

"Be careful," Paulo said. "I have a very detailed way of organizing so I know where everything is."

"You can put it back later," one of the officers said.

Paulo spat at Emily's feet. "I should have known never to trust anyone in your class. You pretended like you cared about Gabriella's story, but it was all an act."

"It wasn't an act," Emily cried. She turned to Matthew. "Officer Thomas, let him go. He did nothing wrong."

"We have to arrest him. We have strong reasons to believe he killed Luther Howard," Detective Durben said.

"I have it, sir!" The youngest of the officers held up a yellow box. Pyrethrin was written across the label. "Half of the contents are gone too."

"Of course they are. I sold it."

"To whom?" the detective said.

"A young wife. She said she was having trouble keeping aphids off her roses, and I knew this would do the trick. She didn't need the whole box for the size of her garden."

"What is her name?"

"I don't know," Paulo said. "I don't ask customers their names."

"Maybe you should start."

The young officer put the box in a brown paper bag. "We will compare this to the powder that we found on Mr. Howard."

Paulo looked around. His eyes were wide, almost crazed. "I'm telling you I didn't kill him. If I did, you would know it. I would shout it from the mountaintops because there was no man who deserved to die more than Luther Howard."

"Paulo, don't say anything more," Emily said.

He glared at her. "Don't tell me what to do after what you have done."

"I will ask my father to help you. He's a lawyer. He will clear all of this up for you."

Matthew glanced at me, but it was only for a second. Then, he marched Paulo into the trees and onto the path.

An officer took a small spade from Paulo's wagon and shoveled dirt onto the flames.

Emily and I walked back to the homestead, and Detective Durben insisted on accompanying us there. While we walked, Emily peppered the detective with questions, all of which he ignored like he had not heard them. It finally got to the point that she gave up.

When we approached the edge of the Dickinson property, Emily spoke again. "Detective, you can leave us here. As you can see, the house is in view. It would be better if Willa and I approached the house alone."

The detective looked as if he didn't like this idea at all, but then Emily said, "Unless you want to be the one to accidentally wake up my father and explain what has occurred."

He frowned. "I will leave you here. But remember, stay out of this investigation. It is over. We have our man. Amherst can be at peace again." He melted back into the woods.

I guessed that he was headed back to Paulo's camp to look for more evidence. I wished I had the nerve to follow him.

Emily stepped out of the woods first with Carlo at her side. Before I could emerge from the trees, she jumped back. "Father! You scared me."

Mr. Dickinson's booming voice broke through the trees. "Emily Elizabeth, what are you doing out here at this time of night?"

Emily turned back to me but made a show of petting Carlo while she did it. "Stay in the trees," she whispered.

I knew what she meant. If Mr. Dickinson saw me, I surely would have been dismissed on the spot for corrupting the eldest Dickinson daughter.

"What are you doing out here in the middle of the night alone? Do you have any sense at all?"

"I wasn't alone. I was with Carlo. You gave me Carlo, did you not, to go with me on my walks."

"On your walks during the day, not at night. What are you thinking to be going on a walk in the woods this late at night? Have you forgotten that a man was killed in this very garden?"

"I have not," Emily said. "The image of his unseeing eyes is etched on my mind forever." She paused. "I just needed some fresh air. We have been very cramped the last few days in the lecture hall. I need the open air. I am not accustomed to sitting for so long in a room with so many people."

Through the trees, I saw Mr. Dickinson hold his lantern high. He wore bedroom slippers and a silk dressing gown over his nightclothes. His hair was flattened on one side where it had been pressed against his pillow.

"What made you come outside, Father?"

"I thought I heard a noise," he said gruffly. "I would have thought that the yardman or stableman would have come out of their cabin, too, when they heard it, but neither one of them appeared."

"They work hard. They must sleep very soundly."

Mr. Dickinson lowered his lantern and let it hang from his fingers at his left side. I could no longer see his face. "You are not allowed to go out like this at night again. It's not safe."

"I'm not a child," she snapped.

"You are as long as you are under my roof, and from what I can tell, you have no inclination to leave."

"You wouldn't let me leave if I wanted to. You wouldn't let Lavinia leave. Perhaps you were so upset at the idea of it that you did something about it."

I clapped my hand over my mouth to muffle my gasp. Mr. Dickinson was so angry at Emily I doubted that he would have even heard it.

He glared at her in the light of his lantern. "Watch your tongue."

"Or what, Father? You will throw me out onto the street? You would never do that to any of us. You can't control us then. You can't control me. You never could. I leave here dozens of times a day in my mind, and I would leave physically, too, if I wanted to. Staying has been my choice, not your directive. Now, please move aside so I can go to bed. I'm tired. Carlo and I had a very long walk, which was quite pleasant until this moment." She brushed past him and went in through the back door of the house.

Mr. Dickinson turned around and watched his daughter walk away.

I shifted my feet, and a small twig under my shoe snapped.

Mr. Dickinson spun around and faced the woods again, holding his lantern high.

I dared not breathe.

Finally, he lowered the lantern and made his way back to the house.

I stood in the trees for several minutes until a small animal ran across my shoes and made me jump. I was too afraid to go into the house until I was certain that Mr. Dickinson had fallen back to sleep. The last thing in the world that I wanted was for him to see me running to the homestead from the woods, the same woods that he insisted his daughter not visit at night.

I skirted the property through the trees and came up behind the farmyard and the barn. The animals were inside for the night. I climbed over the split rail fence into the barnyard and ran into the barn. I opened the door just a crack and slipped inside.

From his corner of the barn, Terror blew air between his lips. I recognized the sound. I let my eyes adjust to the dark and made my way to his stall.

The cows shook their heads as I passed and the sheep kicked and rustled, but other than that, nothing stirred. When I reached Terror's pen, I lifted the latch and stepped inside. "Hi, mind if I hide out here for a few minutes?" I scratched his nose.

He blew hot air in my face, and then lowered himself to the

stall floor. I sat down next to him and leaned my back against his side. I was grateful for his warmth.

"I'll just stay for a little bit," I whispered to the horse. "Just long enough until I know they are all asleep."

That's the last thing I remember saying before I closed my eyes.

CHAPTER TWENTY-FOUR

"WILLA! WILLA, WAKE up!" a harsh whisper broke into my dream. In the dream I was with Matthew, and we were standing on the coast looking out onto the ocean. I have never seen the ocean, but in my mind it was shining and glorious. He was asking me to stay with him. I couldn't make up my mind.

"Willa!" The whisper came again.

Slowly, I opened my eyes, but it was difficult, as I felt like my eyelids were glued together. When my vision cleared, I found Jeremiah standing over me, holding a lantern high. The barn door was open, and I could see the sheep grazing out in the barnyard just as the sky was beginning to change over to a soft gray beckoning the coming morning.

My back was still resting against Terror's side. He was wide awake but hadn't moved all night long. He hadn't moved for me. I placed a grateful hand on the horse's warm flank.

"What are you doing in here? Are you all right?"

I sat up and groaned. Sleeping in a sitting position all night had not been good for my back.

Jeremiah offered me his hand, and I took it. He helped me to my feet. He let go of my hand and asked a second time. "Are you all right, Willa? Are you in any kind of trouble? Because Henry was my best friend, a better friend to me than I ever got a chance to be to him, I would happily help you."

I rubbed my sore back. "I know that, Jeremiah, and I appreciate you saying that. It would mean a lot to Henry, and it does mean a lot to me."

His brow creased in concern.

To ease his mind, I said, "I'm not in any trouble, I don't think. Miss Dickinson and I went to look for Paulo the peddler last night. When we returned to the homestead, Mr. Dickinson was quite angry. We thought it best if he not know I was with her."

Jeremiah nodded. He understood like any servant would in that position.

"I came into the barn to wait until they all went to bed, and fell asleep."

He smiled. "Well, I can say that Terror has been watching over you all this time. If he did not trust me, I don't believe he would have let me anywhere close to you."

Hearing his name, Terror stood up.

I scratched the black horse on the cheek. "Thank you."

Terror blew hot air out of his nostrils.

"Did you find Paulo?"

I nodded. "And he's been arrested."

"What?" Jeremiah asked.

I quickly told him what transpired the night before.

"Then this is over. The police have the killer, and we can go back to normal life at the homestead."

I wished that were true, but I couldn't believe it, not yet.

"I should go. Miss O'Brien will wake soon, and I have to be the first one in the kitchen this morning."

He nodded. "At least you are already dressed and ready for work."

I glanced down at my black dress. It was the same dress that I wore every day working in the Dickinson home. I had another just like it and my Sunday dress. I wore the latter every chance I could, which wasn't often. "You are right."

I left Jeremiah and peeked out of the barn before I made a dash from the barn door to the laundry shed at the back of the homestead. As I ran, I looked at the back of the house, watching for any movement. The curtains in Miss Lavinia's room blew in the wind, or I assumed it was the wind and not Miss Lavinia making yet another note of the trouble that I brought to the family.

I washed up as best I could in the kitchen and hurried to all my morning tasks that had to be completed before Margaret came down. I don't think I had ever moved through the long list of duties so quickly in my life.

I rubbed the back of my neck as I opened the windows around the house. Outside, birds sang, and Jeremiah called the cows in to be milked as day broke. When I returned to the kitchen, I found Margaret boiling eggs for the family breakfast.

She glanced at me. "I hear Miss Dickinson got into some trouble last night. You wouldn't know anything about that, would you?"

I felt all the color drain from my face. "Oh? What happened?"

"I'm surprised that you didn't hear Mr. Dickinson shouting at her during the night for going on a late walk." She studied me as if gauging my response.

"I might have heard shouting," I said, and left it at that. Again, I was telling a half-truth for the second time that week. The first had been to the police about finding Mr. Howard's body.

She pressed her lips together as if she was dissatisfied with my answer. "I have more news."

My shoulders tensed as I wondered what that could be. "When the delivery boy came this morning with the flour and salt I had ordered from the grocer, he said that the killer Paulo had been arrested. But why do I think you already knew that, Willa?"

I busied myself with starting the porridge.

"Good morning," Emily said as she stepped into the kitchen. "Margaret, did the flour come?"

"Yes, Miss Dickinson," Margaret replied. "It came bright and early this morning."

"And it is white flour?" Emily asked.

"Yes, just what you ordered."

"Very good. I am going to make sweet rolls. They are quick and my father's favorite. I need him to be in a good mood."

"Why is that, Miss Dickinson?" Margaret asked.

Emily donned her apron. "Because I am going to ask him to get an innocent man out of jail."

Margaret might question me about the night before, but she would never ask Emily directly. So as long as Emily was in the kitchen making her sweet rolls, I was safe from answering any uncomfortable questions.

When Margaret's eggs were done, I carried them in an egg dish up to the dining room. Thankfully when I stepped inside, I found it empty. I did not want to face Mr. Dickinson in case he could read it all over my face that I had been with Emily in the woods last night.

If he found out, I knew very well it would be grounds for the Dickinsons to dismiss me. They could blame me for Emily venturing in the forest in the middle of the night. It would be much easier for them to believe it was my idea and not their daughter's.

I set the table as quickly as I could so I could escape before anyone appeared. I was just putting the very last spoon in its place when Mrs. Dickinson stepped into the room. She smiled at me. "Good morning."

I bent my head. "Good morning, ma'am. Is there anything else you require this morning?"

Mrs. Dickinson gazed at the room with that faraway look, much like her eldest daughter had a tendency to do. "No, this is all fine."

I nodded and backed out of the room as quickly as possible. While doing so, I bumped into Mr. Dickinson.

He grunted, "Watch your step, girl."

"I am so sorry, sir." I kept my head down.

He scowled at me. "You must be more careful. I will not have a clumsy maid in my home."

"Yes, sir, I do apologize." I wanted to fall through a hole in the floor.

"Go find my eldest daughter and tell her she is wanted in the dining room right away. I need to have a word with her."

I looked at the floor. "I will, sir."

He stepped into the room, and I hurried toward the kitchen, looking over my shoulder, as I wanted to make sure Mr. Dickinson wasn't following me. I hadn't expected him to. In all the time I had worked in the Dickinson home, I had never once seen him in the kitchen or laundry, or even in the barn. However, it was always better to double-check.

In the kitchen, Emily pulled her sweet rolls out of the oven. "They are perfection." She smiled from ear to ear. "There is no way Father can say no to me after tasting one of these."

"Miss Dickinson, your father would like you to go to the dining room right away," I said.

Emily must have caught some anxiety in my voice, as she looked up sharply from the rolls. "Perhaps I should have made a cake instead."

Emily instructed me to bring the rolls to the dining room as soon as they were cool enough to remove from their cooking pan, and she left the kitchen.

"I'd say the two of you stepped in it," Margaret said after Emily left the kitchen. "You might want to think of other places you could work."

My stomach twisted into a knot.

Twenty minutes later, I carried a cloth-lined basket of sweet rolls into the dining room. I stopped just outside of the door.

"Father, I am telling you Paulo didn't do this. You have to represent him," Emily said.

"I will do no such thing." He shook the newspaper in his hands.

"Then I will ask Austin to do it. He is a lawyer too. He can help Paulo Vitali just as well as you can."

Mrs. Dickinson was no longer in the room. It was not uncommon for her to retreat when a conversation became uncomfortable. Miss Lavinia sat in her chair with her head bent over her porridge. She looked like she wanted to be anywhere but there and likely wished that she had followed her mother out of the room.

Mr. Dickinson folded his paper and set it by his plate. "Austin works at *my* firm. He can't take any case without my approval."

I placed the sweet rolls on the table and backed away quickly as if there were a chance that I might be burnt by their heated exchange.

"I thought he was a partner in the firm. Wasn't that part of the agreement for you to keep him in Amherst?" Emily lifted her teacup to her lips.

Mr. Dickinson scowled at his daughter. "You wanted him to stay just as much as I did."

"I know that. I never want our family to be broken up. I have always been clear on that," Emily said. "But as your partner, Austin should be able to choose his own cases, and he might take Paulo up." She arched her brow. "Or is he not a true partner who can select his own clients?"

I slipped out into the hallway. I wanted to stay out of Mr. Dickinson's sight, but my curiosity would not let me move out of earshot.

Mr. Dickinson snorted. "I'm not worried about Austin taking the case. He is trying to build his reputation. He won't do anything that might harm it, and representing an outsider, a foreigner, who I have heard has made it abundantly clear he wanted Mr. Howard dead, is not the way to do that."

"Father, I believe he is innocent," Emily said.

I peeked around the corner of the doorway.

Her father looked her in the eye for the first time. "Why?"

Emily opened and closed her mouth.

Mr. Dickinson narrowed his eyes. "Because you have a feeling or wish his innocence to be true?" He shook his head. "I can assure you neither of those has any meaning in a court of law."

"But—"

"This arguing is giving me a headache. Let us be glad someone has been arrested and we can forget this incident ever happened."

"Do you think Vinnie can forget it happened so easily? She thought she was going to marry Mr. Howard."

Miss Lavinia jerked back in her seat as if she had been slapped.

"Emily," Mr. Dickinson snapped. "That is outrageous."

"You never consider how I feel, Emily. Never. I've spent my life worrying about you. I just wanted it to be reciprocated this one time." Miss Lavinia jumped up from her chair. She ran past me crying, while I stood silently in the hallway.

CHAPTER TWENTY-FIVE

"E MILY, YOU HAVE to pick out your dress to wear to the Thayers' ball," Miss Susan said.

Miss Susan and Emily sat together in the first parlor of the Dickinson homestead. Mr. Dickinson had gone to his office for the day, and Mrs. Dickinson went back to bed. Margaret said that she was resting so that she could attend the ball to-morrow. It would take all of her strength to go.

Miss Lavinia claimed she was headed to the final day of Mr. Emerson's lectures, but I had my doubts, as I had seen her walk in the opposite direction down Main Street. It was clear the younger Dickinson sister was still chafing over the argument at the breakfast table. I did not blame her for it. Her sister and father fought in front of her that morning like she wasn't even there. I felt new compassion for Miss Lavinia as I realized how difficult it must be to be the youngest in the family but also the one expected to care for them all.

Carlo lay in front of the cold hearth, and two of Miss

Lavinia's cats sat in the front window as if they were waiting for her to come home.

I went into the second parlor and began polishing the windows, as I would not do such a task when the family or any of their guests were present. There was a pocket door between the two parlors, and it stood wide open. This allowed me to hear every word of Emily and Miss Susan's conversation. I could not help it if Emily left the door open like that because she wanted me to overhear.

"Sue," Emily said. "How can I worry about what I am going to wear to a ball when I know for a fact that a man has been wrongfully accused of murder?"

"You don't know that," Miss Susan argued. "The only people who know if he is guilty or not are the police."

"I am telling you, if Paulo Vitali is the killer, he would have owned up to it. He detested Mr. Howard, and for very good reason. He was happy that the man was dead. I believe a man with that much vitriol would confess with a little bit of pride."

Miss Susan shook her head. "Emily, you aren't in the real world enough to know how others lie."

"If that is the case, I will gladly stay away from it."

"If the story he told you is true, yes, he did have a good reason to kill Mr. Howard. However, he could still lie about his innocence in order to save his own skin. It's self-preservation."

"Then why tell us his story at all?"

"Us?" Miss Susan asked with heat in her voice. "You and who else?"

I froze with my cloth on the leaden windowpane.

"Carlo and I, of course," Emily said.

Miss Susan said something in a low voice that I could not hear. When she spoke up, I relaxed because it seemed that the conversation shifted back to Paulo.

I continued to clean and listen.

"I'm shocked you think everything he told you was the truth."

"There is one way to prove it," Emily said. "I will write a letter to Viola the seamstress. She will be able to tell me if the story about Gabriella is real. It's the only way I can prove to anyone it is the truth." She paced throughout the room. "I wish I could just travel to Concord and ask her myself."

"That is three days of travel by carriage. If you go, Paulo could be sent to prison in that time."

"Then a letter is the only answer. I will start right now so it can make the afternoon post."

"I wish instead you would just choose which gown to wear so the maid can clean it and brush it out for tomorrow."

"You pick," Emily said. "You know what looks best on me. I have more important things to do." She ran into the second parlor and didn't even acknowledge me before she left the room.

In the first parlor, I heard Miss Susan sigh. "I love her so, but she is the most infuriating person in the world."

For the rest of the morning, I did my best to make myself as invisible as possible. I decided if the Dickinsons couldn't see me, then they couldn't fire me either. I was still very much expecting that it would be found out that I was with Miss Emily in the woods last night. Matthew, Detective Durben, and the other police officers all knew. There was no reason for Detective Durben not to tell Mr. Dickinson about my presence should the topic of that night come up. I very much hoped that it would not.

Even though I did my best to hide, Emily found me outside hanging linens on the clothesline.

"Willa, there you are," she said in an accusing tone. "Where have you been? I have been looking for you all over the house."

"It's wash day," I said, as if that were explanation enough. It really should have been. Emily knew wash day was an all-day, exhausting event. It was my least favorite day of the week. However, since it was keeping me out of the Dickinson family line of sight, I was grateful for it.

"Wash day is not that important. We have much more pressing things to attend to than my father's knickers."

I clipped a clothespin over a white bedsheet on the line. "What is that?"

"You need to come with me to the post office to send this letter to Concord." She held up the letter as if it were all the proof I needed to go.

"You can't post it yourself?" I asked. It wasn't often that I challenged Emily, but I did not want to do anything to attract the ire of Mr. Dickinson until his irritation about the night before blew over.

She dropped the letter at her side. "I want you to come with me. We are in this together." She held up the letter again. "This letter is addressed to the seamstress in Concord whom Gabriella worked for. She can give us the answers we need."

I slapped another damp sheet on the line. "May I ask you a question?"

"Of course. You may always ask me whatever comes to your mind."

If only that were true. Even so, I forged ahead. "Why are you so invested in proving Paulo's innocence? You don't know him, not really."

"Because I know in my gut that he is innocent. Should we let an innocent man go to prison just because it is more convenient for the rest of us? Meanwhile, the real killer—whoever that might be—gets to live his merry life like nothing happened. How is that justice?"

"It's not," I admitted. "I think Paulo is innocent too."

"Good, now go take off your apron so we can leave."

I did as I was told.

Thankfully Margaret was away at the grocer to pick up a few things Mrs. Dickinson had wanted for the evening meal with Mr. Emerson. This would be the last night Mr. Emerson ate dinner with the family, as he had informed the Dickinsons that he would be leaving for Concord right after the ball tomorrow night. Miss Susan had tried to convince him to stay another night, but he had claimed he needed to return home to his wife and children. I personally thought he just wanted to escape from Amherst and the scandal of Mr. Howard's death. According to Margaret, there had been very little coverage of it in the Amherst paper other than mentioning that a man died suddenly while visiting the Dickinson family. It did not mention Mr. Emerson or Mr. Howard by name. She said it was out of respect for Mr. Dickinson. He had done so much to elevate the status of Amherst in the commonwealth, the newspaper refused to paint him in a bad light.

The newspapermen might have felt that way, but from what I could tell of the general public, they didn't mind talking about the Dickinsons in the least. Some of them even reveled in it. Whispers and gossip buzzed through the town. I knew this had to be the reason that Mr. Dickinson was so accepting of Paulo Vitali's arrest. The heat was no longer on the family but on a stranger, and because he was a foreigner, all the better.

Carlo galloped ahead of Emily and me as we made our way down Main Street. She gripped the letter in her hand. I hoped Viola would write back for Paulo's sake, and for Emily's, but there was no guarantee.

Outside the post office, a small group of older gentlemen sat as always. "Miss Dickinson," one called. "It has been a long time since we have seen you down this way. Busy with murder?"

It was all the proof I needed that the town was gossiping about the recent events at the Dickinson home. The old men always knew what was happening in Amherst even though it seemed like they rarely moved. I wondered if they even went home at night sometimes. Did they just sleep outside of the post office so that they were the first to receive every crumb of information each day?

Emily scowled at him. "It is unkind to make light of someone's death. Mr. Howard was a respected man. He aspired to be a writer like his mentor, Ralph Waldo Emerson."

"We all aspire to something. It doesn't mean that thing we aspire to has any chance of happening," one grumped.

"I find that to be a very dark way to look at the world," Emily said.

"Dearie, if you live as long as we have, you will see the world in the same way too."

He laughed. "As for Mr. Howard being a respected man, I

don't know about that. I haven't heard one nice word about that Luther character. He's apparently a user of people and would have done anything to claw his way to the top."

"How do you know that?" Emily asked, gripping the letter so tightly in her hand that it crinkled.

"You sit by the post office all day, you hear things. People forget we are here. They just think we are a group of old washed-up men who can't hear or see." He nodded to his two friends. "Isn't that right, boys?"

They grunted in agreement.

"Did anyone in particular say this about Mr. Howard?" Emily asked.

He tapped his index finger against his cheek. For the first time, I noticed that it was significantly shorter than his other fingers on that hand. At some point the tip had been cut off. "Well, Mrs. Thayer didn't have anything nice to say about him. She ran into another lady just in the spot you were standing and told the woman she was upset he was coming. He would only bring trouble."

"When was this?" Emily asked.

"A week ago, maybe two."

"So before Mr. Emerson and Mr. Howard arrived?"

"Yes, ma'am."

The door to the post office opened, and a young woman stepped out. Her dark hair was parted in the middle and tethered at the back of her head in an intricate braid, and it shone in the bright summer sunlight. She had a round face and piercing dark eyes. "If you don't mind, I would like to pass."

Emily and I stepped to the side.

I noticed a package addressed to Mr. Ruben Thayer in the

woman's hand. Emily must have also, because she asked, "Are you acquainted with Cate Lynn and Ruben Thayer?"

The woman, who was clearly in a rush, paused to glance at Emily. "Yes, my father and I are staying with them."

"They are friends of mine as well," Emily said. "I did not know they had new guests."

"Yes, my father and I came down on a whim from New Hampshire. We came down on my *father's* whim, I should say. He wanted to see his friend Waldo's last lecture here. No one comes to Walpole, where we live, to give lectures. No one comes to Walpole at all, truly. This is a touch closer than Concord, and my father had not seen his friend in over a year."

"Who is your father?" Emily asked.

The dark-haired woman tilted her head to one side. "Bronson Alcott. My name is Louisa Alcott. You may know of me from my writing."

CHAPTER TWENTY-SIX

"Oh, I do," Emily said with her eyes sparkling. "Your father sent us a copy of *Flower Fables*. They are lovely fairy tales."

"He has sent the book to many of his friends," Miss Alcott said. "How do you know him?"

"I've never met him," Emily admitted. "But he knows my father, Edward Dickinson."

Miss Alcott nodded. "I've heard the name. I'm glad you enjoyed the book. Buy a copy and give it to a friend since you have one of your own. I write books to sell them, not to be given as gifts. I wish my father understood that." She started to walk away.

Emily followed her. "You mentioned Concord. Do you know it?" She held up the letter in her hand. "I was just writing to someone there."

Miss Alcott turned and frowned. "It's where I spent my

childhood. I have moved many times. My fondest memories are in Concord."

"Do you know the seamstress Viola there?"

Miss Alcott laughed. "When I was a child, we were lucky to have one dress each. I have three sisters, and we were as poor as church mice. We would still be if it were not for my work. We did not go to the seamstress."

Emily dropped the letter to her side. "Oh, I was writing to her about Mr. Howard."

This last comment got Miss Alcott's attention. "You knew Mr. Howard?"

"Not well, but he was murdered in my garden."

"Seems fitting," Miss Alcott said with little emotion. "Seems more than fitting he would die in such a way." She paused as if she was considering something. "Will you be at Mr. Emerson's lecture this afternoon?"

"I had not decided if I planned to attend."

"You should," Miss Alcott said. "I will be there, and we can talk more."

"About what?" Emily asked.

"About Mr. Howard. Or was there something else you needed to discuss?"

"No," Emily said, surprised. "Just that."

"Then I will see you there." Miss Alcott walked away.

Emily looked at me. "Well, she seemed quite sure of herself."

After Emily dropped off the letter, she was in a hurry to return to the homestead, as she had decided to go to the lecture that afternoon in order to speak to Miss Alcott. She said she needed time to prepare. I wasn't certain what she meant by it. All that was required of her during the lecture was to listen.

However, her plans were dashed as soon as we stepped into the house.

"Emily," Mr. Dickinson said. He was sitting in the front parlor. "Will you come here, please?"

Emily went into the parlor, and I waited in the hallway. I didn't want Mr. Dickinson to see me standing there, but I was so curious as to what he had to say to Emily, I couldn't make myself leave.

"The police were just here," Mr. Dickinson said. "They were looking for you. They also wanted that maid of yours."

My chest tightened. I knew "that maid" could only be me. When Mr. Dickinson spoke of Margaret, he always referred to her by her name.

"What did they want?" Emily asked.

"They told me of your adventures the night before. This is not acceptable. I have raised you to be a proper young woman, but you have been anything but. I let you stay home for church, I let you write, and still, you push the boundaries."

"I do not need your permission to do those things."

"As long as you are under my roof, you do."

"Then it is no wonder Vinnie wanted to marry Mr. Howard in order to escape you," Emily snapped.

"This is not about Vinnie. This is about you and your defiance."

I pressed my back against the wall as I listened. I needed to go, to hide in the kitchen and make myself useful. I needed to avoid Mr. Dickinson at all cost, especially when he was this angry and could dismiss me on a whim.

"Your brother, Susan, and I will go to Waldo's last lecture today, but I wish for you and Vinnie to stay home with your mother. Home is the place you should be. I'm afraid including you in the symposium has given you an inflated belief in your ability. The police informed me you don't believe the peddler is the killer. I have already told you to stop saying such nonsense."

"You can't tell me what to say."

The sound of a chair scraping across the floor spurred me into action. I ran into the dining room just as I saw Mr. Dickinson's shadow in the hallway. Through the dining room, I went into the kitchen. I held on to the edge of the sink. I was surely going to be fired. Mr. Dickinson was so angry at Emily. He knew I had been with her last night. It only made sense that the blame would be put on me.

The back kitchen door opened, and Margaret stepped through. Cody followed her carrying the box of supplies she had bought at the market.

"Put them there," Margaret said, pointing to the old wooden table in the middle of the room.

Cody set the crate on the table.

"Willa, what have you been up to while I was gone?"

"I—"

"Margaret," Emily said as she came into the room. "Vinnie and I have received an invitation from Cate Lynn Thayer for afternoon tea at the Thayer home. We won't be home for luncheon, I gather."

Margaret nodded. "What about Mrs. Dickinson?"

"She was invited, too, but Mother plans to stay in her room. She has a headache. Can you take a tray up to her after a little while? She must eat something, even when she doesn't want it."

Margaret nodded.

Emily cleared her throat. "Also, I would like to take Willa with me."

Margaret frowned. "Why?"

"We have not had many high teas in our home since Willa came to work for us, and I would like her to see how it is done. There is no doubt Cate Lynn will have impeccable service, and we would wish that for ourselves if we were to host one. I hope I can convince Mother it is a good idea. Susan isn't the only hostess in the family."

Margaret removed the two pounds of salt from the crate. "I don't know why I bother to argue with you on this point any longer. You always do what you want."

Emily grinned. "You need to tell my father that." She looked at me. "Willa, go put on your Sunday dress. The Thayers are of another ilk."

A half hour later, I stood outside on the wide side porch of the Dickinson home in my Sunday dress. I had been so proud when I'd earned enough money to buy it at the dress store. I had saved for over a year and bought it in the spring. It was dark green linen and had a black velvet band at the waist. The sleeves and hemline had been a touch too short for me, which was the case with most store-bought clothes, so I had added black cuffs and a hem of my own. I wanted to make the best impression possible on the Thayers. It seemed important to Emily that I did.

"I don't know why I have to go to this tea," Miss Lavinia complained as she and Emily came out the front door.

"Because Father would not let me go if I went alone. He has it in his head that I will get into some sort of trouble."

Miss Lavinia snorted. "And he would be right."

"Besides, you cannot mope in your room all day and night over Mr. Howard. From what I have learned about him, you are lucky you didn't become more deeply involved with him."

Emily and Miss Lavinia walked over to the spot at the corner of the house where Carlo and I waited.

"Are you ready to leave, Willa?" Emily asked. Emily held a beautiful bouquet of late summer flowers from the garden. They were sunflowers, asters, dahlias, and snapdragons. All in shades of yellow and purple and arranged to their best advantage.

"Willa is coming?" Miss Lavinia asked.

"I want her to learn how to serve high tea. If Susan really wants our homes to be the center of Amherst society, it is something Willa will have to know."

"You have the most ridiculous ideas," Miss Lavinia complained, and then marched down the steps.

"Don't mind her," Emily said.

If I only knew how to do that.

Carlo followed Emily down the steps.

"No, Carlo, you have to stay. I don't believe Cate Lynn wants you in her home." Emily pointed back to the house.

The big dog sighed, trudged back up the steps, and lay on the porch rug at the front door.

I walked behind Emily and Miss Lavinia down Main Street in the direction of the Thayers' home.

"I don't know how you convinced Father to let you go to this tea after he was so angry with you over what you did last night."

"It wasn't that hard. He had forbidden me from going to the lectures this afternoon, and then the invitation arrived. He thought high tea was the proper choice for a lady." Emily chuckled.

"Just don't bring up the murder or Mr. Howard while we are there," Miss Lavinia said.

"Vinnie, you must be joking. Why else would I be going?" Emily quickened her steps.

CHAPTER TWENTY-SEVEN

O N THE WALK to Thayer Manor, as it had been renamed by Ruben Thayer, Emily and her sister bickered about everything from Emily investigating the murder to how many cups of sugar should go in a lemon cake. Emily said three, and Miss Lavinia said two. It got quite heated, and I was glad to see it. It was a sign to me that Miss Lavinia was beginning to recover from the shock of Mr. Howard's death.

As she said she didn't love him, she must have loved the idea of having her own life outside of the family. It seemed that she was giving up on that hope now and was falling back into her sisterly role.

"Really, Emily," Miss Lavinia said. "There is no reason that you should have brought the maid."

Emily stopped in the middle of the path. "Her name is Willa. I wish you would stop talking like she wasn't with us."

"I wish that you recognized the class distinctions in society," Miss Lavinia said.

"I don't recognize anything that doesn't serve me. Whether it be classes or religion or anything else this society has conjured up."

Miss Lavinia gasped. "Emily, you shouldn't talk like that. There is a proper way of doing things. What would Father say?"

Emily twirled in the middle of the path, and her skirts flew out around her. "I don't care. I would say all of this to his face and have. I don't think any of it would come as a surprise to Father."

Miss Lavinia threw up her hands and marched in front of us in a huff.

I bit my lower lip. "Is she all right?"

Emily laughed. "She will be fine. Do you see how she had the fight back in her? That's how I know that she will recover. Vinnie needs to have some fight in her. She needs to be disagreeable for the sake of it." She smiled. "That is how I know that she is being herself."

Emily skipped ahead to catch up with her younger sister. She looped her arm through Miss Lavinia's. At first Miss Lavinia tried to pull away, but when Emily wouldn't let go, she relented and the two sisters walked arm in arm the rest of the way to Thayer Manor.

I hung back, giving the sisters plenty of space to talk without me overhearing, but when we reached the tall black iron gates of the manor, I hurried to catch up.

I thought the Dickinsons' homes and estate were large, but they did not compare to the Thayers' property. The front lawn was the length of the college green and was a pristine blanket of grass. There wasn't a single dandelion to mar the surface. The walk leading to the house was made with flat polished bluestone that shone in the sunlight. The stones glistened so much they appeared to be wet, but when no one was looking, I bent to touch one and it was perfectly dry.

Two large elm trees flanked the white Georgian home, featuring pillars that rose thirty feet in the air. The house was large enough to put both the homestead and the Evergreens inside.

"Did you know they had *this* much money?" Miss Lavinia whispered.

The front door opened, and instead of the housekeeper greeting us, it was Isadora Foote on the other side. "Good afternoon. Cate Lynn is still getting dressed. You know how she is. She has to look her best, even when she is having a simple tea in her home with friends." Isadora laughed and held the door open wide.

Emily and Miss Lavinia stepped inside, and I followed a few paces behind them.

Isadora raised her brow at me. "You do seem to go everywhere with your maid," Isadora said.

Emily said, "She's a good companion to both Vinnie and me."

Miss Lavinia made a snorting sound at this comment, and even to my ears, Emily's reasoning sounded a bit far-fetched.

"The Thayers have a lovely home. The only place I have ever seen anything quite like it was when I went to Mount Vernon," Emily said. "Of course, Washington's house was even grander than this, but the look and feel are the same."

"Wait until you see the rest of the house," Isadora said. "We will be having tea in the grand parlor." She glanced at me. "What should we do with your maid?"

I squeezed my arms at my sides, wishing I'd insisted on staying home with Margaret. Wash day would be more enjoyable than this.

"May she observe while we are in the parlor?" Emily asked. "I'm hoping she can gather some pointers on how to serve tea. Before coming to work for us, she was a maid at a boardinghouse. As you can imagine, serving high tea was not part of her duties there."

The way she said "boardinghouse" made it sound like a brothel. However, instead of speaking up and saying something about it, I held my tongue like I always did, like every servant did.

"It's up to Cate Lynn, of course, but I don't see her having any objections to it. I believe we all want our servants to be well trained," Isadora said.

"Excellent," Emily said, and smiled at me.

All the while I was wondering what my mistress had gotten me into again. She seemed to have a knack for putting us both in uncomfortable positions, and unfortunately, I was the one most uncomfortable with them.

The parlor was a room out of a fairy tale. Everything was brocade or trimmed with lace. Every surface was decorated with white, gold, and rose. The settees were covered in deep rose velvet. I wanted to reach out and touch them to see how soft they were.

"Oh my!" Miss Lavinia said. "What a lovely room. I have never seen so much adornment before."

Isadora chuckled. "It's a lot to take in at first, but it is definitely Cate Lynn. She loves frills, and she has the money to indulge herself in them."

"Yes, I do on both counts," a sweet voice said as Mrs. Thayer came into the room. She was dressed in what I could only say was a ball gown. It was rose satin with ruffles on the skirt and rosettes wrapping around her tiny waist.

"Cate Lynn, are you wearing your gown for the ball?" Emily asked.

"This?" Mrs. Thayer laughed and fluffed her skirts before sitting down. "No, this is ten years old. I have something much better to wear to the ball. I hope you are both coming." She nodded to Emily and Miss Lavinia in turn.

"We are," Emily said, speaking for both of them.

"I wish I didn't have to go," Miss Alcott said as she came into the room. "I hate balls. There is so much time standing, dreading, and hoping someone will take pity on you and ask you to dance. It's intolerable. And when someone does ask you to dance, he steps on your feet and has foul breath."

Mrs. Thayer laughed. "Louisa, you never hide how you feel. That's what I love most about you. I'm so glad that you will be here for the ball if only to hear your disgruntled opinion about everyone attending afterward."

"It's nice to have something to look forward to." Miss Alcott wore the same traveling dress she had been wearing at the post office.

"Miss Alcott," Emily said, "when I met you earlier today, you mentioned that you were going to the lectures, but you are here."

Miss Alcott leaned back in her chair. "Call me Louisa, please, because I will call you Emily no matter your preference. I still plan to go, but Cate Lynn guilted me into staying through the tea."

Mrs. Thayer laughed. "Don't put it like that, Louisa. I wanted you to meet the Dickinson sisters. You have much in common."

"We will see about that," Miss Alcott said.

Emily held out her bouquet of flowers to Mrs. Thayer. "These are for you as a thank-you for your kind invitation. We know that you are in the middle of preparing for the ball tomorrow, and to have this tea is an extra bother for you."

Mrs. Thayer didn't take the flowers from Emily's outstretched hand and placed a lace handkerchief at her nose. She sneezed and then she sneezed again. Her eyes watered. "It's not an extra bother at all. I have been looking forward to this tea so very much even if my invitation was last minute." She sneezed again. "I just wanted to make sure that I felt up to it before I sent the invitation out. Summer with its pollen in the air is quite difficult for me."

Emily pulled the flowers back to her chest. "Are you quite all right?"

"I will be fine, but I can't accept your flowers. You can see how they affect me. It pains me so much because they are truly beautiful, perhaps the most beautiful flowers I have been given."

Her eyes continued to water, but I didn't know if it was because of her reaction to the bouquet or because she was teary over not being able to accept the flowers.

"I'm so sorry. I didn't know," Emily said, aghast.

Mrs. Thayer smiled. "Eugenia, will you take the flowers and give them to the cook? She could use some cheer as she bakes for the ball."

A young blond maid appeared at Emily's side and took the bouquet.

"Would that be all right with you, Emily, if I gave the flowers to the cook?" Mrs. Thayer asked.

"Of course," Emily said. "They are a gift and yours to do with whatever you wish."

"Thank you." She smiled and patted the handkerchief on the corner of her nose.

The maid left the room with the flowers.

"That was my fault," Isadora said. "I let Emily in with the flowers. I wasn't thinking. I wasn't thinking about your reaction to them."

"No one is at fault," Mrs. Thayer said. "I will feel better in no time. I just have to breathe some cool fresh air." She looked to Emily. "You likely don't remember, but I missed a lot of school when I was younger from being ill. We were in school together for such a short time."

"I didn't remember," Emily admitted.

"Well, I don't blame you; I was no more than nine when my family moved to Boston." Mrs. Thayer smiled. "Yes, well, the doctors told me that I had weak lungs. It wasn't until we were in Boston, and I saw a specialist that could tell me the outside influences that were making me sick. He said that my body saw flowers, grass, and leaves as something that would hurt me, so I cough and sneeze in defense. I wish there was some way to convince my body not to believe that."

"Was that one of the reasons that your parents decided to move to the city, so you had access to the doctors there?" Miss Alcott asked.

"That was precisely the reason, and there certainly are not as many plants in the city as there are in the country. Knowing what I had to avoid, I was thriving in the city."

Eugenia returned without the flowers but with a tea tray, which she set on the table. With shaking hands, she served Mrs. Thayer first. The teacup and saucer rattled as she passed them to her mistress. If Emily wanted me to learn how to serve high tea from this poor girl, it would not go well at all. I would do better making it up as I went along.

The maid moved on to Miss Alcott next.

Miss Alcott held up her hand as if to block the tea from coming in her direction. "Do you have coffee?" Miss Alcott asked.

The maid started. "Ma'am?"

"It's fine, Eugenia," Mrs. Thayer said. "I'm sure there is some coffee in the kitchen, will you bring it for Louisa?"

Eugenia, who couldn't be more than sixteen, nodded with wide eyes. She quickly served the other ladies. "I will go collect your coffee, miss."

"Thank you," Miss Alcott said. "If you could just put the cream in it, it will save me a great deal of trouble."

After the girl left, Isadora chuckled. "You always have to be contrary don't you, Louisa?"

"I see no reason to drink tea when I want coffee, assuming both are available. If I were a man, coffee would have been offered at the start," Miss Alcott replied, and helped herself to one of the tiny cheese sandwiches on the tray.

Miss Lavinia cleared her throat. "You have a lovely home, Cate Lynn."

Mrs. Thayer smiled. "Thank you. I am happy that it was something I could bring to my marriage with Ruben."

"Oh?" Miss Lavinia murmured.

"My father owned part of the railroad through Boston. He

sold it shortly before he died. My mother died when I was a child, so when Father passed away, it was left all to me, a single woman living in Boston." She smiled at Isadora. "That is how Izzy and I became such good friends. We had a grand time in the city as two unmarried heiresses."

"We did, until you fell in love with Ruben and got it in your head to marry him," Isadora said.

"He was charming."

"How did you meet your husband?" Emily asked.

"He was my father's accountant of all things. He helped me so much after my father died with understanding my accounts and what I had. He was the one who said I had this home in Amherst that I didn't even know of at the time of my father's death. I assumed that my father sold it years ago since we never returned. It was a welcome discovery. I have very fond childhood memories here in Amherst, and I knew when I married this is the place I would want to live and raise children. Boston is no place for children." She smiled. "And you and Isadora met at Mount Holyoke?"

Emily nodded. "Yes, I was there one year."

"What a small world it is," Isadora said.

"Quite," Miss Alcott said, accepting a steaming cup of coffee with cream from Eugenia the terrified maid.

"Emily and I both had a passion for writing at Mount Holyoke," Isadora said. "But we will never be as accomplished as you are, Louisa. I must say I'm so impressed by all you have achieved."

"You could be just as successful." Miss Alcott blew on her coffee. "You just have to have the right motivation. I can assure you, poverty is a great motivator."

The other ladies laughed uncomfortably. All except Emily, who asked, "What do you mean?"

"I do enjoy writing. I might even say I love it sometimes, but there is a great difference between writing to live and living to write. I write to live. It's my livelihood, and I do it under many names and hats to make money. I do not apologize for that."

Mrs. Thayer placed a hand on her cheek. "But it is art. Shouldn't it be pure?"

"Art for purity's sake is the advantage of the rich. The difference is not having money and knowing you have to make your talents work for you. I can't depend on my father or family to provide for me. They depend on me. I do it openly and honestly. Not everyone does."

"What do you mean?" Mrs. Thayer asked.

"Your Mr. Howard is an example, a perfect example. He had talent but wanted shortcuts because he wouldn't put in the time." She leaned back in her chair. "And that probably got him killed."

Mrs. Thayer, Miss Lavinia, and Isadora all gasped, but Emily was quiet. She seemed to be studying Miss Alcott with newfound respect in her eyes. Miss Alcott was blunt and straightforward and perhaps rough around the edges. I believed Emily admired that.

It did not hurt that the conversation about Mr. Howard was the very reason Emily had agreed to come to this tea in the first place. She had to be grateful that Miss Alcott had been the one to bring up the subject.

Miss Lavinia shifted in her seat.

Isadora eyed her. "Is there something wrong, Lavinia?"

"I—I just have a small headache. I need to step outside for a moment. A bit of fresh air will help." She got up from her seat.

Emily started to stand too.

Miss Lavinia waved her away. "No, Emily, I will be fine. I just need a moment." Miss Lavinia hurried out the door.

"What is wrong with her?" Miss Alcott asked, and then sipped her coffee.

Isadora glanced at Emily. "I noticed Mr. Howard paid extra attention to her when he first arrived. Were promises made?"

Now Emily shifted uncomfortably in her seat.

"Wouldn't be the first time," Miss Alcott said in her frank way. "He's a social climber and jumped from woman to woman in order to raise his station in life. I have no respect for that. I work to improve my life and the life of my family. Trust me; it was not a skill that I learned from my father." There was bitterness in her voice.

"Have any of you heard of a young woman named Gabriella that Mr. Howard was attached to?" Emily asked.

"No, but I know he was attached to a rich woman the last time I visited Concord," Miss Alcott said. "He bragged about it to me. I believe he was smarting that I had published *Flower Fables* under my real name. Although it wasn't my first book. I have written under other names. All he had to show for his life's work, he carried about in Waldo's satchels."

"Louisa," Mrs. Thayer said. "That is quite harsh."

"Sometimes the truth is harsh. I do not apologize for that." She touched the side of her mouth with a cloth napkin.

I bit the inside of my lip and slipped out of the room. I hoped my leaving wouldn't upset Emily, but I wanted to check on Miss Lavinia to make sure she was all right. Even though she would not be pleased that I was the one to go and look for her, she was hurting, and I knew what a broken heart felt like.

The Thayers' home was open and spacious with high ceilings and large windows, but I took a deep breath when I stepped outside onto the front porch. I felt like I had been let out of a cage, and a gilded one at that.

I looked around for Miss Lavinia. I didn't know how I would find her. The grounds of the estate were expansive, with so many barns and outbuildings. She could be anywhere. I glanced back at the house. I didn't want to go back in there and listen to the women's small talk. I just had to trust that if anything important happened, Emily would share it with me.

I stepped off the porch and followed a path to the back of the house, thinking Miss Lavinia would most likely have taken it. It was made of pebbles and large stones, looking as if it had been freshly raked. Horace and the other men at the homestead took good care of the Dickinson property, but it could not compare to the immaculate grounds of the Thayers' estate. There wasn't a petal or leaf out of place on any flower or plant I saw. I wondered whose job it was to make sure everything was perfect all the time, and how exhausting it must be.

As I neared the stables, I heard horses neighing inside. The stables were grand like everything else belonging to the Thayers. They were even larger than the town stables where Henry had worked at the end of his life. This was the kind of place a majestic horse like Terror should live.

I couldn't resist taking a peek inside and told myself that Miss Lavinia very likely did the same thing. She was fond of horses and all animals. It was one of the few things she and I had in common.

As I stood just inside the door, my eyes adjusted to the dim light and I spotted Mr. Thayer standing outside an open horse stall. I stepped into an empty one and ducked down to hide. I leaned my ear closely to the stall wall.

"It's not a problem anymore," Mr. Thayer said. "The Italian is in jail. They aren't going to let a man like that out."

"But what if he didn't do it?" a high-pitched male voice replied. The voice had a slight Irish accent, but I knew many of the yardmen in Amherst were Irish. Even so, I felt nervous and hoped I was wrong in thinking I recognized the voice.

"That doesn't matter. We had a deal," Mr. Thayer snapped.

"I didn't know anyone would be arrested," the Irishman said. "I didn't know anyone else would be accused."

"You think the police would just let the death of Mr. Howard go unsolved when he was attached to a man as powerful as Emerson? Maybe the country you come from is lawless, but it is not that way here."

"I—I didn't think about it. I don't know that I can live with what has happened, with what I know I've done."

I peeked over the edge of the stall, hoping to see the Irishman's face.

"That is your problem, not mine," Mr. Thayer said. "Here is the money I promised you, and the pyrethrin. Do what you want with the former and dispose of the latter. Now, get out of here." He dropped a brown paper bag into the other man's hand. But I still could not see the Irishman's face.

"That should be enough for your girl's safe passage," Mr. Thayer said.

My stomach twisted even tighter. I knew who it was, but I very much wanted to be wrong.

"I don't know if I can take it. I don't know if it is right to spend the money on my Colleen when another man will suffer for it."

"Take it. You don't have a choice. We are in this together, and neither of us can breathe a word about it to anyone. Do you understand?"

In a shaky voice, the Irishman said, "Yes, I understand."

"Now get out of my sight." Mr. Thayer's voice was full of venom.

I ducked behind the stall door just as Cody Carey ran by me carrying the brown paper bag.

CHAPTER TWENTY-EIGHT

I WAITED BEHIND the stall door until I was certain Mr. Thayer was gone, and then I stumbled out of the stables into the bright sunlight. I covered my eyes.

"Emily sent you to look for me, didn't she?" Miss Lavinia asked me in a bitter voice.

I spun around, as I was still reeling after hearing Mr. Thayer and Cody. Was Mr. Thayer paying Cody for putting the blame for the murder on Paulo? Did that mean Cody was involved in the murder? Cody, whom I had protected from the very beginning?

"Lavinia?" I asked.

She narrowed her eyes. "Miss Lavinia to you."

She was holding a small black kitten that looked no more than a few weeks old.

I swallowed. "I know. I'm sorry. I— You surprised me."

"You didn't surprise me. I knew you or Emily would come

out here to look for me. It's just like Emily to send her maid, rather than do it herself."

I lowered my hand from my face. "Miss Dickinson didn't send me. I came to look for you myself."

She frowned and held the kitten under her chin. "Why?"

"Because I wanted to make sure you were all right."

"Why?"

My brows knit together. "What do you mean? You were clearly upset by what the women at the tea said."

"Why do you care? I have never been kind to you. Why would you have any sympathy for me at all?"

I couldn't argue with her on that point. I swallowed. "Because I know what it feels like when a person you love dies."

She snorted. "You think I loved Mr. Howard? I barely knew him before he was dead. There wasn't enough time to love him."

I blinked. "But you were so upset."

"Because it was an opportunity lost. There was a chance I could come to love him. He said he cared for me. How he did in such a short time, I don't know. Now, listening to the women, I know what a fool I was to believe him for a second. He was a flirt. He was just using me to advance himself, and if someone else came along who was better connected or had a more powerful family, he would have moved on to her. I was saved from that embarrassment."

I pressed my lips together. She was saved from that embarrassment because Mr. Howard was dead. I wanted to say it, but I held back. There was no reason to make her feel worse.

"I think I'm just coming to realize that being a daughter and sister is my life. I lack nothing. There is no reason this melancholy feeling should wash over me because of it. I am better off than many." She looked me in the eye. "I am better off than you, a servant with no family."

Her words were as sharp as a wasp's sting, but what she said wasn't untrue.

"It is all right to mourn something that is not to be," I said. "But you are still young. There is much time in your life for love."

"Soon I will be of an age that is no longer desirable to a young suitor. The older I become, the less chance there is for me. My only option would be to marry a widower, a man left with children who need caring for. I don't want that. I have my family, my cats, and a comfortable home." She looked down at the tiny cat. "A stray just had kittens here, and as I came outside, the stableman was threatening to drown this one because he's black and thought to be unlucky. I said I would take him. He will still need milk for a few weeks, but I will be able to care for him. It will be good to have this little creature to distract me until I am content again. I suppose that was the worst part of Mr. Howard's visit. He stole my contentment because he opened my eyes to other possibilities."

The kitten purred as if he knew how lucky he was that Miss Lavinia saved him from a terrible fate.

"I named him Zeus because he will be powerful, but I will call him Z for short. My Baby Z." She tucked the kitten into her shawl. "I need to take him home and feed him. He will need milk every few hours. Don't tell Emily I have taken another cat inside of the house. You know how she feels about them. She will not like it."

The tiny black head popped out of her shawl.

"I won't say a word," I promised.

She nodded and walked toward home.

I could not help but wonder if she would run into Cody on her way back to the homestead.

As I watched Miss Lavinia leave, I was torn. Did I go back into the house with Emily, or did I return to the homestead and try to find Cody to learn what he knew? It seemed to me both Mr. Thayer and Cody knew Paulo didn't kill Mr. Howard. Had one of them committed the crime instead? Cody had found Mr. Howard; however, Mr. Howard had been feeling ill at dinner. Had Cody seen him before dinner? Had Mr. Thayer, for that matter?

I realized that if I could discover the person or persons who saw Mr. Howard before his final meal, I could narrow down the suspect list.

In the end, I decided to go back into the Thayer house, if only to tell Emily that Miss Lavinia had gone home. I would say nothing of her new kitten Baby Z though. I loved all animals, including cats; Emily felt differently.

Inside of the house, to my surprise, I found Miss Alcott sitting on the stairs with a pencil and a piece of paper. She was scribbling away.

I hesitated, wishing to speak to her but fearing her sharp tongue would chase me away.

Finally, I asked, "Miss Alcott, is everything all right? Do you require assistance?"

She looked up and blinked at me. "What?"

"Are you all right? You seem to be in pain."

"Just creative pain. I left the room for a moment to get my thoughts down on a story I'm writing."

"Miss Dickinson often does the same thing."

Miss Alcott grunted at this and continued to write. She then folded up the piece of paper and tucked both it and her pencil into her skirt pocket. "There. Now, the story will keep until I can get back to it. It is a ridiculous tale of a rogue and a fallen woman."

"Oh," I said.

She stood up smiling. "This surprises you? I have written many works under different names. Each of my salacious stories is more outrageous than the last one, but people love them. Who am I to refuse to write them just because they are petty and silly? They pay well. That is reason enough to continue."

"May I ask you something?"

She studied her hands. They were stained with pencil lead, much like Emily's often were. "What is it?"

"About Mr. Howard. You seemed to know him."

"I didn't know him well. I know he tried to steal my work once."

"And pass it off as his?" I asked.

"Yes, I even wrote Waldo to tell him this, but I don't think he believed me. Mr. Howard was a charming, handsome man and could easily talk himself out of any situation except for possibly the very last."

"I think Mr. Emerson would believe you now," I said. "He came to the realization that Mr. Howard was attempting to steal his own work not long before Mr. Howard died."

"That is a shame. Something Mr. Howard never understood was a good editor would surely be able to tell when he turned in work that sounded completely different from his own, making it obvious it could not have been by the same writer. I must admit, I am a little shocked he would go as far as to try to steal Waldo's work. It is one thing to pass off a lesser-known author's work as your own; it is quite another to do so with the best known writer in the country."

"Was he ever published?" I asked.

"No." She said this as though Mr. Howard were something no better than a worm. "He was not yet good enough to be paid for his work."

"There you are, Willa," Emily said, coming into the hall. "I was getting worried about you. Where is Vinnie?"

"She went home," I said, and winced inwardly as I waited for Emily's reaction.

Emily nodded. "I expected as much." She turned to Miss Alcott. "I could not help but overhear your conversation, and I do not agree. Being paid for your work doesn't necessarily make you a writer. Being able to contribute to the world in any manner of written word, on the other hand, does. Simply making money seems like a very narrow view of things."

Miss Alcott shrugged. "Perhaps that is true. However, if no one reads your contribution to the world, is it truly a contribution, or self-indulgence? In my mind, one must be practical about these things. Writing is a business, and a successful business makes money. Unsuccessful businesses shutter their doors after a year or two. That won't happen to me."

Emily seemed to consider this.

"You say you're a writer, Emily. What is it that you write?" Miss Alcott asked.

"Poems," Emily said.

"Poetry is nice, but it does not afford a good living. Poetry is not lucrative," Miss Alcott went on. "Since it is not profitable, poets are made weak by their art. If you want to make a name for yourself and earn a livelihood, you need to write novels."

"Novels are finite when they are published," Emily argued. "My poems are living things and as such they can always change."

"The same cannot be said for my writing. It is etched in stone. It should be read at face value for the story that it is, not for the story the reader wishes it to be."

"But you also write fairy tales," Emily argued.

"Fairy tales have the power to tell truths," Miss Alcott said.

"As do poems."

Miss Alcott cocked her head. "But in an understandable way for the masses? A poem will have a hundred meanings. A story has just one."

"I don't know if I agree with you," Emily said. "A story can have many meanings depending on the reader."

Miss Alcott shrugged as if it was no concern of hers. "Few people agree with me on most topics. However, I learned a long time ago not to care about anyone else's opinion but my own." She brushed pencil lead from the sleeve of her shirt. "Now, I am off to Waldo's lecture even though I have missed most of it." She walked out of the Thayers' home with her head held high.

CHAPTER TWENTY-NINE

EMILY AND I found Mrs. Thayer still in the grand parlor and gave her our apologies. "I'm so very sorry your lovely tea has been cut short. Vinnie is not feeling well; I should go home to check on her."

Mrs. Thayer held out her hand to Emily. "Oh, Emily, not to worry. We have been friends for ages, and I know your sister must come first."

"Where did Louisa go?" Isadora asked.

"She went to the lectures," Emily said.

Mrs. Thayer gave a little laugh. "That is just like her, to go and do as she pleases. I wish I were that brave."

"Your husband would never allow it," Isadora said with a touch of scorn in her voice.

Mrs. Thayer frowned. "I suppose you're right. Speaking of which, he will be home soon, so I must dress for dinner. Isadora, will you join me upstairs?"

"I believe you and Ruben should have an evening alone, Cate Lynn. I have made too much of a nuisance of myself these last few days. I think I will grab an apple from the kitchen and then head to the lectures myself. After that, I might stroll around the campus. It is so peaceful here. As much as I am looking forward to going home to Boston, I will miss the peace and quiet of Amherst when I am back in the middle of the hustle and bustle of the city."

Mrs. Thayer shook her head. "You're not a nuisance at all! I have been delighted for the company these last few days. Ruben works so hard at the college, and even in the summer, he is not at home as much as I would like him to be."

"All the more reason for the two of you to have an evening alone," Isadora said.

"Very well," Mrs. Thayer said. "I can see your mind is made up."

"We will walk with you, Isadora," Emily said. "The campus is just across from my home."

Isadora smiled. "Wonderful. Let me go gather my things, and I will meet you outside."

A minute later, Emily and I stood on the Thayers' front porch. The sprawling lawn lay before us and was meticulously trimmed. If I had a ruler with me and measured each blade of grass, I was certain every one would be a perfect match to the ones next to it.

"It is beautiful," Emily mused. "But where is the wildness? Growing things should not be cultured so. They need to be able to choose the direction they want to spread. You can ease them into doing your will, but this is forced, as if any seedling that dare threaten to grow out of line will be plucked and tossed into the fire. How is that a real garden?"

I didn't have an answer for that question, and I wasn't certain Emily even wanted one. I was saved from making the choice as Isadora Foote arrived. In one hand, she held a large brown leather satchel.

Emily eyed the case. "Is that for your apple?"

Isadora chuckled and adjusted her grip on the wooden handle. "My apple is inside, but this is for my work. I didn't mention it to Cate Lynn because I know it is a sore spot with her, but I carry my writing in here. Mr. Emerson has agreed to review it after the lecture this afternoon."

"Why would that be a sore spot for Cate Lynn?" Emily asked.

Isadora pressed her lips together. "She gave up aspirations of her own when she married. Sometimes, I believe, pursuing mine reminds her of that."

"Meeting with Mr. Emerson is why you won't be joining the Thayers for dinner," Emily said.

"Precisely. Either the meeting will go very well and I will be overwhelmed with excitement, or it will go terribly, and I will be somewhere on the campus licking my wounds. My career hinges on what Mr. Emerson says."

"I don't believe it does," I blurted out, and then clapped a hand over my mouth.

Both women stared at me.

"I apologize for speaking out of turn," I said.

"It is quite all right, Willa," Emily said. "What is the point you are trying to make?"

I cleared my throat. "Just because one person doesn't like your writing doesn't mean someone else won't like it. My brother and I had very different tastes in books."

Isadora arched her brow. "Perhaps I should have you and your brother read my manuscripts then."

I snapped my mouth shut. I wasn't going to tell her that Henry was dead.

To my surprise, Emily didn't share this information either.

"Emily, you are always writing. You should share your work with Mr. Emerson as well. You can't miss out on this opportunity."

Emily pulled her black shawl up higher on her shoulders. "I have considered it, but I think I have upset him too much now. His opinion would be swayed."

Isadora cocked her head. "Upset him how?"

"I wanted to know what he knew about Mr. Howard's murder. I don't believe the Italian peddler is behind it. Mr. Emerson took issue with that and believes I should leave well enough alone."

"I don't disagree with him on that point," Isadora said. "You should leave it alone. It had nothing to do with you."

"He died in my garden."

"Yes, but you weren't responsible for that," Isadora said.

"The powder used to kill him took thirty minutes to cause even a mild reaction," Emily said thoughtfully. "Someone could have exposed him to it before the meal started."

"Are you implying it was someone at the dinner party?" Isadora asked. "It's no wonder Mr. Emerson was offended. He was the only one at the table who really knew Mr. Howard, so he might have the most reason to want him dead."

The large stone building that served as the college's main lecture hall came into view, but it was still a few hundred yards away.

"All I am saying is," Isadora went on, "you have to think before you speak, Emily. Just because something crosses your mind doesn't mean you have to say it aloud. Save that kind of honesty for your poetry. Don't waste it on spoken words where it could give the wrong impression."

"I can't hide who I am."

Isadora arched her brow at her. "You already hide who you really are quite well."

To my surprise, a blush filled Emily's face. It was the first time I had ever seen my mistress blush. I hadn't known anything could be said to ever embarrass her. Perhaps that was the gift of living in her own thoughts so much of the time.

"Even if Mr. Emerson is miffed at you, still, you should show him your work. When will you get another opportunity like this? He is a gatekeeper of the literary world. If that is where you want to enter, you will need someone like him to show you the way."

"I will think about it," Emily said.

"Don't think too long. You might miss your chance altogether."

Emily didn't say anything back.

We watched as Isadora walked confidently to the lecture hall.

"I admire women like Isadora and Louisa," Emily said. "They know their value in the world and they are comfortable with it. They make no apologies for it, and don't let anyone hold them back."

I glanced at her. "You don't let others hold you back either."

"I try not to, but if you could spend one day in my mind, Willa, you would want to leave. It is so crowded up there. I promise you that." She shook her head. "But Isadora might be right. Showing Mr. Emerson my work might be the best and fastest way I can receive recognition."

"Then what is the delay?" I asked.

She smiled at me. "The same as it always is. I don't know if I can stand someone tearing apart my work if he doesn't understand my words in the way I wrote them."

I didn't have an answer for that.

Emily wrapped an arm around my shoulders and guided me in the direction of the homestead. "My dear Willa, at times, I think solving a murder is easier than comprehending a poem."

Margaret was more than a little relieved when I returned from the tea sooner than expected, and then put me through my paces for being gone. As I scrubbed the family bathtub, I can't say I blamed Margaret. I had been absent quite a bit recently. Also, cleaning gave me time to let my mind wander. The trip to the Thayers' had been enlightening, and not in the way I'd expected. I thought we might learn something from Isadora or Mrs. Thayer about Mr. Howard since they knew Mr. Emerson. Instead, I saw Cody, the Dickinsons' yardman, seemingly being paid off by Mr. Thayer. For what? Had Cody somehow contributed to Paulo Vitali being arrested? If that was true, I wasn't sure that I could ever look at him the same way again.

After scrubbing the bathtub, I polished it with a white

cloth until it shone. I stood up and admired my work. It was the cleanest I had ever seen it. Even Margret would be impressed . . . maybe. Although I knew she wouldn't tell me even if she was.

I stepped across the room to open the small window looking out on the gardens. Below, Cody was pruning in the rose garden. Before I could change my mind, I gathered up my cleaning pail, brushes, and cloths, and headed down the back servants' stairs.

I dropped my cleaning supplies in the laundry room, went out the back door, and hurried into the garden. I prayed Margaret wouldn't look out the kitchen window and see me. As long as she thought I was still polishing the bathtub, she would leave me alone. She hated polishing anything.

Cody was bent over a rosebush shaking a yellowish-white powder onto the plants.

"What are you doing?" I asked.

Cody jumped, and the box of powder fell into the wood chips beneath the roses. The box sat on its side, but I could clearly see the word "pyrethrin." "Guaranteed to kill pests!" it read underneath, with a drawing of a dead bug below the writing.

"Willa, you scared me to death."

"What are you doing?" I asked again.

He blinked at me. "The late summer beetles are overrunning the roses. I had to do something."

I looked down at the roses. I didn't see any beetles. "Did Horace ask you to do that?"

He scowled at me. "I understand plants too. I don't need Horace's permission for everything I do in the garden."

I was certain Horace wouldn't agree with that. If the gardener had it his way, everyone, including Mr. Dickinson, would need his permission to touch anything in the gardens.

I pointed at the box. "Where did you get that?"

He frowned. "Willa, what has gotten into you?"

"Are you trying to get rid of the evidence?" I wrapped my arms around myself as if I had caught a sudden chill on this summer afternoon.

"What are you talking about?"

"Where did you get that box of pyrethrin? Are you using it on the roses to make it go away? Because you used it to kill Mr. Howard?"

He scooped up the box. "I got this from the garden shed."

"We do have some in the shed. I bet if I go to the garden shed right now, it will still be there on the shelf." I turned. "I'm going to check."

"Don't!" he cried.

I turned around and stared into his pleading face.

How could I have been so naive?

I had trusted him because he reminded me of Henry. That wasn't reason enough to stick my neck out for him. I had been a fool.

"Cody, I helped you," I said. "I left your name out of things when the police questioned me about Mr. Howard's death. You would have been a suspect in his murder if it had not been for me, and now I'm wondering if that was a mistake because you're guilty. You have to tell me the truth."

"You had better tell both of us," a voice behind me said.

I spun around and saw Emily standing at the edge of the rose garden.

"I—I can't," Cody said.

"Why not?" Emily asked, walking up to us.

He looked us both in the eye in turn. "Because I am afraid. So afraid."

CHAPTER THIRTY

EMILY GLANCED BACK at the house. "Here, let us talk in the orchard so that we can't be seen."

Cody and I followed Emily.

While we stood amid the rows of apple and pear trees that were just beginning to show the signs of fruit, Cody wrung his hands, and his accent was so thick I had to concentrate on his words to understand what he was saying. "It doesn't matter where I go. He will find me. There is no escape for me. He can hold this over my head forever. I will never be free unless I leave here. And if I do, will I have to give up my dream of my sweetheart coming to America? She trusted me to bring her here, and in my haste, I ruined everything."

Emily studied him with her appraising gaze. "Who is he of which you speak?"

Cody looked in all directions, as if the trees themselves had ears and could report back to his tormentor. "If I tell you, you will be in danger too."

"What danger can I be in?" Emily asked. "I'm a Dickinson. No one would dare touch my family in Amherst."

"This man would."

"Who is it?" Emily asked forcefully.

"Mr. Thayer."

Emily's eyes went wide in surprise, but since I had witnessed Cody and Mr. Thayer together just hours before, it was the answer I was expecting.

"He killed Mr. Howard?" Emily asked.

"I—I think so. Yes, yes, it had to be him."

"But why?" Emily asked.

"I do not know. All I know is he asked me to buy the pyrethrin for him from the peddler. He wanted me to do it at night when no one was there, so I would not be seen. He gave me the money for it. He said he'd pay me handsomely because it would look odd for a man of his stature to buy from the peddler."

"Why didn't he ask one of his own servants?" I asked. "It wouldn't have been odd then."

"I don't know. I didn't ask him."

"Why not?" Emily asked.

He stared at her. "It is not my place to question a gentleman."

"He is right," I said.

Emily cocked her head as if she hadn't considered this before. She was comfortable questioning anyone, even Ralph Waldo Emerson himself. As a woman of her class, she had that privilege, but it was not the privilege of Cody or me.

"Did he tell you anything at all?" Emily asked.

"He only said he needed it to fix a problem. I thought at the time he was having an issue with insects. Why else would someone buy that? We use it for the garden here. I didn't know it could be used in any other way."

"But you did not ask him what it was for," Emily said.

"I just told you, it was not my place. Had I known that he had ill intentions for it, I would not have gone along with his plan."

Emily folded her arms.

Cody wiped sweat from his brow. "I'm sorry. I shouldn't speak to you that way, Miss Dickinson. The last week has been so difficult for me."

Emily nodded for him to go on.

"Mr. Thayer was paying me good money. More money than I had ever seen. It wasn't until Mr. Howard died, and I heard the police detective mention the insect killer, that I became nervous. It seemed too much of a coincidence. When I asked Mr. Thayer about it after Mr. Howard died, he said it was best if I didn't know, and told me to keep my mouth shut. Then he gave me the box and ordered me to dispose of it. Very little had been used, so I thought it'd be best to sprinkle it on the plants to protect them from insects. August is the very worst time for bugs, so it seemed the sensible use for it."

"And an easy way to get rid of it," Emily said, shaking her head. "He didn't confess to the murder to you?"

"No," Cody said. "And I—I don't know what he wanted the powder for. I really don't."

"But you suspect you might know."

Sweat trickled down the side of Cody's face. "Isn't there a chance that it was an accident?"

"Then why did Mr. Thayer ask you—who works for *my*

family—to purchase the incriminating substance and then dispose of it after Mr. Howard died? Was he hoping to point the blame in my family's direction to cover his tracks? It makes a wicked kind of sense. To make matters worse, you are now disposing of it in our garden." Emily narrowed her eyes. "Did you think for one second how this would affect my family?"

Cody opened and closed his mouth as if he couldn't think of anything to say.

"You were just thinking of yourself," Emily accused, before grabbing the box of pyrethrin from his hand and stomping away.

During the entire encounter, Cody's face had been so red his freckles had vanished. Now, all the color drained from his face, and his freckles were more pronounced than ever.

"What is she going to do? Is she going to the police? To Mr. Thayer?" He grabbed at his waist. "I may be ill."

"Cody, please," I said. "You have to calm down. I will speak to her."

Tears welled in his eyes. "Why? Why would you help me now after I lied to you? After I put you at risk?"

"Because it's the right thing to do." I walked out of the orchard.

I glanced at the house, knowing I should return to my work there. Margaret knew how long it took me to perform each task she assigned and that by now I would be near the end of my list for the day. Even so, I needed to find Emily. If she went to her father about what Cody had done, Cody would be sacked immediately. Despite everything, I didn't want that. Also, Mr. Thayer would likely hear about it before we could discover the extent of his involvement in Mr. Howard's death and his reasons for wanting the secretary dead. It was his motivation that I struggled with the most. Why would Mr. Thayer want to kill a man he didn't even know and in such a premeditated way? To poison someone would take thought and patience. It seemed like an odd choice.

I found Emily sitting on a stone bench facing the perennial garden. There was still an indent in the black-eyed Susans where Mr. Howard had fallen.

She glanced at me. "If you are coming here to say I was too hard on Cody, you can save your breath."

"I wasn't going to say that." I folded my arms across my waist. "But Cody knows that he made a terrible mistake."

She glanced at me. "Willa, I wish I had your compassion at times. I think seeing the good in people would be a gift. I see all parts of them. The good and the bad."

She scooted over so I could sit next to her.

I took that to be an invitation. But I couldn't relax, as I worried Margaret would stomp out of the kitchen at any moment and shout my name.

Emily stared wistfully at the black-eyed Susans that bobbed and dipped their heads in the light and fleeting breeze.

"I was quite a good botany student at Mount Holyoke," Emily said. "It was one of my favorite subjects. I always loved plants and have been diligent in keeping up my herbarium with specimens I find in the garden and the woods around Amherst. When I saw Isadora, I was most excited to speak with her about plants again. She and I worked together often in school, as we both had a passion for them." She shook her head. "But she is too preoccupied now with her writing to have such conversation. I suppose being lost in her work is a better fate than being lost in a marriage. Look at what it has done to Cate Lynn. Her whole life is focused on her husband's happiness now."

"Is this why you didn't want Miss Lavinia to be attached to Mr. Howard?"

She stared out into the garden. "I don't want anything to change. I feel like a corrupt person."

"Why?" I asked.

She looked at me. "I was relieved when Mr. Howard died because his attention to my sister could have changed the family forever. It was the last thing I wanted."

"And now you want to find his killer to make amends for that."

She stared at me. "How do you know this?"

I watched a large bumblebee heavy with pollen make a lazy trip from one bright coneflower to the next. He rested on the second flower as if he could not believe that he had flown so far. "I think if I had been in the same position with Henry—if he'd become attached to someone who I believed was not good for him and that person passed on—I would have felt the same way."

She squeezed my hand. "Thank you, Willa. You are kind. Sometimes I think you are too good for this place."

I wanted to ask her what she meant by that, when she said, "We have to tell the authorities about Cody."

The bumblebee took off for the sky. I was sad to see him go.

I placed a hand on Emily's arm. "We have to remember the position Cody was put in, and we don't know the extent of Mr. Thayer's involvement."

She folded her hands on her brown skirt. "You're right.

Assuming what Cody told us is true, we're going to need something more before we tell Detective Durben. He and Mr. Thayer are old friends. He won't believe us without evidence."

"How are they close?" I asked.

"From what Austin said, they are old childhood friends. Because of this, we can't accuse Ruben of anything until we are sure the pyrethrin that killed Luther was the same one purchased from the peddler."

The box of pyrethrin was at her feet. "The box of pyrethrin he made Cody buy for him isn't enough on its own?" I asked. "I saw Mr. Thayer give it to Cody in a paper bag."

"When was this?"

Quickly, I told her about my eavesdropping on Mr. Thayer and Cody in the Thayers' barn.

"Very good, Willa. You are becoming a proper detective," she said. "But we have to be careful. You saw Mr. Thayer give something to Cody in a paper bag. He can claim it was anything."

"But they were talking about Mr. Howard's death and Mr. Thayer said he would give Cody money."

Emily shrugged. "You are still a servant, Willa, and a female one at that. We need something else. We have to see the peddler."

"How do we do that? We can't talk to Paulo now."

She looked at me. "We can't, but your Matthew can."

I bit my lip. "He is not my Matthew."

She shook her head as if she couldn't bring herself to have this argument with me again. "He is your friend, and you can speak with him about what we know." She stood up. "I will send him a note and ask him to meet us at the college tonight, if it will make you more comfortable."

"Why at the college?"

She arched her brow at me. "Do you want to meet here and take the risk of being seen with him?"

I sighed. "When do you want to meet him?"

She stood up. "Meet me at the laundry room door at midnight. I will handle the rest."

CHAPTER THIRTY-ONE

THE DICKINSONS ALL dined with Mr. Emerson at the Evergreens that evening for the last time. Tomorrow night would be the ball at the Thayers' home, and Mr. Emerson had already expressed the need to leave for Concord right after the ball to go home to his family.

I was grateful the family was away. Margaret had a light dinner of leek soup, and I caught up on the mending that'd been piling up in the laundry since I had started helping Emily in the gardens.

I perched on a three-legged stool with a spool of thread, a needle, and Mr. Dickinson's socks needing to be darned. I had already mended my own apron, a pair of Emily's stockings, and the hem of Miss Lavinia's Sunday dress. I was pleased with the fact they all looked like new from my handiwork.

When I was a young girl, I'd felt bitter that my mother had forced me to learn to sew on Sundays after church while Henry had been free to run wild through Amherst with his friends. It was the only day of the week we did not have school or work to do for another family. Now, I was grateful to her, because she had turned me into, if not a great seamstress, at least quite an adequate one.

Margaret stepped into the room carrying a reed basket filled with sheets just as I was finishing the last stitch on Mr. Dickinson's sock.

"Oh, I didn't expect you in here," she said.

I smiled up at her. "I thought since the family is away this evening, it was a good time to catch up on the sewing pile."

"Quite," she said. Her voice dripped with suspicion, as if she wasn't sure whether she believed me. She examined the sewing pile, which was twice as high as the pile I had already finished sewing. "Are you doing this all tonight?"

I looked up at her. "I hope to."

She frowned. "I didn't ask you to do it."

"It needed to be done, and with the family away, I had the time."

She shook her head. "I am continually surprised by you, Willa."

I was too cowardly to ask her if that was a good thing.

Sewing into the evening and night helped me pass the hours until it was time to meet Emily. As every hour ticked by, I became increasingly nervous. What had Matthew thought when he received her note? He had plenty of reason to tell his superiors about it. If he did, I knew the police would be knocking on the Dickinsons' front door.

The knocks never came.

Finally, I finished the last garment to be mended and folded it into the wicker basket. It was late, and I would put the clothes away in the various bedrooms around the house the next day when the family was otherwise occupied.

The house would be abuzz tomorrow with the ball approaching. I knew Emily planned to attend, but I had not yet heard if Miss Lavinia also planned on going.

I stretched, stepped into the kitchen, and looked at the clock on the windowsill. It was five 'til midnight. I had finished just in time.

I went back into the laundry and waited.

I didn't have to wait long. Emily soon appeared in the doorway. She wore a black dress and her cloak. Again, it was a warm night, but I didn't bother to question her clothing choices this time.

Carlo was by her side. She held a lantern in her small pale hand, and in the light of it, her eyes shone with excitement. This would be our second nocturnal investigation in Amherst that week, and she clearly enjoyed it. I hoped it didn't mean she planned to make a habit out of it.

"Everyone else in the house is asleep. Are you ready?" she asked.

I nodded even though my stomach felt like a thousand lightning bugs were dancing in it. In recent weeks, the only time I had seen Matthew was in his official capacity as a police officer. He had given me the space I asked for last year. I wasn't sure how I felt about seeing him at night with only Emily and Carlo as witnesses.

"Then let us go."

"What about your father?" I whispered.

She looked at me. "My father?"

"He caught you the night before when we went to find

Paulo. I'm afraid what he would do if he knew that you snuck out of the house on a second night."

"Nothing. Nothing is exactly what he would do. I am not a child," she said forcefully.

I'd heard her say the same to her father the night before. "All right," I said, knowing there was no point in arguing with her when her mind was squarely made up.

I followed Emily out the door. We walked around the side of the house and through the main gate. She walked with her head held high, as if nighttime walks with her dog and maid were something she did all the time. We crossed Main Street and into the Dickinsons' fields. There were rows and rows of corn around us. I had to admit it, the tall crops made the perfect cover in case anyone happened to look out the window.

We came out the other side of the field, and Emily held her lantern higher. We were now on the college grounds but still quite far from any buildings. "Are you all right, Willa?"

I dusted corn silk from my shoulders. "I'm fine. Where are we to meet him?"

"I told him to meet us by the lecture hall at twelve thirty. I guessed it would give us enough time to be there before him. Also, no students and professors live on that side of campus, so it is the best place to remain undetected."

"How do you know where people live?"

She grinned at me. "Willa, you act like this is the first time I have left my house in the middle of the night to go for a simple stroll."

My eyes went wide. I wouldn't call this a simple stroll by any means.

The lecture hall appeared to be even more formidable at

night. The stones shone in the moonlight, and the large window loomed over us like giant eyes. Carlo must have had the same idea because he whimpered when he stared up at the building and stepped behind his mistress. Not that the petite Emily was much cover for the giant dog.

"We will wait at the picnic tables," Emily said.

I held on to Emily's arm, as I could just make out the shape of someone sitting at the table.

Emily held her lantern high. "Who's there?"

"It's Matthew," he said in a strong, clear voice.

Emily lowered her lantern, and I felt the two of us relax. I dropped my hand from Emily's arm.

"I asked you to come at twelve thirty," Emily reprimanded.

He nodded. "I always arrive early when it's something important. Your note said it would be, so here I am."

Emily dropped the hood of her cloak. "Very well. We need to speak to you about Paulo Vitali."

Matthew rubbed the back of his neck. "So everything about Willa being in trouble is a lie?"

"You said I was in trouble?" I asked.

Emily glanced at me. "I had to say something to guarantee that he would come."

"But, Emily, it's not true," I said.

"Isn't it?" She challenged me. "If the real killer discovers we know that Paulo is innocent, then we could be the next target."

"Emily, don't say that," I gasped.

She shrugged. "It's true."

"There is no other killer. Paulo has confessed," Matthew said.

I placed a hand to my chest. "What?"

"He's confessed to the murder. We found out about what happened to his niece. He had a good motive. He had access to the powder because he sold it from his wagon. It all makes sense. Now that he has confessed, we can finally put this all behind us."

"I don't believe it," Emily said. "Why would he confess if he's not guilty?"

"He's guilty," Matthew said. "He said that he is, and we have to take him at his word."

"Would you take him at his word if he said that he was not guilty?" Emily asked.

Matthew pressed his lips together and did not respond to that.

A memory came back to me from one of the many times Henry had been arrested. One of the many times Matthew had been able to get him out of trouble. I knew now he had done that for me.

"Willa," Henry had said at the time. "There was a man there accused of stealing a carriage on the road into town. He said he didn't do it. He swore to me that he didn't. They took him out of the cell we shared. He came back hours later bloodied and battered and said he confessed to them."

Henry didn't have to spell out for me what had happened. I was just grateful that either Henry's crimes were not large enough to make the police want a confession so badly, or perhaps Matthew had gotten him out before it came to that point. Matthew protected Henry for me. However, he had not protected Paulo.

I licked my lips. "Do you think Paulo is guilty?"

Matthew stared at me. "What?"

"What do you think? Do you think in your heart he is guilty? Because he also told Emily and me about Gabriella and what Mr. Howard did to her. He was honest about being happy that Mr. Howard had paid for her death. He denied killing Mr. Howard though. I think if he had killed him, it would have been a point of pride."

Emily set the lantern on the table. "Willa is right. What is your answer?"

"I don't have an answer. I'm just an officer. It's not my job to interrogate any of the suspects at the station."

"Whose job is it?" Emily asked.

"Detective Durben's," Matthew said.

"The same Detective Durben who would go to any length to protect his friend Ruben Thayer?"

Matthew jumped up from his seat and blew out the lantern. "Hush!"

Carlo gave a low growl deep in his throat as the three of us stood silently in the dark. With the lantern out, the only light was that of the moon, and it was little more than a crescent half cloaked by thin cloud.

"Why did you hush us?" Emily whispered. "And why did you blow out the lamp? Is someone here?"

"If you want to talk about Ruben Thayer, the college is the worst place for it. This is his domain. Anyone could be out and hear us," Matthew hissed.

"So we are close to something," Emily said excitedly. This time, she did little to control the volume of her voice. "Ruben is up to something."

"I cannot tell you."

Emily wrapped her cloak around herself, and for a moment

she looked like a statue. It didn't appear she was even breathing. After a few minutes, she spoke again. "You must tell us, or we will keep digging."

"You can't do that. You will put Willa and yourself in danger."

"You give us no choice. We can't let Paulo—who I know is innocent—be framed for this crime just to protect ourselves."

Matthew groaned. "I promised I wouldn't tell."

The hairs stood up on the back of my neck. Emily was right. There was something very wrong and possibly corrupt going on. I shivered, and it wasn't due to the outdoor air.

"You leave me no choice," Matthew said. "Come with me." He started to walk away from the lecture hall, back in the direction of the homestead.

Emily and I shared a look, and then she followed him. I had no choice but to do the same.

CHAPTER THIRTY-TWO

I'D FOUND WHEN I follow someone and I didn't know where I was going, the trip felt like it took so much longer. The same proved to be true while Emily and I trailed Matthew through campus and the Dickinson field to the churchyard.

We could have walked on the road—which would have been a much more direct way to reach the church—but I was certain Matthew didn't want us to be seen. Back through the corn we went.

In the churchyard, Horace Church sat on the little stool staring at his fully bloomed moonflowers. The delicate white blossoms glowed in the moonlight. The cloud that had been obscuring the moon moved to the side.

He stared at the flower. "I didn't expect you tonight, Matthew."

"I wasn't planning on coming, but Miss Dickinson and Miss Noble forced my hand," Matthew answered.

Horace turned around on his stool then, but he didn't

appear to be surprised to see Emily and me there. "I had a feeling you would be able to put it all together, Miss Emily." He stood up. "Let's go speak in the church. No one will hear us there."

Emily, Matthew, and I followed Horace to the back door of the church and through the winding halls to the sanctuary. The only light in the massive room was moonlight that shone through the windows. It dusted every surface in a silver glow.

Horace sat in the third pew, while Emily and I sat in the one in front of him, turning to face him.

"Horace, what is going on?" Emily asked.

"You know I agreed to be sexton of this congregation," he began. "Because of what it stood for. The church has always taken a firm stand against slavery. My family has been fighting for that cause since I was a child. Have I ever told you the story of Angeline?"

Emily gasped. "You never told me, but I remember Father speaking of it when I was a little girl."

He nodded. "When you were ten, there was another young girl about your age in Amherst. Her name was Angeline Palmer. My mother got word that she was going to be sold to the South. I was a teenager at the time. Four good men of this community saved her from that fate by bringing her to my mother, Sarah. We hid her in our house until it was safe to move her again. The four good men were arrested for abduction, and your father, Miss Emily, represented them at the trial. I don't always agree with Edward's views." He stared at the cross in the middle of the simple altar at the front of the church. "I think he should take a firmer stance on slavery. He stands too much in the middle and depends on compromise.

There is no compromise in this arena, none at all, but I respected him for representing those men."

"I do remember that time," Emily said. "Father worked long hours on that case, and so many people were coming in and out of the house. Austin and I tried to sneak down to overhear what was being said, but our mother always caught us. I did know that a Black girl my age had been in trouble and my father was trying to help."

Horace nodded. "It would have been good conversation to overhear. I think the young should know what is going on in this country. Protecting the children from the truth doesn't help. Showing what the world is really like is the only way to truly encourage them to change it."

Emily held on to the back of the pew. "It is an important story, but what does it have to do with Ruben Thayer and Luther Howard?"

Horace's brow furrowed and he clenched his jaw. "Ruben Thayer is a traitor of the worst kind."

"A traitor?" Emily asked.

"He's a liar." He smacked the back of the pew so hard both Emily and I jumped. Matthew, standing in the aisle, flinched as well.

"He says he is an abolitionist," Horace went on. "He goes to all the meetings for the cause, but the opposite is true. He sends money to the South to finance slavery, not destroy it."

"But he's Northern," Emily said, as if that would be reason enough for Mr. Thayer to be innocent of such an accusation.

Horace shook his head and looked at the cross again. "It's for the same reason the institution of slavery was created. Greed. He's greedy. A greedy person can be of any ilk or culture. He doesn't want slavery to end. He doesn't want the money to dry up."

"How is he getting money from it?" I asked.

Horace looked at me for the first time, like he just remembered I was there. "He's an investor in a cotton mill in Georgia. It was planned to be the biggest in the country. It would never make the money it does without slavery. Without slavery, they would actually have to pay their workers."

Emily sat back. "I thought he was a college professor."

"He is. He's a professor of economics. He knows how money works and where to put it to make the most, but it's not his money, of course. Thayer also knows how to pad the pockets of the men in Washington, so they will continue to keep slavery intact."

"Does Cate Lynn know?" Emily asked. "I can't believe she does. Cate Lynn is one of the most outspoken abolitionists."

"I don't know if she knows. I like to think that she doesn't," Horace said with sadness in his voice. "It would break her heart."

Emily scowled. "If this is true, why has no one told her? She has a right to know what her husband is doing."

Horace stared at her. "She is his wife."

Emily gripped the back of the pew. "You are telling me that she has not been told because she is a woman. That is outrageous."

Horace stared at Emily as if he didn't know what to make of her. I knew Emily's argument, although it was right, was difficult for Horace to understand. Horace would believe a woman like Cate Lynn Thayer was too delicate to hear the truth about her husband. But women aren't nearly as delicate as most men believe.

"This is awful," I said. "It truly is, but it still doesn't answer the question as to why he bought the pyrethrin to kill Mr. Howard."

"What's this?" Matthew asked.

I winced, wondering how I could continue to protect Cody even though he lied to me.

Emily, however, didn't have the same qualms and told Horace and Matthew what we had learned from Cody that afternoon.

"It does not surprise me that Ruben Thayer would do such a thing. If you can support slavery, you are capable of anything," Horace said.

Emily, Matthew, and I left Horace in the sanctuary. He'd said he needed to pray. I felt like I could say a few prayers, too, and most of them would be asking for clarity. The murder of Mr. Luther Howard was more confusing than ever. How could what we learned from Horace about Mr. Thayer be tied into all of it? What was the connection to Mr. Howard?

Matthew stood at the foot of the church steps with us. "I'm sorry if that didn't give you the answers you were looking for."

"It didn't give us the right answers. Why did you have us speak to Horace?"

"Because I wanted both of you to understand what a dangerous man Ruben Thayer is," Matthew said.

"Then arrest him and throw him into prison for what he has done." Emily folded her arms under her cloak.

"Even if what he is doing by investing in a cotton mill is morally wrong, it's not illegal. I can't arrest someone just for being a rotten human being. If that was the case, the jails and prisons across the commonwealth would be full to bursting." Matthew sighed.

"I'm sure you can find something he's done wrong," Emily said. "You just have to try harder."

"However," I spoke up. "There is also the issue that Mr. Thayer and Detective Durben are good friends. If Matthew started poking into Mr. Thayer, the detective would hear about it."

Matthew nodded. "I wish that weren't true, but Willa is right."

"In any case, I have to talk to Cate Lynn," Emily said. "She has to know what her husband is doing."

"Tomorrow is the ball," I said.

"Then I will just do it there." Emily's tone left no room for argument.

"I don't think that is a good idea. It might spur too many questions," Matthew said.

"No," Emily said. "It is the perfect place. There will be a lot of people around. Ruben will be reluctant to make a scene."

I bit my lower lip. I didn't think it would go as smoothly as Emily expected, but I knew there was no way I would be able to change her mind.

CHAPTER THIRTY-THREE

THE NEXT MORNING at breakfast, Miss Lavinia was putting her foot down. The only problem was, her father would not hear of it.

"I have already told you I'm not going to the ball. I have no interest in it. Balls are dances to find a husband. Since I am not looking for such a thing, I have no reason to go," Miss Lavinia said, and sipped her tea. Baby Z, the tiny black kitten that she had saved from the Thayers' groundskeeper, was on her lap. She set her teacup down and fed Baby Z scraps of her toast.

Emily walked into the room and pulled up short. "Lavinia Dickinson, did you get another cat?"

Lavinia picked up the kitten and held it protectively under her chin. "It is not your concern, Sister."

"Not my concern," Emily yelped. "You already have four or five, and they tramp all over the grounds and the grounds of the Evergreens. They chase the birds and scratch the trunks of the trees." She looked to her father, who was hiding behind his newspaper. "Father, are you going to allow her to keep this cat?"

I stood near the sideboard and was adding more toast to the spread. Mr. Dickinson was very fond of toast. I worked as quickly as I could because I could feel the tension in the room building. I didn't want to be caught overhearing yet another family argument.

"I said that she could have it," Mr. Dickinson said. "Lavinia takes good care of all her animals. I don't see how having one more is an issue."

Emily fell into her chair with a groan.

Miss Lavinia smiled at her sister. "His name is Zeus, but I call him Baby Z."

Emily snorted. "That is a ridiculous name for a cat."

"What kind of ridiculous name is Carlo for a dog?"

"He's named after a dog in *Jane Eyre*," Emily said. "At least my dog is named after an actual animal. He's not named after a Greek god."

"He could have been," Miss Lavinia said smugly and lowered the kitten back to her lap. "You missed the opportunity on that."

Carlo looked up from his spot on the rug. When no one said his name again, he lowered his head with a great puff of air out of his mouth that ruffled the long fur over his eyebrows.

"Girls!" Mr. Dickinson snapped. "You are acting like spoiled children, not the young ladies that you are. I said that the cat stays, and that is the end of it."

Emily scowled. "What were you discussing before I came into the room? I thought I heard raised voices."

"They weren't raised voices," Mr. Dickinson said. "I was

just telling your sister that I expect both of you to go to the Thayers' ball."

"But, Father, there is no reason for me to go to the ball. It is very unlikely that I will even dance," Miss Lavinia argued.

"She just wants to stay home and be with her cats," Emily grumbled.

"You will both go," Mr. Dickinson said to his youngest child.

Miss Lavinia sat up straighter in her chair. "Father—"

"There is no argument. The ball is in honor of Waldo and his work. He is a guest of your brother and, by extension, our family. No one from my family will snub him by staying home. Not even Emily."

Emily looked up from something she was writing on an envelope. "Oh, I'm going. I'm looking forward to it. I would never consider snubbing Mr. Emerson."

Miss Lavinia narrowed her eyes at Emily as if she suspected that there was another reason she wanted to go to the ball. Mr. Dickinson, too, didn't seem to take her answer at face value. His bushy eyebrows went way up. Surely, he was surprised that his less social daughter was the one who was more excited to attend the ball.

"Everyone in this family is against me." Miss Lavinia got up and marched out of the room with her kitten on her shoulder.

Mr. Dickinson shook his head and went back to his newspaper, and I slipped out of the dining room.

The rest of the day, Margaret and I went through our normal chores of keeping the large house in order. By late afternoon when I came into the kitchen, she was making a light supper. The Dickinson family would be eating at the ball.

She sliced a large red pepper from the garden. "This is the first day you or Emily hasn't asked if you can leave the house for some fool's errand Emily thought up. I hope you noticed how much more smoothly our chores went with you here."

"I did, Margaret, and I'm sorry I have been gone so much." I washed my hands in the sink.

She sniffed.

The kitchen door opened, and Emily walked in. "Willa! There you are. I have been looking for you everywhere. Father said you can come to the ball tonight."

I stared at her and held a tea towel limply in my hands. "The ball? You want me to go to the ball?"

"Yes, I told him I needed you there for support since I couldn't take Carlo. Isn't it wonderful?" She clapped her hands.

"What will I do during the ball?" I asked.

"You will stand there and keep watch. Now, you must come with me so we can find you something to wear." She grabbed the tea towel from my hands and tossed it into the sink.

I glanced at Margaret, and she scowled at me. I didn't blame her. I would have been just as annoyed in her position.

"Do you think this is a good idea?" I asked.

"It's the best idea," Emily said, and grabbed my hand. "Come." She pulled me out of the kitchen.

I heard Margaret grumbling as we left the room. At least I had finished Margaret's chore list for the day and she couldn't complain of that, but I knew she would find something else to complain about.

Emily took me up to her room, which surprised me. The bedroom was her sanctuary. The rose blossom wallpaper was bright and pink, and seemed to jump off the walls. Every time I was in the space, I stared at the wallpaper for a little while as if I expected the roses to begin to dance. I came in the room only when Emily was in another part of the house, so I could tidy up as best I could. I made the bed, picked up scraps of discarded poems from the floor, put away garments, and dusted the fireplace and dresser.

I never touched her desk. It was too sacred a place. Her tiny writing desk sat in front of the window, looking out on Main Street. From there she could see the road and the Dickinsons' field across the street while she was writing. She could even see a bit of the college just beyond the field.

There were two dresses on her bed. One of brown gingham, and the other blue satin. "These are old dresses of mine. Perhaps you can wear one of them tonight."

I stared at them. The waist was twenty inches if not less, and they were hemmed to Emily's height, which was nearly eight inches shorter than me. "That is very kind, Emily, but there is no way these dresses will fit me. I am tall and broad. You're the opposite."

Emily picked the brown gingham up from the bed, held it up to me, and frowned. "Oh, I see." She dropped it back on the bed. "We will think of something."

"Are you sure you want me to go to the ball? A ball is no place for a maid."

"You have to go! Tonight everything will become clear about Luther's murder, I'm sure of it, and you have to be there when I speak to Cate Lynn about Ruben."

"I don't see why my being there will help," I said.

"It will help me," she said.

She looked me in the eye, and I realized that she was saying the truth. I thought about how apprehensive she must be about going to such a large event when by her very nature she would much rather sit alone in her room and write all day.

I nodded. "All right. But I still don't understand why Mr. Thayer would kill him. He had no connection to Luther, no motive."

Her face cleared now that I had agreed to go to the ball. "No connection and no motive that we know of. But I can assure you it exists," she said with feeling.

"Won't it bring more attention to the fact you are up to something if I am there?" I asked.

"Maybe it will," she said with a shrug. "And maybe it will make Ruben more nervous because he will know we are onto him."

I sighed. "I will wear my Sunday dress."

"We will put a ribbon in your hair to make it special," she said with the confidence of someone who knew she had won the argument.

CHAPTER THIRTY-FOUR

AT SIX O'CLOCK in the evening, Jeremiah York pulled the family's largest carriage up in front of the house. Emily, Miss Lavinia, and their parents waited outside of the homestead. All were smartly dressed. Mr. Dickinson wore a freshly brushed coat, and the ladies were in ball gowns. While Mrs. Dickinson's gown was the most subdued brown, both Emily and Miss Lavinia wore bright colors. Emily was in teal, and Miss Lavinia was in yellow. If they were willing, they would be asked to dance many times by the young men at the ball.

I felt Margaret watching me from the parlor window, while Cody and Horace watched me from the yard. My attending this ball would be the talk among the servants for days to come. When I returned home, I might receive several cold shoulders as a result of it. The most notable would be from Margaret, of course. I wished us to find a place where we could be friends, but I knew it was not to be as long as Emily kept singling me out.

I stood behind the family as they prepared to climb into the carriage. Miss Lavinia looked over her shoulder at me. "Why is *she* coming? Can we ever be rid of her?"

I tried to remind myself that when Miss Lavinia was being disagreeable, she was being her natural self, or so Emily had said.

"Your sister asked if she could come, and I granted her permission," Mr. Dickinson said. "That is all you need to know."

Miss Lavinia scowled. When Jeremiah opened the carriage door, she was the first one inside.

Mrs. Dickinson and Emily climbed in next. Mr. Dickinson glowered at me. "I'm sure you will be happy enough riding with the driver."

"I will, sir," I said.

He climbed into the carriage. Jeremiah closed the door, hopped onto his seat, and gave me a hand up to sit next to him. In truth, I was much more comfortable sitting on the driving seat next to my friend than I would be inside the carriage with the family.

Jeremiah flicked the reins, and we were on our way. He did not speak until we turned onto Main Street. In a low voice, Jeremiah asked, "Why are you here, Willa? A ball is no place for people like us."

I took no offense to his remark because I knew all too well he spoke the truth. Other than Emily, Jeremiah was my most reliable friend at the homestead. He had been Henry's friend, so he deserved my trust.

"Can they hear us?" I asked in a whisper.

He shook his head. "Not over the rattle of the carriage, but the windows are open because it's so warm. It's actually much more pleasant for us out in the open than it is for them in the stuffy carriage. At least Thayer Manor is not far."

"I'll whisper just in case. Emily and I believe the Thayers are connected to Luther Howard's death."

Jeremiah jerked his head back. "I can't believe that. Cate Lynn Thayer is one of the biggest advocates in Amherst for the cause."

When he said "the cause," I knew he spoke of abolitionism.

"I can't believe she would have anything to do with murdering anyone. She would not hurt a gnat," Jeremiah continued.

"We don't know if Cate Lynn is aware, but her husband is involved in some suspect business dealings." I decided not to tell Jeremiah what Horace had shared about Ruben Thayer. It would upset him, and I still had not confirmed it was true. I would not be the one to start a rumor that would affect the Thayers' reputation.

"It's too hard for me to believe." He shook his head and slowed the carriage, because ahead of us, a line of carriages waited to turn in to the long lane leading to Thayer Manor. The wrought-iron gate stood open, and large torches stuck in the ground glowed on either side of it. The sun would not set for well over an hour, but I could imagine how dramatic those torches would appear when we left at night.

The excited chatter of ladies and gentlemen floated back to us from the carriages up ahead.

Every time a horse and driver dropped off their finely dressed guests, Jeremiah tapped the reins and Terror moved forward a few feet. We made slow progress, but at a certain point, I could see the ladies and gentlemen disembarking from their carriages. The men were in frock coats with high collars. Some carried canes they clearly didn't need for walking. The ladies wore jewel-colored dresses with wide hoopskirts and low necklines. Their garments were made of silk, satin, and velvet. Around their pale wrists they wore small reticules, many of them with intricate beadwork. I looked down at my Sunday dress. It was the nicest possession I owned, but against the finery of the ladies ahead of us, I might as well have been wearing a tobacco sack.

I touched my blond hair, which Emily had divided in the middle into two braids and bound in a net at the nape of my neck.

Jeremiah bumped my shoulder with his. "I think you look as nice as any of those ladies. You look like a real person, just a bit more shiny than normal. I'm sure Matthew will take note."

I pressed my lips together. If Jeremiah was trying to cheer me up, that wasn't the way to go about it. And this was the first time that I thought Matthew might be at the ball. He was not a lowly servant like I was, but he was of the working class. Would Mrs. Thayer invite him? My palms began to sweat. I was less nervous to come face-to-face with Mr. Thayer, who likely killed a man, than I was with Matthew. I refused to consider what that might mean.

At last Jeremiah parked the carriage in front of the grand home and its soaring white pillars. Two footmen stood on either side of the carriage. One stepped forward and opened the door. Mr. Dickinson was the first one out, followed by his wife, Miss Lavinia, and, finally, Emily.

Emily looked up at Thayer Manor. "It's even more breathtaking in the evening."

Jeremiah started to get up. "I will help you down, Willa."

I stood up. "There is no need. I can get down very easily on my own." As if to prove my point, I hopped off the driver's seat. However, I miscalculated and nearly jumped onto the footman who was assisting a lady onto the walk. "Watch yourself," he snapped.

I shuffled back and bumped into Miss Alcott, who was walking between the carriages.

"That's how I would disembark if I could get away with it," she said.

"Miss Alcott, I'm so sorry. I did not see you there." I could feel my cheeks growing hot.

"I should hope you didn't, since you almost flattened me against the side of the horse."

Miss Alcott was also wearing a fine dress with a hoopskirt, but the collar was a bit higher. While most other women chose to wear bright colors, she had selected a gray so dark it almost looked black.

She must have noticed me looking at her dress, because she said, "I think possessions with multiple purposes are much more practical no matter how much money a person may have. This is a gown I could wear to a ball or a funeral. I go to many more funerals than balls."

I didn't know what to say, and it was just as well, because she moved off to join the line of guests who were to be greeted by Cate Lynn and Ruben Thayer at the door. I looked around for Emily and saw her five people ahead of me. I dithered as to whether I should run ahead to join the Dickinsons. Would the Thayers even allow me into the ball if there wasn't someone to speak for me?

Skipping ahead in the line seemed like it would bring too much attention to me, so I went to the end of it and prayed that Mrs. Thayer would remember me from yesterday's tea.

"Louisa, I thought you were already in the house," Cate Lynn Thayer said to Miss Alcott, who was three people in front of me.

"I was, but I went out for a stroll. The way your servants were running this way and that with fear in their eyes just before the first guests arrived grated on my nerves. I was much more comfortable outdoors."

Mrs. Thayer laughed. "I'm sure Isadora was putting them through their paces. She is a good one to have here when planning such an event."

"Much better than I," Miss Alcott agreed.

"Be sure to see the silent auction in the library of some fine pieces of my mother's jewelry. I know it might not be the couth thing to do, but all the money raised will go to the abolitionist movement. It was Mr. Emerson's wish to have some type of fundraiser for the cause, and I thought it was the very best use of jewelry I don't need."

"Then I will certainly bid on a piece or two. My youngest sister, May, adores shiny baubles of all kinds," Miss Alcott said.

"We are very glad to hear that," Mr. Thayer said and smiled at Mrs. Thayer. "My wife is just about the most generous person in the world. I learn so much from her."

"It is gratifying to hear you say you learn from your wife," Miss Alcott commented, and then went into the house.

The Thayers had similar conversations with the next two guests in front of me, and I could feel myself begin to sweat under my linen dress. What if they turned me away because I was clearly not one of their guests? It would be mortifying not just for me, but for the entire Dickinson family.

"Aah, Willa," Mrs. Thayer said. "Emily told us you would be joining her. I'm so glad you could come and be with her. Large parties have never been her favorite, but I am so happy she came regardless. The least that I can do is let her maid stand with her."

Relief swept over me. "I'm very happy to be here and help Miss Dickinson."

"It is so kind of you to care for your mistress so much that you would be here tonight to support her." She smiled.

"I don't think Miss Dickinson needs that sort of support," Mr. Thayer said. "But her father is an important benefactor of the college, so if this is his wish to let in a maid, I will allow it."

Mrs. Thayer placed a hand on her husband's arm. "Do not worry, Ruben. Willa is just here for Emily to be a person to lean on. I have told you of her peculiar ways, haven't I?"

"Yes," he said, but he didn't sound like he was completely happy with the arrangement.

That made two of us.

With the Dickinsons at the ball tonight, I could have retired to my room early, and curled up with Emily's copy of *The Scarlet Letter*.

"Please go in," Mr. Thayer said. "And keep yourself out of sight as best you can. It is clear from what you are wearing that you are not one of the guests."

His words stung, but before he changed his mind, I slipped into the grand house. I had always believed the Dickinson home was grand—and it was, compared to any other place I had lived throughout my life—but the Thayer Manor was so much more. The ceilings were several feet higher, and each one had ornate paneling. The floor in the entryway was marble. There were faces of cherubim engraved into the banisters.

Although I had been in the Thayer home just the day before, I had only been in the grand parlor where Mrs. Thayer had tea with the ladies. That door was closed tonight, and beyond the one room and the entryway, I did not know the layout of the house. Thankfully, the partygoers were all traveling single file through the home to where I assumed the ballroom would be.

After several turns, I stepped through double doors into the most opulent room I had ever seen. The floor was intricately patterned, and the wallpaper had a metallic sheen to it. The ceiling looked to be made of gold. Or perhaps it was only gold plated. It was overwhelming. When I'd gone to Mount Vernon with Emily last year and toured President George Washington's house, there hadn't been a room so grand and large there, and he was the first president of our country.

The first person I saw upon entering the room was Matthew. He was in uniform and stood along the wall. He looked very handsome. Even though he was clearly at the ball in his capacity as a police officer, I could tell that he had taken care to brush and mend his uniform before arriving. That made me smile.

He was scanning the crowd, looking for something. A killer maybe? That was what Emily and I were in search of.

I was afraid to walk further into the room. If I did, Matthew would notice me, and I wasn't sure I was prepared for that. I didn't want him to see me in this place and compare me to all these beautiful ladies in ball gowns, jewels, and flowers in their hair when I was in my Sunday dress with an added ribbon.

My face reddened as I thought on it more.

"Miss, please go in," a gruff male voice behind me said.

I turned to find an old man in an army officer's uniform trying to get into the room. I blocked the door and therefore his path.

His harsh tone attracted Matthew's attention. Matthew turned in our direction just as I moved out of the man's way.

Matthew walked over to me and tucked his hand under my elbow. "Step over here, Willa, before you get trampled."

I did as he asked and leaned against the wall with my hands folded in front of me. I didn't know the last time I felt this terribly out of place, and that included my trip to Washington with the Dickinsons the year before.

Matthew quietly stood next to me. He seemed to sense that I needed a moment to collect myself. I clenched and un-clenched my hands.

Finally, he spoke. "I didn't expect to see you here."

"I could say the same for you."

He smiled down at me. "Yes, balls are not my typical rounds. As you know, Ruben Thayer is a good friend of Detective Durben. The detective assigned me to come and keep an eye on things."

"Because of the auction?" I guessed.

He nodded. "There are a lot of jewels in the library. You will have to take a peek before you leave. I have never seen so many shiny pieces."

"I'm sure that I have never seen anything like it." I watched as more guests entered the ballroom. It seemed that each one was more finely dressed than the last. The ladies wore a dozen petticoats under their skirts to make their dresses as full as possible and their waists appear to be no thicker than a man's arm. The colors were rose pinks, peacock blues, and emerald greens. They wore their hair up or falling into ringlets on one side. I felt like a fool.

Matthew leaned down. "You look beautiful tonight."

I looked up at him, half expecting to see some teasing in his eyes. How could he seriously believe that when there was all this finery around us?

His eyes were serious. "You are the most beautiful woman in the room."

I wanted to argue with him because I was *never* the most beautiful woman in the room. I was too broad in the shoulders, too tall in height, and too plain in face, but looking at Matthew in that moment, I believed him. His expression was so sincere, and I could have easily said to him that he was the most handsome man in the room if my tongue had not become lodged in the back of my throat.

When I didn't say anything, he took pity on me by asking, "Why are you here?"

"Emily," I croaked.

He chuckled. "It seems to me Emily is always the answer."

"She just might be," I said and looked around the room. "She is in here somewhere. She and the family came in before I did."

"Why did Miss Dickinson want to bring you here?" he asked, and studied my face.

"She is not comfortable at these grand types of events. She grows nervous and unsure. I am here to help her." This was partially true. However, the murder was Emily's main reason. If it weren't for the murder, I had little doubt that she and I would both be back at the homestead right now. The puzzle of solving the crime was a great motivator for Emily.

He arched his brow. "Because Carlo the dog can't be here?"

I lifted my chin up just a hair. "Well, you can't imagine Carlo in this ballroom, can you?"

He grinned. "No, but it would have been worth coming just to see that. I'm sure that he would have been the talk of the party."

Despite myself, I smiled. "He would," I said.

"But even with Carlo absent, it's worth being here just to see you and talk to you. I have missed our talks, Willa."

I could feel him looking at me, and I couldn't bring myself to look up at him. Instead I stared down at my hands. They had to be the only ladies' hands in the room without gloves covering them, and instead, the palms were calloused from washing, the fingernails chipped from gardening, and the skin freckled from the sun.

"Willa, I do want to talk about our future."

My breath caught in my throat, and I finally made eye contact with him. I realized that I wanted to talk about our future too.

Someone grabbed my hand.

"Willa, what took you so long to get in here? Did you forget we have a murder to solve?" Emily hissed. She waved at Matthew. "Hello, Matthew! Keep an eye out!"

Behind me, Matthew groaned.

CHAPTER THIRTY-FIVE

S HE PULLED ME across the room behind a partition where it turned out the food was located, and I stared at the spread. I had never seen so much food in my life. There were lobster puffs, figs, caviar, shrimp tails, and more. There was every kind of delicacy a person could want and many that I had never seen before but was more than willing to try. Even with all the people here, I could not believe all this food would be eaten tonight. My stomach growled, as I had missed out on my simple dinner with Margaret to prepare for the ball.

"What is our plan?" Emily asked.

I blinked at her. "Were you expecting for me to have a plan? It was your idea that I come here in the first place."

"You have many good ideas, Willa. Surely, you have thought about how we should proceed."

I bit my lip. "I—I think we should find out from Mrs. Thayer if she knows about her husband's business, and if she knows of the connection between Luther Howard and her husband. If she doesn't know, do you plan to tell her what Horace shared with us?"

"Yes, I do," Emily said with feeling. "Too often women are kept in the dark about their husbands' behavior. Cate Lynn is my friend. I would not wish that on her or anyone I cared about. She should know." She paused. "But it might be difficult to get her alone. She is the hostess."

I looked around the room. An eight-man orchestra sat in one corner. They played softly as the guests arrived. They all wore matching black suits and white shirts and appeared to be quite young. I supposed since Mr. Thayer worked at the college they were music students that the professor could hire at a discount or convince to play for free. Even so, they were quite talented, and several of the ladies in their wide hoop dresses swayed to the music.

"Maybe we should pursue this tomorrow after the ball," I said.

"No, it must be tonight," Emily said. "Ruben can't deny what he has done in front of all these people. He needs to be held accountable."

"Yes," I said. "But we don't know he killed Mr. Howard."

"We don't know *yet*. I will find out," Emily said.

I didn't like the sound of that.

"I will speak to Cate Lynn as soon as I can get her alone," Emily said. "There has to be at least one moment throughout the night when she will want to leave to catch her breath. When she does, I will tell her what we know."

"What do you want me to do?"

"Do what you do best, Willa. Watch everyone." She peeked around the partition. "There's Isadora. Since she has been staying with the Thayers this last week, she is the most likely to know anything at all. Good luck!" She hurried away.

I stood on the side of the partition and looked around it. Ladies and gentlemen moved about the room. The orchestra was beginning to play more loudly. Everything was perfect and looked perfect. I had never felt so out of my element in my life.

"Can you offer these to the guests?" a footman asked me, holding out a tray of wine in short glasses.

"I don't—"

"Just take it," he said, and forced the tray into my hand. I had to accept it to keep the glasses from spilling. He gave me a nudge, and I found myself on the other side of the partition.

"Oh, thank you," a gentleman said, taking two of the glasses from the tray before walking away.

I started to relax. With the tray in my hand, I was far more comfortable in my usual role as servant. I scanned the room for Isadora, but didn't see her. In fact, I hadn't seen Isadora at all.

The dancing began, and I watched as young men approached young women and asked them to waltz. A handsome young man stepped up to Emily and held out his hand, but she walked by as if she didn't even see him. Knowing my mistress, she might not have.

Miss Lavinia stood in one corner of the room as if trying to blend in with the drapery behind her. Austin and Miss Susan joined the other young couples on the dance floor. Since the younger Mr. and Mrs. Dickinson were there, I assumed Mr. Emerson had also made his appearance. I soon spotted him on the other side of the room speaking to none other than

Isadora. Carrying the tray with me, and stopping every so often as a guest took a glass, I made my way across the room.

"I do appreciate that you trusted me to read your work. Cate Lynn Thayer is a good friend of my family's, and her parents were such wonderful people," Mr. Emerson said.

"Cate Lynn speaks highly of you as well," Isadora replied. "She is passionate about the abolitionist cause. As passionate as her parents were. God rest their souls."

"It is good to see she married a man who supports it too," Mr. Emerson said.

"Yes," Isadora murmured. She cleared her throat. "I hate to corner you at the ball like this, but I know you are leaving shortly after. Did you have a chance to read my pages?"

"I did. They were very concise and well written. I can see a clear grasp of the English language there." His tone was measured.

Isadora smiled. "Thank you. I was hoping you would say something positive."

"But," he began.

Isadora's face fell.

"They are familiar to me. What you have written sounds very similar to the pages written by my late secretary, Luther Howard. He asked me to write a foreword for a book he was working on, and it felt as if I was reading the same words." He studied her face.

Isadora flushed.

"I cannot pass your work onto my publisher if I am not certain you are truly the author. I do know that Mr. Howard could at times borrow or be influenced by others' work." He cleared his throat. "But since, in this case, I don't know who wrote what and can't ask Mr. Howard to clear it up for us, I cannot endorse your work. It would be best if neither version was published. If you truly wrote this, you have talent, so you should be able to come up with something new that can be published. However, you must understand after what happened to Mr. Howard that I can't be involved in any of this."

Isadora balled her fists at her sides. "Those are my words; that is my manuscript. He promised me that he would show it to you, but he never did. Now you are telling me that he stole it and passed it off as his own?"

Mr. Emerson held up his hands. "Please, Miss Foote, do not raise your voice. Luther did a great many things that upset a great many people. I wish that I had seen it sooner. If I had, I never would have brought him on the trip to begin with. That was my mistake."

I didn't know that Isadora was even listening to him at that point. She gripped her reticule so tightly I hoped that it was empty, because surely whatever was inside would be crushed.

"I'm sorry." He paused. "When you write your next piece, you might have better luck using a man's name. That's my advice to give you the best chance of being published," Mr. Emerson said, and stepped away.

Isadora stood on the edge of the ballroom with her hand clenched around her reticule. She then spun on her heel and left the room.

CHAPTER THIRTY-SIX

"MISS, MISS," A young man in a shiny frock coat and purple waistcoat called out to me. "May I have some wine?"

"What?" I asked, and then I remembered that I had the tray of wine the Thayers' servant had handed me. "Oh, oh, yes, of course."

He gave me a strange look and took two glasses from my tray as if he was afraid if he asked a second time that I would say no.

I walked around the ballroom and offered glasses of wine to guests. All the while, I thought about the conversation that I had overhead between Mr. Emerson and Isadora, and my mind was whirling. She said that Mr. Howard had promised to share her work with Mr. Emerson. That meant that the two of them had to know each other somehow, but at luncheon on the first day of the symposium, Isadora and Mr. Howard acted like they were meeting for the very first time. Why would they behave in such a way?

"Have you spoken to Isadora yet?" Emily asked.

I jumped and almost dropped the tray of glasses. Thankfully, there were only two left; I was able to catch them before they toppled over. "Emily, you gave me a fright. I didn't know you were there."

"I'm sorry." She cocked her head. "What are you doing with that tray? Do you work for Cate Lynn and Ruben now?"

"I—I was just helping out. A waiter needed help," I muttered.

She shook her head and took the tray from my hands. She set it on a nearby windowsill. "Is it possible for you to not be a servant just for one second?"

"Apparently not," I said. "And in my defense, it was a very good cover. I look much more convincing as a servant than a guest, even in my best dress."

"I suppose you're right," Emily said. "I have news. I spoke with Cate Lynn, and I am certain she doesn't know what her husband is up to. She believes he is just as strong an abolitionist as she is."

"Did you tell her?" I pulled nervously at the black cuffs of my dress.

"I started to, but we were interrupted by another guest." Her brow furrowed in irritation. "She needs to know. I hate to be the one to tell her, but it appears that I am the only one brave enough to do it," she said.

"What is her connection to Mr. Howard? Did you find that out?" I asked.

"She doesn't have one." Emily leaned toward me. "But this is where it gets interesting. Mr. Howard and Isadora Foote were connected in Boston. There were even rumors they might marry, but Isadora always claimed that wasn't true. Cate Lynn has been worried about her since Luther's death."

"Because she thinks Isadora will mourn him?" I asked, thinking this all fit with the conversation I had just overheard between Isadora and Mr. Emerson.

The orchestra picked up the tempo and played a faster song. The dancers in the middle of the room held hands in a large circle and skipped to the right and then to the left. Then, as one, they all broke off into partners and twirled. The women's wide skirts flared out, and laughter filled the room. It was so loud that Emily and I could no longer hear each other and had to wait until the noise died down enough to continue the conversation.

Miss Susan and Austin were among the dancers, and they were laughing and spinning together. Miss Susan's eyes sparkled, and Austin beamed at his young bride. Next to me, Emily was very still, and she had her eyes trained on them.

When the music stopped, Miss Susan and Austin left the dance floor before the next song began. Emily clenched her fists at her sides.

"Emily, what else did Cate Lynn say about Isadora and Mr. Howard?"

She was still staring at her brother and sister-in-law.

"Emily?" I asked in a low voice.

She looked at me, but it was like she was seeing through me. "Are you all right?"

My question seemed to bring her back to the present. "Yes, why wouldn't I be?"

I didn't know the answer to that.

"What is it that you asked?" Emily wanted to know.

I tugged on my dress sleeve again. "What else Mrs. Thayer said about Isadora and Mr. Howard."

"Nothing. We were interrupted."

I told her my impression that Isadora and Mr. Howard acted like they didn't know each other at the luncheon.

She tapped her index finger against her cheek. "You're right. Why would they lie about knowing each other?"

"And if Mrs. Thayer knew about their relationship, why did she go along with the lie?"

"We need to ask her." Emily looked around the room. "But she is on the dance floor. If we grab her now, it will cause a scene."

"This still doesn't answer the question as to why Mr. Thayer would want to hurt Mr. Howard. I did not think he was especially close to Isadora. Isadora is his wife's friend, not his." I paused. "And anytime Isadora speaks about Mrs. Thayer's husband or about their marriage, she seems to be disparaging of it."

Emily looked at me with newfound respect. "Those are very keen observations, Willa."

"Taking them under consideration, would Mr. Thayer want to hurt Mr. Howard because of how Mr. Howard treated Isadora? It doesn't seem likely."

"I don't know," Emily said. "Only Ruben and Isadora can answer that."

"Is Mr. Thayer here?" I asked. "I haven't seen him since he greeted the guests at the front door. He's not dancing with his wife."

"Cate Lynn said he was in the library guarding the auction items. He is quite nervous about having all those jewels out on display with so many people coming and going from the house for the ball, so he has taken up his position as guard. We need to speak to him, and now seems like the best time."

I looked over at the party. Mrs. Thayer now danced with Mr. Emerson. It was a tradition for the lady of the house to dance with the guest of honor.

Emily started for the door. "Are you coming?"

I nodded.

I assumed Emily had been in this house before we met Mrs. Thayer for tea, because she seemed to know where the library was. We stepped inside, and there were three tables set up in the middle of the room with jewelry on them. Two footmen stood in the room and nodded at us. I knew they had to be there to make sure no one walked off with the jewels. Mr. Thayer was not in the room.

"I thought Mr. Thayer would be here," I whispered.

Emily glanced at the two footmen. "It seems he put hired guards in his place."

There was a piece of paper and pencil below each piece where someone could bid on the jewelry. The starting bids were all more than my wages would allow.

Emily bent over a sapphire necklace. "I knew Cate Lynn's family had money when we were children, but nothing like this. If all these bids come through, she has already raised quite a bit of money for the abolitionist cause. Her parents would be very proud of that."

"My wife is very generous in that way," Mr. Thayer said as

he entered the room. He was holding a short glass of amber-colored liquid in his hand. He smiled. "I leave for just a moment, and you come into the room."

"I wanted to see the jewelry that Cate Lynn was putting up for bid," Emily said.

"Are you interested in any of the pieces?"

"Me?" Emily placed a hand to her chest. "Oh no. I'm not much for jewelry, and I don't personally have the kind of money that people are bidding here."

"Then ask your father to bid."

Emily laughed. "Edward Dickinson would never spend money on something so extravagant and impractical."

Mr. Thayer nodded. "I have heard that about your father, that he is tight with the purse strings."

"It is no secret in Amherst. He is careful with his money, the money of the college, and the money of the church. Not a penny goes unaccounted for by my father."

"Well, it seems that it is no matter. By the looks of it, there are plenty of people who are ready to bid and help the cause."

Emily studied a bid sheet beside an emerald ring. "I can see that." She looked up at Mr. Thayer. "How do you feel about your wife making such a generous donation?"

He frowned slightly as if he was trying to decide if Emily was asking this question to make conversation or she was hinting at something else. "They are Cate Lynn's pieces left to her by her mother and grandmothers. It is her choice as to what she wanted to do with them."

"Don't you have a say in it as her husband?"

He narrowed his eyes. "Would I have made a donation to

any cause in this way? No, but I'm not nearly as giving as my wife. Her parents raised her to do this sort of work. It is admirable." He said "admirable" like it was some sort of insult.

Emily must have heard the tone of his voice, too, because she said, "You don't seem like you are pleased with it."

He forced a laugh. "Maybe it's just jealousy. Sometimes I think she cares more about her cause than she does about me. Should she not put her husband first? Is that not a wife's duty?"

Emily arched her brow at him. "I believe this is why I would not make an adequate wife. I don't know if I could do that."

"It is best to know that before you join in a marriage," he said.

"I thought perhaps you weren't pleased with your wife's involvement in the cause because her donations were canceling out your investments in the South."

A black cloud fell over Mr. Thayer's handsome face. He turned to the footmen. "Leave us."

The two young men looked at each other and then dutifully left the room, closing the door behind them. To me, the sound of the heavy door closing sounded like the sealing of a tomb.

"Does Cate Lynn know about your business ventures in the South?" Emily asked.

"Aah, I had thought you might have heard something about that," he said.

"I have heard," Emily said as she raised her chin to look him squarely in the eye. It was no small feat, as she was considerably shorter than the professor. She folded her arms defiantly. "It must be difficult for you to see her give all this money to a cause you are trying to stop."

He stood in front of the door, and I knew it was with intention. He didn't want anyone leaving or entering this room.

I glanced at the windows. They appeared heavy. It would take too long to open them and make our escape if the need arose, and there was the issue of the large prickly bushes that we would fall into if we managed to get out before Mr. Thayer grabbed us.

"Cate Lynn is naive to think she or anyone can stand in the way of commerce. If slavery were to end, the country would be ruined. We depend on it. Our whole society would fall apart, and England would swoop in to make us a colony again. Is that what you want? To be in the service of a monarch?"

Emily lifted her chin. "I don't believe that would happen."

"I don't expect a woman to understand," he said. "What do you understand about money? You said yourself that you don't have money of your own. It's all your father's, as it should be. Women are not capable of managing money. You can't even have a bank account without a man's signature. That is law for a reason."

"Louisa Alcott would argue with you on that point."

"I don't care what that woman thinks or what Isadora Foote thinks, either, for that matter. I have told Cate Lynn time and time again that these friends are bad influences on her. Because of them, we have come to this."

"To what?" Emily challenged.

"To the fact that I have to make a hard decision to secure my future."

"Your future? Don't you mean the future of you *and* your wife? She is the reason that you have such a comfortable life, is that not true?" Emily asked.

Mr. Thayer loosened the silk tie at his throat and shrugged as if it wasn't a concern.

"What I don't understand is why you killed Luther Howard," Emily blurted out.

I winced. I wondered when she was going to come right out and say it. To be honest, Emily had used a lot of restraint holding that bit back for so long.

He had lifted his glass to his lips, but lowered it again when she spoke. He laughed. "I didn't kill Luther Howard. I didn't even know the man."

"You paid Cody Carey to buy the pyrethrin from Paulo. You knew Luther had hay fever."

"I knew no such thing. I knew my wife had hay fever." He allowed the words to hang in the air.

"You were going to kill Cate Lynn," Emily said with a gasp.

"What choice did she give me? She is spending my money, getting so close to ruining us. She has no idea about our finances. She always had everything that she ever wanted from her father."

"What happened to the money? I can't believe that she would give it all away so that the two of you would be destitute."

"You have to spend money to make it. Have you never heard that? Maybe you haven't because you are a woman. You don't understand the complexities of the economy. You're not capable of understanding."

"I can assure you that I am more than capable of understanding a great many things, such as the fact that I can ruin you with one word to Cate Lynn."

He took a step forward.

Emily glared at him and held her ground. In truth, I wished that she would have taken a step or two back from him. I didn't like the fact that she was within striking distance of his hand.

It seemed that during the argument both of them had forgotten I was even there. I inched toward the end of the room. Perhaps I could run out and find the footmen or someone to help us.

"You squandered away her money?" Emily asked. "Didn't you marry her for the inheritance? You ruined it for yourself by making risky investments."

"They would not have been risky investments if the fools in Washington would just stop trying to force their will on Southern states," he snapped.

Emily studied him with disgust on her face. "How did Luther get the powder on him if you meant to kill your wife?"

"That is something you will have to ask Isadora." He lifted the glass to his lips and took a drink. He seemed to regain his composure while he said this. "I have done nothing wrong. Cate Lynn is living, is she not?"

"Isadora?" Emily shook her head as if she were trying to make sense of it.

"Don't tell me that you haven't put that part of the puzzle together. After all this time of trying to convince me of how clever you really are? Not that it matters. What you do know will ruin me, which is why I will have to do away with you and your maid. If there weren't so many people in my house right now for this awful ball, I would just shoot you and be done with it." He sighed. "I will have to be more creative than that, I'm afraid." He sipped from his glass.

By this time, I had made it all the way to the door behind Mr. Thayer. I was torn between running out to find help and staying to make sure Emily wasn't hurt.

I placed my hand on the door, ready to run, when I was distracted by Mr. Thayer. He doubled over and dropped the glass. The remainder of the drink soaked into the rug. He fell to the floor.

"What's happening?" Emily asked.

"He's ill."

"Go get help," Emily ordered.

I ran from the room and almost collided with Miss Alcott and Mrs. Thayer, who were walking together. "Mr. Thayer is sick. He's on the floor in the library."

Mrs. Thayer gasped and ran to the library. Miss Alcott turned to a footman. "Go find a doctor."

He didn't move.

"Now!"

Miss Alcott and I returned to the library. Mrs. Thayer was kneeling by her husband, who was convulsing.

"What did he eat?" Miss Alcott asked.

"I don't know," I replied. "He drank from that glass."

Miss Alcott picked up the glass and smelled it. "Oleander. He's been poisoned. It is oleander poisoning. We have to make him vomit. Cate Lynn, do you have any vomiting syrup?" Miss Alcott asked.

"I—I don't know."

"We do, ma'am," her housekeeper said, who at some point

appeared in the doorway. "I will fetch it." She ran from the room.

While we waited, Ruben convulsed on the floor. Cate Lynn—with tears running down her face—tried to hold him. My heart broke. I realized she really did love him. She didn't truly know who he was, but she loved the person she thought he was.

CHAPTER THIRTY-SEVEN

THE HOUSEKEEPER RETURNED with the medicine, and I looked away as they gave it to Mr. Thayer. He vomited on the carpet while his wife cried for him. She had no idea he had plotted to kill her.

Emily touched my arm. "We have to find her. I know where she would have gone."

I knew she was speaking of Isadora. Emily and I left the room. In the hallway, guests had poured out of the ballroom, all whispering about what had happened to Mr. Thayer.

Emily and I walked past them all and out the door.

When we were outside, she turned to me. "Why would Ruben blame Isadora for Luther Howard's death?"

"I think I might know," I said.

"You can tell me in the carriage." She headed straight for our carriage, where Jeremiah was snoozing in the driver's seat. "Jeremiah, you need to take us to the lecture hall on the campus."

Jeremiah jumped. "What? What? I wasn't sleeping."

"You need to take us to the lecture hall," Emily repeated.

Jeremiah stood in the driver's seat. "But what about the rest of the family?"

"You can drop Willa and me off at the lecture hall and come back for the rest of them. Tell them I had a headache and decided to head home early."

Jeremiah looked at me.

"Please, Jeremiah. It's very important," I said.

He nodded and held the door for Emily and me to climb into the carriage.

Its wooden wheels bumped down the Thayers' long drive and onto the gravel road.

"Tell me what you know."

"I overheard Mr. Emerson saying he wouldn't share Isadora's writing with his editor because it was too much like Mr. Howard's."

"Luther stole her writing?"

I nodded. "That's what she said."

"And she killed him for it."

"I—I don't know."

The carriage bumped, and being so tall, I knocked my head on the roof of it. I wished we could tell Jeremiah to slow down, but I knew we had to reach Isadora Foote quickly.

"Emily, how do you know she went to the lecture hall?"

"Because it's a place where she would want to be revered as a writer just like Mr. Emerson was this week. She craved the recognition he enjoys," Emily said, as if it made perfect sense to her.

I shook my head. I would have to trust her on this. If I were

Isadora, I would be making my way to the frontier by now to get as far away from Amherst as possible.

The August moon shone on the lecture hall, bathing the stone in a ghostly white. Before the carriage even came to a full stop, Emily had the door open and was poised to jump out.

Jeremiah climbed down from the driver's seat. "What are we doing here?"

"Go back to Thayer Manor," Emily said. "Find Officer Matthew and tell him Isadora Foote is the killer. Tell him where we are."

His eyes were huge behind his glasses. "I don't know if I should leave you here."

"Go. It is an order."

"I will keep her safe," I reassured Jeremiah.

He nodded and jumped back into the driver's seat and flicked the reins. He would be back at the manor within minutes.

I stared up at the hall. "How do we even get inside?"

Emily walked up to the door and opened it. "This way."

"They leave it unlocked?"

"They do on some nights when it needs to be cleaned." She went inside, and I followed her.

The hall smelled musty. I pressed my hand against the cold stone wall, and despite the heat in the room, the damp cold sank into my skin. I shivered. Emily walked in front of me and down the aisle. There was a slim form behind the podium. A flame ignited, and a lantern on the table by the podium glowed.

"I thought you would come here eventually, Emily," Isadora Foote said. She was in her ball gown, the same one she had been wearing when she'd confronted Mr. Emerson at the start of the ball.

"I know what Luther did to you," Emily said as she walked up the steps to the platform. She stopped about ten feet from Isadora. "If I had been in your place, I would be just as angry. I had been upset when he asked my maid to take some of my work to show him. She never did, but if she had, I might be in the same position you were that night."

I stayed where I was at the foot of the steps. I didn't know if I would have to run for help at a moment's notice or not.

"You would understand, wouldn't you, Emily?" Isadora held on to the side of the podium. "We talked about our dreams at Mount Holyoke. You knew how important writing was to me."

"It's important to both of us," Emily said.

"So you can't blame me for killing him, can you? He stole my dream. Even now that he is dead, he has still stolen my dream. Mr. Emerson said that the book I had been working on for a decade can never be published because Luther already claimed that it was his. He said that he doesn't know whom to believe." She held on to the podium even more tightly. "It doesn't matter that Luther tried to do the same thing to Mr. Emerson. He doesn't know whom to believe because one of us is a thief and another of us is a woman."

"Mr. Emerson is not the only way to be published. There are many ways."

"But how long will they take? In the meantime, what should I do with my life? Be a mistress to a home? A wife or a mother? I do not want those things. I would have thought that if anyone would understand, it would be you."

"I do," Emily said.

"Mr. Emerson had the audacity to tell me that I should write something new, and if I wanted great success, choose a man's name to write under. I wanted to be published under my own name. Why should I take a man's name? Why should I hide my identity in order to be taken seriously?"

"I don't know," Emily murmured.

Isadora began to pace. "Do you know he promised to marry me?" she said with a snort. "I was so naive. I thought by marrying him, I would be welcomed and have a chance in the literary world. However, when he came here and saw your sister, he changed his mind. He saw someone who could raise his status even more than I could. He would have even offered marriage to you, if you were open to it. I was furious, rightly so.

"I wasn't furious at the fact I was losing the chance to marry. I was mourning my chance to publish. He told me he would share my work with Mr. Emerson, and Mr. Emerson would be just as impressed with it as he was. It was all a lie. He was stealing my work and passing it off as his own. But he made a misstep when he did the same to Mr. Emerson. He came crawling back to me then, knowing he had no chance with your sister if he had a falling-out with Emerson. He wanted to marry me again."

"When did he tell you this?"

"An hour or two before dinner that night. He sent me a note and begged me to forgive him. I sent a note in return asking him to meet me in the garden just before dinner so we could talk."

"But you arrived earlier than your assigned meeting, so you killed him with the pyrethrin then. He began to suffer from it during the dinner, when you were sitting right there and had the perfect alibi," Emily said.

"I did not use pyrethrin in the way you believe." She lifted a glass bottle from the table. "Oleander is the most dangerous plant in the world. One taste of it can kill you. When I realized what Ruben was planning for Cate Lynn, I already knew I was going to give Luther oleander. It was a painful and fitting way for him to die."

"Where does the pyrethrin come in? Why did you take it from Ruben?"

She scowled. "I took it from him to save my friend's life, not just from death but from that marriage. If I could kill Luther and frame Ruben for the crime, all the better." Holding the bottle near the lantern, she studied the liquid inside. "I already had the oleander, and when I overheard Ruben sharing his scheme with your gardener, I knew I had the perfect plan."

I shivered at her tone. Luther Howard had not been a good or kind man, but I would not have wanted to see him suffer. I didn't want to see anyone suffer. I supposed that was the greatest difference between Isadora and me.

"When he arrived in the garden, I told him that he had lost his chance with me and I blew pyrethrin into his face. I didn't even give him a moment to speak. I knew there wasn't much time before the meal."

"What happened?" Emily asked.

"He started to sneeze and cough. I told him to stay there, and I ran to the back door of the Evergreens like I was going to get help."

"But you didn't go get help," Emily said. "You snuck up to his room to search for your writing."

Isadora smiled. "Very good, Emily! You were always so clever." She frowned. "Sadly, I couldn't find it. I knew I didn't have much time, and there was always a chance Luther would do something stupid like go into the house. I ran back to him as if I just found cough syrup that would cure him." She smiled at the memory. "Little did he know I had brought the cough syrup with me and tinctured it with oleander."

I shivered at the coldness in her voice.

Isadora's smile faded then. "But it fell apart. The peddler was arrested instead of Ruben Thayer. He would always know what I did. However, I knew I had time; at least as long as the peddler took the blame. Ruben promised me that the peddler would confess because he is friends with the detective. He said Detective Durben had ways to make the strongest of men confess to the crimes for which they are charged. But I knew Ruben would not stay silent forever, so I had to give him some oleander as well." She sighed. "I had my revenge; I thought that it was over. At the end of the week, I knew I would have to disappear. Then I heard you were asking questions and didn't believe the peddler's confession. Now I have no choice but to completely give up on my dreams." She held up the bottle as if she was ready to drink from it.

"Don't!" Emily cried. "The world will not get to appreciate what you will write in the future if you are dead."

"I can't write after this. I'm finished."

"If you are a writer, a true writer, you can always write if only but a little. You thrive on it. You need it, and it needs you."

Isadora looked at the bottle. "What good does that do in jail? Do you think a printer will publish my story of being a murderer?"

"They might. They will publish a great many things," Emily said.

From where I stood, I looked for a way that I could help Emily. I inched toward the stairs. Did I just jump on the platform and run at Isadora? I was much larger than her. It would not be difficult to knock her over, especially if I caught her off guard.

I dithered in making the choice, and it seemed that I dithered too long. The back door to the hall opened. "Police!" Matthew and another officer ran inside.

Isadora was momentarily distracted with their entrance, but then she came to her senses and lifted the bottle to her lips. Emily jumped on her, knocking it from her hand. They fell in a heap on the hard platform. Isadora scooped up the bottle again.

I ran up onto the platform. "Emily!"

She and Isadora rolled around, fighting over the bottle clutched in Isadora's hand.

I yanked the bottle from them and threw it down. It shattered, and the contents ran over the floor.

Isadora tried to crawl to it, reaching for the poison, but Emily held her long enough for the officers to restrain her.

I helped my friend to her feet. She had a growing bruise on her cheek. She smiled at me. "Whoever said poets were weak?"

"Not me," I replied. "Never me."

EMILY LOOPED HER arm through mine, and we walked through the garden. She had that faraway expression that I knew so well. I had noticed over the last few months that it was becoming more and more frequent, as if she was slipping into the safety of her mind more often. I was torn between knowing that she was happiest in her own thoughts and the fear of someday not being able to reach her. I don't know if the family felt the same. Like Mrs. Dickinson's illness, Emily's far-away stares were something that wasn't spoken about, at least not in my presence.

Carlo was a few feet in front of us, galloping and hopping in the garden path. His massive tongue hung out of his mouth, and every time he looked back to check on us, he showed his toothy grin. He had been extra attentive to Emily these last few days since our confrontation with Isadora in the lecture hall. Ever since that time, I had had a sour taste in my mouth over it. I knew what Isadora did was wrong, and she was paying the price sitting in a jail cell awaiting trial. Maybe in her mania over her dreams she didn't know that murder was never the answer. I knew she was desperate, and as a woman, had few options to succeed. Not every woman could be a Louisa Alcott and break down all the barriers on her own.

However, every woman could be strong in her own way. Cate Lynn Thayer was crushed by Isadora's arrest and her husband's betrayal. Ruben Thayer was arrested for conspiring to murder his wife, but was quickly released because of his close friendship with Detective Durben. I knew if I came across the detective again, I had to consider what he was capable of. I considered myself warned.

After his release, Mr. Thayer tried to return to Thayer Manor, only to find a guard on duty and the locks changed. Cate Lynn would not allow him back in her home or her life. She was in the process of divorcing him and recommitted herself to her parents' abolitionist ideals. I overheard her tell Emily that she was considering going to Washington in the fall to lobby for the cause. She planned to pour all her pain into helping others. I commended her for that; I didn't know if I could do the same in her place.

I touched the prickly leaves of a sunflower as we walked past it. The lower leaves were yellowed and withered, but the leaves near the top by the shining flower were green and strong. I thought of Cody. Thinking of him was much more painful than thinking of Cate Lynn Thayer and Isadora. Of everyone involved in the crimes, he was the only one whom I knew well. I didn't believe that he knew what Mr. Thayer's plans were when he was asked to buy the pyrethrin from Paulo Vitali, but he still should have come forward when he suspected that Mr. Thayer was somehow connected to Mr. Howard's death. Although not the killer in the end, Mr. Thayer did play a large role in how Mr. Howard died.

I tried to argue Cody's case with Emily so she would tell her father, but it was no use. Mr. Dickinson would not abide a disloyal servant, and in his eyes, Cody had been disloyal for not telling the Dickinsons what he knew. He was dismissed, and he told me when he said goodbye that he planned to go back to Boston to find work, as the city was far less dangerous for Irishmen than the country. I didn't know if that was true, but I hoped for his sake that he was right.

As he was leaving on foot, Matthew appeared on the street and gave Cody the goldfinch figurine that the detective had confiscated. "Send it to your sweetheart," Matthew said.

With tears in his eyes, Cody said that he would. The small crack in the shell around my heart opened a tiny bit more when Matthew did that. I'd yet to see him and thank him. It was the first thing I planned to do when Sunday came around again.

At the very least, Paulo Vitali was free. I liked to think he was somewhere far away selling his wares. I would not blame him if he never returned to Amherst again. I hoped that he was happy wherever he was, but I knew he would always miss his niece Gabriella.

As if she could read my thoughts, Emily murmured, "I understand why she did what she did."

As just a week had passed after all that had happened, it was difficult to believe that any of us could be thinking of anything else. I didn't ask whom she meant. I knew it was Isadora. I waited. Usually when she began a discussion in such a way, she had much more to say on the matter, and I only needed to be patient.

"Luther stole the most precious thing she owned. Her thoughts. He took her thoughts and tried to pass them off as his own. There was very little she could do about it since she is a woman. He was a man and had the support of the most powerful figure in the literary world. She didn't feel like she had a choice. Now, she is in prison awaiting trial. Sadly, I don't believe the jury will rule in her favor."

"Mr. Howard wasn't her only way to share her work with the world," I argued. It was a conversation that Emily and I had had many times since Isadora's arrest, and every time I made this statement.

"You're right. There are ways, but not as many ways for a woman as there would be for a man, and not just any man, but a wealthy one. Think if Cody wanted to write and be published. He would be no better off than Isadora, maybe worse. At least she is respected for the wealth she inherited from her parents."

I didn't argue with her on that point. "What is the solution?" I asked.

She stopped in front of the orchard and turned to look at me. "Not what Mr. Ralph Waldo Emerson told her, I can tell you that."

I wrinkled my forehead trying to remember what he said.

Emily shook her head as if she could not believe that I didn't remember. "He told her to write something else and to get it published under a man's name."

"Other women have done that."

"Yes." Emily folded her arms. "And is that fair?"

I didn't have an answer for that. I was certain that my lower station meant my understanding of what was fair was quite different from my mistress's. Instead I asked something else. "Since you disagree with Mr. Emerson on this point, will you share your work with him?"

She lifted her chin. "No, and if Mr. Emerson ever returns to Amherst, I plan to tell him that too."

I couldn't help but smile. I didn't doubt that she would, and I hoped that I was there to see it.

Her tone softened again. "Isadora was right when she said that I might have done the same thing. I might have killed a man for my art. I don't know what I would do if someone took my poems and passed them off as their own. It would destroy me. Perhaps this is why I hold them so close to me and why I hide them away in my room."

"You wouldn't have killed anyone. I know that," I said. "As much as it would hurt you, you would never make the decision to take another person's life."

"Are you sure, Willa? Everyone is capable of terrible and great acts if given enough reason." She started walking again.

"Your conscience and faith would stop you," I said, refusing to believe that my friend could commit a crime as awful as Isadora had done. In two steps, I caught up with her.

"I don't believe in the same God that you, my father, and brother do. What I believe is wholly different. My rules are different. It seemed Isadora's rules were different as well."

"Will you ever share your work when you find the right person? I think you should. I have read it in parts on the scraps of paper on the floor, on the napkins in the kitchen, on the newsprint in the parlor. It should be shared . . ." I bit my lip to stop myself from saying more. I did not know how Emily would react to my reading those slips and scraps of paper, and what she would think if she knew I saved them and tucked them away in my single drawer in my room. In the last year, I had collected hundreds upon hundreds of words.

"Sharing your soul is the most terrifying act," Emily said quietly. "I don't know that I am brave enough in this life. But I do believe, Willa, that someday my name will be known. Not by just my family and friends, not by just Amherst or the commonwealth, but by the world."

In the end, she was right. But of the two of us, I was the only one to witness it.

AUTHOR'S NOTE

THERE IS NO evidence that Emily Dickinson ever met Ralph Waldo Emerson, but it's hard to believe that she did not. Emerson stayed at the Evergreens as the guest of Susan and Austin Dickinson many years later than the time of this novel, when Emily had pulled away from society. I moved the timeline of this visit up in order to have Emily interact with the "sage of Concord," as he was called.

As Susan wanted to make her home the social and intellectual hub of Amherst, Massachusetts, I don't believe she would mind that I messed with the timeline. Emerson, I'm not so certain about. He might have found it improper.

I most wanted to include Emerson in this story to share his lifelong mission with readers, which was to encourage American literature and a truly unique form and way of writing. Ralph Waldo Emerson was on a quest to write and to find writers who wrote in an American voice that was separate from the English style. He was the founder of the *Atlantic Monthly* and a writer, philosopher, lecturer, and rock star of that time. If Emerson had given a lecture in 1856 in Amherst, the hall would have been packed as though a celebrity had come to town. Emerson was one of the few writers in the nineteenth century who actually found financial success with his writing, and one of the few who made it to old age to enjoy that success.

Emily admired him and his work immensely. She was very well read, and her father was kind enough to keep her always well stocked in books on the subjects of literature, history, and botany. He thought all of these were the basis of an education for his daughters.

Emily also read for pleasure. She loved the popular fiction of the time. She enjoyed popular fiction so much that her dog Carlo was named after St. John's dog in the novel *Jane Eyre*, one of Emily's favorites. She would have certainly known about Louisa May Alcott.

Emily and Louisa were both women writers of the time, but in their approach to their work, they could not have been more different. Louisa had a pragmatism about her that Emily lacked. Her father, Bronson Alcott, was not a practical man and failed financially many times, causing the Alcott family to move often. At a young age, Louisa and her sisters worked as teachers and governesses to help the family. Louisa, unlike Emily, knew what it was like to be truly poor and have to work to eat. Although Louisa was extremely driven for her own sake and her love of writing, it was the need to take care of her family and the fear of poverty that kept her going. Emily wrote for the expression of her art. Louisa wrote for the money. Neither motivation is wrong.

The Dickinson family, Ralph Waldo Emerson, and Louisa

May Alcott aren't the only historical figures in this novel. Margaret O'Brien was the Dickinsons' maid at the time, and Horace Church was their gardener. The story of the young girl, Angeline, Horace Church tells to Willa and Emily is true and happened when Emily was about ten years old. Because of his upbringing by his strong mother, Sarah, Horace was a staunch abolitionist and was often at odds with Emily's father, Edward Dickinson, on the topic of slavery. Although both men believed slavery was wrong, Horace and Edward had different ideas about how freed enslaved people should be treated after being released from bondage.

In the 1850s, the Irish were scorned in the United States. Thousands, like fictional Cody Carey, came to the United States to escape the Great Famine. Italian immigrants, like fictional Paulo Vitali, were also treated poorly. Either of these men would have been an easy scapegoat at the time for a crime.

ACKNOWLEDGMENTS

I want to thank all my amazing readers who gave *Because I Could Not Stop for Death*, my first historical mystery, a chance, which made this novel possible. I hope that you enjoy this story as much as you did the first book.

Special thanks to my super-agent Nicole Resciniti, who believed in this series from the start, and to my editor, Michelle Vega, and the team at Berkley for their enthusiastic support. With your edits, guidance, and support it became possible for the first novel in the series to be a Mary Higgins Clark Award–nominee and winner of the Agatha Award. I am so honored and grateful.

Thanks to Kate Schlademan, owner of the Learned Owl Book Shop in Hudson, Ohio, and Cari Dubiel of the Twinsburg Public Library for an amazing launch to this series. Thanks also to all the other librarians, booksellers, readers, and friends who spread the word about the series. Books are still sold by word of mouth in many cases, and I could not be more grateful to each and every one of you who read, talked about, and reviewed the first novel.

Thanks, too, to Kimra Bell, for reading this manuscript.

Love and gratitude to my family, who support me as I pursue my dreams, especially to my wonderful husband, David Seymour.

Finally, I would like to thank God for allowing the dreams I dream to come true.

DAVID M. SEYMOUR

Amanda Flower is the *USA Today* bestselling and Agatha Award–winning mystery author of more than forty novels, including the nationally bestselling Amish Candy Shop Mystery series, Magical Bookshop Mysteries, and, written under the name Isabella Alan, the Amish Quilt Shop Mysteries. Flower is a former librarian, and she and her husband, a recording engineer, own a habitat farm and recording studio in Northeast Ohio.

VISIT AMANDA FLOWER ONLINE

AmandaFlower.com
AuthorAmandaFlower
AmandaFlowerAuthor
AFlowerWriter